Flowing Water,
Falling Flowers

流水, 落花

X.H. Collins

MWC Press
Rock Island, Illinois

MWC Press
An imprint of the Midwest Writing Center
401 19th Street
Rock Island, IL
www.mwcqc.org

Cover Design by Chris Xi

ISBN: 978-1-7334802-3-9

For my parents

FAMILIES IN THE NOVEL

The Han Family

Zhuo Han

Chang (Old Ancestor) — ..Yu-wen (Master Han)

..Iris   ..Pearl

De-chen   Shan

..Daisy   ..Hong-mei   ..Elsie

Peony (Lady Han)

Ching-yu   ..Lily

..You-jun   Alvin   ..Rose

Others: Green Jade, Cook, Tutor, Madame Zhao (match maker), Liang Fei

Harriton

The Wang Family

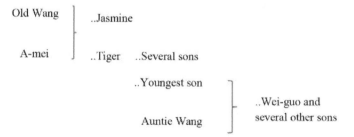

Old Wang   ..Jasmine

A-mei   ..Tiger   ..Several sons

..Youngest son

Auntie Wang   ..Wei-guo and several other sons

Others: Wu Er, Yan (Wu Er's mother), Auntie Wang's nephew

The Fang Family

Mrs. Fang   ..Jian-da

PEONIES

Dazzling peony,
  Beloved of spring,
Half-reclines on the red balustrade
  and waits to bloom.

Under heaven, no flower can compare;
Among men, only nobles are fitting company.

Stealing fragrance: black ants creep
  Slanting through the leaves;
Espying blossoms: golden bees hang
  inverted from the stems.

A mind awakened to Chan will not be moved,
But the youth of Wuling may be driven mad.

  By Lingquan Guiren, a Chinese Zen monk in the tenth century

PROLOGUE
THREE RIVERS, 1891

Pure Brightness: Fifteen days after the Spring Equinox and the fifth solar term of the twenty-four seasons. Time to remember the ancestors.

It was a moonless night. The air was cool and damp from the non-stop rain of the past several days.

The darkness hung like a dense canopy over the three rivers, the steep steps leading from the water up to the narrow city streets, and the houses on those streets.

The rivers hummed their gentle swishing tunes as the breeze brushed across their surfaces, while people tossed and turned in their slumber.

A cry came from a house on the bank where the three rivers joined their waters. It was the sharp, urgent cry a baby would make, a baby leaving his mother's warm and safe womb and entering a cold and unknown world.

Just then, the sound of the night watchmen inundated the city. Dong—! Dong! Dong! Dong! Dong! One slow beat followed by four fast ones: the rhythm of the fifth two-hour period in the night. There were two of them. One held a bamboo clapper, the other a bronze gong. Going from street to street, they struck their instruments in unison, and they called out to everyone in the city: Early to bed, early to rise, makes a man healthy, wealthy, and wise!

Then their voices were drowned by the songs of the boat-trackers, the Yangtze River tow men. Pulling towing ropes thick as a small child's arm, the tow men sang as the boatmen rolled the first barge of the day through the city:

Seeing the southern checkpoint, my eyes are full of tears
I want to return to Sichuan and buy an earthenware jar,
Seeing the Binshu Gorge, my thinking is undone,
I miss mom and dad, because my money's gone.
After going past Bream Stream I feel a little hungry,
I think of my son and daughter, but haven't brought any rice,
Getting to Longevity Pagoda the earthenware jar breaks,
There's still a long way to go, two nine one hundred eight!

The sounds passed with the boat, and quietness reclaimed the city. The sky over the horizon started to show a grayish-white color like the belly of a carp. In the fine mist of the dawn, two men, one older and one younger, emerged from a small fishing boat docked at the pier and climbed the winding steps. They hurried towards the house where the baby's cry had come earlier, making their way to the side door used for delivery. The door opened soundlessly.

A young woman handed a basket covered with black cloth to the older man and whispered something in his ear. Then she reached into her jacket, took out five silver coins, and gave them to the younger one. The men turned around. The woman stood unmoving, as if waiting for the men to return. Then she raised her sleeves to wipe her eyes, went back into the house, and closed the door behind her.

She went through the kitchen, turned right onto the covered, stone-paved walkway, and passed the servant's quarter and the school teacher's room. No one stirred. She entered the garden in the back of the house. The rockery at one corner loomed like shadows in the dim morning light. The pagoda across from the rockery looked deserted. The pond was bare, and carp jumped as the woman walked by, but the pair of mandarin ducks did not move. The wind was calm, and the stalks of bamboo did not make any rustling sounds. It was the twenty-seventh day of the second month. Pure Brightness came early this year; it would be another month before the rose bushes started budding, the lilac and magnolia trees came in full bloom, and various annuals woke up and came back to life. The woman took care not to slide on the moss made slippery by the morning dew. On the other side of the garden, she stopped at the door of the first room, and lightly tapped on the door.

"Come in," a voice said, hardly audible.

The woman went in.

"It's done," she whispered.

There was no answer.

4

The woman waited, as if not wanting to break the stillness. Then she spoke again.

"The new girl is young but clever and a hard-worker. I have shown her everything. She knows her way around the kitchen, makes serviceable tea, has met the delivery people, and knows what to do. She is very good with Iris, and right now she is staying with her."

After another long silence, the voice sighed, and then said, "Thank you."

"Do take care, my lady. Send for me when you are ready," the woman said. She stood for a little longer and was backing out of the room when the voice said, "I...I..." But the voice couldn't finish.

The woman went to the bed, lowered herself so her hands could hold the other woman's hands, and her eyes met those of the other woman, deep and wounded as a pair of old wells.

"Peony," the woman said, her voice shaking. "Don't worry, everything will be fine. I promise! You take care of yourself!"

A long pause. Then the woman on the bed let go of the other woman's hands. "Are you heading to the temple?" she asked. But before the woman answered, Peony whispered again, "You should go," and turned her head to face the wall. The woman tucked the comforter one more time and went out.

The house was quiet, but the woman could hear sounds from the streets outside: the city had come out of its sleep and begun a new day of its bustling life.

CHAPTER 1
CHICAGO, 2017

I closed down the PowerPoint presentation. I was satisfied with how it turned out. Lots of images, minimum text. It should go well at the conference. It should impress Harriton.

Thinking about Harriton, I opened my e-mail to see if he'd gotten back to me. I'd e-mailed him the day before to tell him that I'd submitted paperwork for the conference to my dean at the college, and I would be reserving a hotel room in the coming days. Told him I couldn't wait. But there were only a few messages trying to sell me various things. I deleted them and shut down my laptop. I should go for a quick run.

It was a beautiful spring day. Lake Michigan shimmered in the afternoon light, and my thoughts flew like its water as I jogged.

Women are made of water. So says a Chinese proverb. Water is so soft that it changes itself to fit whatever shape it is allowed to be. But water can also turn an angled and rough rock into a round and smooth pebble, erode the mountain that blocks its flow and capsize a ship it carries.

If I were an ideal woman, by this notion, I would be soft yet persistent enough to turn Harriton, my angled rock into the round pebble that I could hold on to.

I met him at an annual conference of our disciplines. We connected instantly, as if we were long-lost friends. We sat next to each other in the audience, during the panel discussions, and at the lunch table. We visited a used book store on the last day of the conference, while his wife was at a flower-arranging workshop. He kissed me between shelves filled with dusty history books, some of them hand-bound. I kissed him back.

Of course, I knew what I did was wrong. Returning home, I tried to forget the whole thing. I wanted to forget the kiss and my fascination with him. I planned to crush the crush. Rose, he's got a wife, for God's sake! I kept telling myself. And how inferior I felt from a glimpse of her slender, aristocratic frame, inherited from some Scandinavian royal ancestor in her bloodline. She didn't work because of poor health. She never even finished her degree. But she had perfect upbringing. While she was with Harriton at the conference, she scouted out the city, visited museums or crafts workshops, and picked out restaurants for them to have dinner. I imagined the kind of elegant parties she could throw. What a perfect academic wife!

But try as I did, I failed in all my efforts. How could I not? He was the man I had dreamed of since I was thirteen but never had the luck of meeting. He was tall and lean, strong-looking, but not thick like a football player. His dark-framed glasses and mop of messy black hair showed he spent more time with books than with a treadmill. We read the same books, liked the same movies. We told each other about our families, our childhood. And we could talk. Oh, how we talked!

I tried to confine my writing to my journal. This will not go anywhere, but I don't want to forget it, either.

But my heart hijacked my brain. One night when I couldn't sleep, I wrote him an e-mail, thinly veiling it as a way to share a picture of the conference.

But I wore my heart on my sleeve, as they say, and Harriton was not fooled.

We poured out our hearts and souls in our e-mails to each other. Written words had always held enormous power over me. If I was smitten at the conference, I fell in love through his e-mails. At some point he signed, "Love," and that was my jail and my sentence.

When we returned to the conference the following year, his wife did not accompany him. She never again went with him in the years that followed. He did not say why, and I never asked. Nor did I ask why he did not wear his wedding ring.

We were like long-separated young lovers. It went on like this for five years. For a whole year, we looked forward to being in the same place for a week so we could absorb the essence of each other: to hear each other's voices articulating new ideas about our work, to touch and caress the curves of each other's bodies, and to inhale the smells and the breath of each other.

Then we returned to our lives until we were slowly depleted of that essence we had soaked up and tucked away. Or that was how I felt, at least.

In between, we e-mailed. And in the nights when sleep eluded me, my longing for him grew out of my bones and spread to the rest of my body.

Or at a time like this, facing Lake Michigan.

My phone beeped. It was a weather alert. Scattered storms would start around nine in the night. There was no new e-mail. I started jogging back home.

#

On Monday morning, I received an email request for a meeting with the vice president of instruction.

I was bewildered. I could not think of anything I needed to discuss with the VP. My contacts were with students, in classrooms and the clubs I advised. I rarely needed to talk to my department chair or my dean.

The VP's spacious office had a huge south-facing window. The faculty offices in my building had no windows. I was surprised to see the people there: the VP, the dean, and the department chair. I felt like a student getting called into the principal's office.

"Dr. Ming, have a seat, please," the VP said. She was an elegant woman who seemed to have an endless wardrobe of skirt suits. I was distracted by the bright coral color of this one when I heard her repeating my name.

Dr. Ming? Uh oh, this was not good. I was usually just Rose.

"How's the semester going?" she continued.

"Pretty well," I said, uncertain where this was headed. I sat down, hands in my lap.

"Dr. Ming, you must have heard about the state budget crisis. There has been no budget for two years now, and we still don't see the light in the coming year."

"Yes, I heard that," I said, shifting in the chair. "Is this about the travel funds for the conference? I..."

No travel funds. My heart sank. No conference. No Harriton.

"It's true we have no travel funds this year, but I'm afraid it's more serious than that." She sighed. "There are some very tough decisions we have to make."

She turned to my dean, as if giving him a cue.

"Rose," said the dean, clearing his throat. A cheerful old guy who always wore a bowtie, he had been the one who hired me thirteen years ago. He had never looked this grim as long as I had known him. "The college has made the difficult decision of reducing our studio art offering, and as a result, your position has been eliminated, and your last day will be May 31. I'm so sorry."

"But I'm not a studio artist! I'm an art historian! I teach art history," I said, stunned. "And I'm tenured!"

"We know. It's an extreme circumstance and this is workforce reduction. I'm sorry, Rose, but you have the least seniority. I'm very sorry!" The dean looked withered—he himself was a historian. "You're brilliant, Rose. I'm sure you'll find something better. I'll be more than happy to write you a glowing letter of recommendation."

I walked out of the office, dizzy and disoriented.

"Rose!" My department chair, also a close friend chased after me as I walked out. "Rose, I fought for you, I really did. But it was not in my hands. I'm so sorry!"

"I believe you. It's okay." I offered her a tight smile as we walked together.

"What are you going to do now, Rose? I'll give you all my connections. Let me know if I can help you. I'm not sure if you want to teach as an adjunct professor after this, but if you do, I have the authority to hire adjuncts. But you know the paycheck is much slimmer, and there are no benefits…"

"Thank you." I stopped, facing her. "I'm fine, really. Don't worry. I'll figure it out."

I walked back to my windowless office and closed the door. Now what?

I called Harriton's office. It was late afternoon. I wasn't sure he was in. I had never called him before, as we often had different office hours, and calling his home was not an option. He did not use a cell phone. He said that he had the means to reach people when he needed to and he did not need a cell phone.

"Hello!" said that deep, gentle voice that played in my head so much.

I froze.

"Hello?"

"Harry…It's Rose."

A pause. Then, "Oh, hey," cool, detached.

"I can't come to the conference this year. I…"

What should I say? No travel funds. And no job.

"It's for the better," he interrupted. "Actually I'm in the middle of writing you one last e-mail. My wife found out. She might have known for a while. She asked me point-black last night if I'm having an affair, with you. I can't lie to her. We have to work things out. We have a counseling appointment tomorrow. She has asked me to not contact you."

She asked? What about you? But no sounds came out of my mouth.

"Please don't contact me again. I…I'm sorry. Truly I am. Bye…Rose." As if my name was a difficult foreign word. Then he hung up.

I stared at the receiver for a while, listening to the static buzzing sound, before putting it down. What had just happened? A moment ago, he was at the other end of the line, so close and so clear. And then he was not.

When I finally locked my office, the campus police officer was making his last rounds of the buildings. He waited with me until my Uber arrived.

That night, I had a stack of papers to grade, which I did. That's the sad fact about me: as a student, Rose always showed up in class, no matter what; as a professor, Rose always got her papers graded within the week she received them, no matter what. It was after midnight when I went to bed. But sleep did not come easily. Instead, tears flooded me, my pillows, my sheets.

A woman made of water, at last.

CHAPTER 2
THREE RIVERS, 1898

The Waking of Insects: the thirteenth day of the second month and the third solar term of the twenty-four seasons. Spring thunders awaken sleeping insects.

The city of Three Rivers got its name from the rivers that weaved through it: Jialing River, the largest of the three, coming from the North, the first and one of the major branches of the Yangtze; Fu River, from the snowy Ming Mountain in the West; and Qu River, from the northeast. The Fu and Qu rivers merged into the Jialing River at the center of the city.

On one side of the willow-covered river banks, at the merging point, stood a white pagoda tower. Its presence would calm the river spirits and tame the river dragons, so the city would be safe from flooding. On the other side, steps paved with black stones led a winding path from the riverbank to a street. A large cypress tree had stood on that spot for more than one hundred years. Next to that cypress tree stood Number One Cypress Street, the house of the Han family.

That morning, before the morning river mist dissipated, the Han house was already in a state of anticipation. Days had been unusually cold leading up to the Waking of Insects, and the spring seemed slow in coming after the Lunar New Year celebration. But this day was warm enough for children to play outside and farmers to bring out their plows.

After breakfast, Lady Han gathered her own children, nine-year-old Iris and five-year-old You-jun, and waited in the front hall. The maid Green Jade was also there.

Lady Han was twenty-eight-years old, with a kind, lovely face. Her long black eyebrows, a pair of perfect arches as if drawn carefully with charcoal twigs, framed her large, deep-set, dark eyes. Her face was smooth as porcelain, and her soft, long hands folded neatly on her lap as she sat on one of the two high-backed nanmu armchairs, on one side of the nanmu table, under the shelf that held an altar to the ancestors. She wore a simple long indigo silk dress, matching pants, with no adornment except for a thin jade bracelet on her slender wrist. Her perfectly bound three-inch feet were protected by a pair of exquisitely embroidered silk slippers.

Although Lady Han spoke in her usual gentle voice, Green Jade sensed unusual enthusiasm in her tone.

"Today is a special and happy day. My old friend A-mei is coming back. You remember A-mei, Green Jade?"

"Yes, Ma'am. She taught me all I know about the household," Green Jade answered.

A-mei was Lady Han's long-time maid. When Lady Han left her parents' home in the village of Cloud Gate and married into the Han family in Three Rivers, she brought A-mei along.

Seven years ago, A-mei went to Cloud Gate to sweep the tombs of her ancestors, as she had always done with Lady Han. Lady Han did not go that year due to illness. The plan was for A-mei to stay in the village to help her husband with farm chores during the busy planting season. It seemed, however, that she had become pregnant during her visit home at the end of the previous year, in preparation for the Chinese New Year, a fact concealed by her bulky winter jacket. And so she sent the word to Three Rivers that her stay would be longer. It in fact extended much longer: she had a girl, and less than two years later, a boy. The children kept her tied to the village. Now the children were older, and she was returning to serve her lady, two children in tow.

Lady Han turned to her children. "Iris, you were only two when A-mei left for her village. You-jun, you were not even born. I want you to be on your best behavior when A-mei and her children come. You will have new friends. Her daughter Jasmine is seven, and her son Little Tiger is four."

14

"Will they stay or just visit, Mother?" Iris asked. She stood almost at her mother's shoulder height.

"They will stay. I want you to treat Jasmine like your sister. A-mei is like my sister. Having a sister is the best thing a girl can hope for."

Iris nodded. She was very curious about this new girl, Jasmine. Her mother talked about her so much that Iris felt like she already knew her. When Lady Han traveled to Cloud Gate to visit the Guanyin Temple, she visited A-mei and her family and took gifts to the children. Iris and You-jun were too young to travel with their mother.

Iris thought about what her mother said. Her mother was right. The same old family tutor who had taught their father taught her and You-jun how to read and write, and she could recite all the books better than You-jun. But because she was a girl, she could not do everything as she pleased, like You-jun could. Life was getting more boring each day as she grew. How much more fun it would be having another girl in the house!

"What about me? I want a sister, too!" You-jun was running around in the room and came to his mother after he heard her words.

Lady Han smiled. She picked up You-jun, who instantly struggled to get down. "Silly boy! You already have a nice sister. Now you are about to have another one! And you will also have Little Tiger to play with." She almost chuckled at this pleasant thought.

She let go of You-jun and said to the girls, "All right, then. Green Jade, you go check with everyone in the house to make sure that the furniture is dusted, the floor and courtyard are swept, and the room for A-mei is ready. Iris, you go tell Teacher there's no class today, and I hope he will enjoy a day off! From tomorrow, he will have two more pupils."

The girls left. Green Jade took You-jun so she could keep an eye on him.

Lady Han sat back on the high-backed nanmu armchair. She closed her eyes. For seven years she had been thinking about this day. She had seen this day so many times in her dreams. She said a silent prayer to Guanyin—Bodhisattva, the Goddess of Mercy and Compassion, the Savior of all sentient beings, especially women and children. And she thanked Her for the blessing.

Around noon, a hubbub of voices and footsteps came from the river, up the winding steps and towards the Han house on Cypress Street. Lady Han and her children, Green Jade, and the other servants all rushed through the black stone-paved courtyard, went around the short stone shadow wall, and stopped at the gate, which was already open. Someone shouted, "They are coming! They are coming!"

In walked a woman about thirty years of age. She had a cloth sack strapped on her shoulder and held a child in each hand, one girl and one boy. A man about the same age followed, carrying a pair of square bamboo baskets on a pole across his shoulders.

"My lady!" the woman cried when she saw the mistress of the house. She nudged the two children forward and said, "Kowtow and pay your respects!"

Lady Han caught the children as they were about to lower themselves. "Oh, no no! No kowtow! Let me take a good look at you two!" She held them both at arm's length and said, "Jasmine! You are more beautiful than the last time I saw you! And, you, Little Tiger, quite a bit taller!" Then she drew them both in with a tight embrace.

She turned to the adults. She took hold of A-mei's hands and squeezed them hard. Then she nodded to the man, who had laid the baskets on the ground, and slightly bent her knees to greet him. "Come in, Brother Wang! Come in!" she said warmly. "You all must be tired! Let's rest a bit in the front hall before lunch." Then she called out, "Green Jade! Serve tea!"

They all went to the front hall. A-mei was reluctant to sit on the nanmu chair. "I'll be okay sitting on a stool, Lady," she said. "I shouldn't be sitting on Master's chair."

"Master is not home today," Lady Han said. "Had he been here, I would have wanted you to take my chair. I want to make sure you are comfortable. It was not easy to travel with two little children! I have never taken Iris and You-jun to Cloud Gate."

Finally, they all sat down. Lady Han sat on her own chair, with Iris by her side. A-mei sat on the other chair at the other end of the large, long table, the girl named Jasmine by her side and Little Tiger on her lap. A-mei's husband, Old Wang, sat on a chair brought in by Green Jade, who returned to the kitchen and came back with a teapot and three teacups. A-mei nodded her head: yes, this girl was clever and a good worker. She was proud—one more thing she did well for Lady Han, her dear friend Peony, since childhood.

Green Jade was happy to see A-mei. "Auntie," she said, "you look happy and prosperous! What good luck to have two such beautiful children!" A-mei thanked her for the kind words.

Old Wang asked about the health of the Old Lady Han, mother of the Master of the house.

"Thank you," Lady Han said, shifting slightly in her chair as if trying to get more comfortable. "We are blessed that Old Ancestor is still in good health. She has always been devoted to the Buddha, as you know. Now she spends more time in the temple in the Diaoyu Mountain near the Fortress than she does at home. There she prays, meditates, and eats only vegan food. This happens to be one of her stays. The older she gets, the more she does to get ready for the West Pure Land."

"May Buddha bless Old Ancestor, so she will live to a hundred years!" Old Wang said.

"I hope the kids won't annoy Old Ancestor," A-mei said, looking at Lady Han, then Jasmine. "They can be quite noisy."

"Oh, you know how Old Ancestor loves boys," Lady Han said. "The more rambunctious they are, the happier she is. As for the girls, you and I can just keep them to ourselves."

Old Wang asked about Master Han and wished his granary business to thrive more and more each day.

"Thank you, Brother Wang," Lady Han replied. "Master said he's sorry to miss you. He had to get the orders negotiated now so we will have plenty of grain in the fall. He said that he knew you were busy, but he asked you to please visit us more often! He was grateful for you to take care of business for him in the village, and he plans to visit Cloud Gate soon."

The adults chatted about the trip. The Wang family had risen before dawn, walked from their village to the river port in the time it took for the sun to rise to the bamboo tops, and then they took a fishing boat for about half a day. It was a good thing that the weather had been nice. Old Wang showed Lady Han what he carried in his baskets: two fat hens A-mei and Jasmine raised; pork belly from their own pig and smoked by Old Wang himself; sweet rice ball fillings made of pastes of sesame seeds and sugar infused with rose petals, and dried long beans. Lady Han praised the farm goods and thanked him profusely.

While the adults talked, Iris and Jasmine studied each other.

Iris thought that Jasmine was beautiful. Her lacquer-black braids reached her lower back; her face was a perfect oval shape, clear as the moon; and her large eyes were full of curiosity and inquiry. She wore a simple cream-colored cotton jacket and red pants. Her feet were bound, as were Iris's. Iris instantly knew that she had found a friend and confidant.

Jasmine looked at Iris. She loved how elaborately Iris's hair was braided and admired Iris's lilac-colored jacket with its broad white trim and matching pants. But most of all, she loved the gentle and genuine smile on Iris's soft, baby-like round face.

When Lady Han told Iris to take Jasmine to their room—the girls were to share a large room on the east side of the house, next to the Master and Lady's room—both went happily, hand in hand.

"Where is You-jun?" A-mei asked. Little Tiger seemed to be not as sure as his sister about the new place and new people. He held on tightly to his mother.

"Oh!" Lady Han seemed to be shocked that she had forgotten about her other child. "You-jun!" She raised her voice to call him and gave A-mei an apologetic smile.

"You-jun is playing with Jian-da. Jian-da came for class, and since there's no school today, they started playing. I couldn't get You-jun to come in, so I asked one of the day-labor men to keep an eye on them," Green Jade said.

"Tell him to come in because Little Tiger is here. He'll get a new toy if he does," Lady Han said.

Green Jade went out. Soon, two boys with mud on their faces stormed in. They both pretended to ride horses with bamboo sticks and made noises, "Ja ja ja!" Little Tiger widened his eyes upon seeing them. "Do you want to go play?" his mother asked him.

"Yes!" He slid down and joined the boys, and they ran back to the yard. You-jun had forgotten about the promise of a new toy.

"Is Jian-da the Fang boy?" A-mei asked.

"Yes," Lady Han said. "He is such a good boy, very obedient to his poor widowed mother. His father was Master's best friend before he passed away when Jian-da was still an infant. Master and I treated him as our own son, and You-jun is good friends with him. The old teacher taught the three of them, and Jasmine and Tiger will now join the class. There will be three boys! Three boys running around! Oh my, I'm getting a headache just thinking about it!"

They all laughed.

The boys stormed back to the room and ran straight into Iris and

18

Jasmine, who were walking back from their room to the front hall.

"Who are you?" You-jun came to an abrupt halt in front of Jasmine, and his eyes met hers. Jasmine turned bright red, not knowing what to say. She tried to hide herself behind Iris. But You-jun wouldn't let her out of his sight. He followed her and pulled her sleeve and said, "Are you a fairy coming from Heaven?"

Everybody laughed. Jasmine wished that she could vanish like a fairy.

Jian-da was also transfixed by Jasmine, but he did not make any comments like You-jun had. He just smiled at her and hoped she would notice him.

"I'm glad to see the kids get along with each other so well and so quickly." Lady Han smiled.

After lunch, Old Wang left for the village. The Waking of Insects was early this year, and the plowing and seeding needed to be done immediately, so he had to turn around and go home the same day. Proper timing was everything for farm work.

Lady Han asked him to stay for a day or two but he said that the farm work couldn't wait. "Please send my respect to Master Han," he said. He hugged his children, telling them to listen to their mother and the Master and the Lady. Then he nodded to his wife and went out. He refused Lady Han's offer to call a sedan chair and insisted that he would walk to the port and get on a fishing boat.

Jasmine and Little Tiger were sad that their father was leaving. Old Wang assured them that he would come back and promised to take them to Cloud Gate to fish and catch fireflies when the summer came.

"I want to go, too," You-jun said.

"Me too," Jian-da said. "If my mother allows me."

It was agreed that all would go. And indeed, from then on, the three families were forever connected, as branches of a tree that emerged from the same root. Mothers and daughters, sisters and friends, they blossomed and withered, as seasons changed and the rivers flowed.

CHAPTER 3
CHICAGO, LOS ANGELES, AND CHENGDU, 2017

The Friday night of the week when my life fell apart, I called my mom. She lived in Los Angeles.

Usually I did not call Mom on Fridays. I couldn't say, "Gotta go, Ma, have class tomorrow morning at eight," if she started to ask why I was home on a Friday night alone. "Are you not going out with friends?" she would ask. And by friends she meant boyfriends. She never let me forget that I had moved away from her, half-way across the country, to the middle of nowhere, among cornfields. I pointed out more than once that Chicago was not exactly nowhere; it's the third-largest city in the country, and we most definitely did not have corn where I lived.

I suspected the move would have been fine had I become a doctor or an engineer. Or married with children. But I did none of the above.

"History!" she cried. "What do you do with a degree like that? Teach at a high school?"

"Art history," I said. "And there is nothing wrong with teaching at a high school. I thought Chinese respect teachers!"

"But this is America," she said.

When I became tenured faculty, I told her that I was teaching at a college, not high school, and that I had job security.

"Very nice," she said over the phone. I was expecting her to say, "Still, teaching," but she did not. Instead, she said, "I'll tell people you are a professor! You know how people always ask. Every time, they ask where you are and what you do!"

But that Friday I just needed to hear her voice. It did not matter what she would say.

"What time is it there again, Mei Mei? How come you are not in bed? Or out with friends?" She still calls me Mei Mei, younger sister, even though she is my mom, not my sister, and I am her only child. In China, men also call their sweethearts Mei Mei, or Jie Jie, if she's older. What a strange language. It used to embarrass me, but that night upon hearing those words, I wanted nothing more than to go back home to my mom. I was all of a sudden so tired.

"Mama, your trip to China, when is it? I think I would like to come."

"Tai hao la, wonderful!" She never stopped talking to me in Mandarin, even after I began talking to her in English only, starting in kindergarten.

If my mother was surprised, I couldn't hear it in her voice. During Christmas break, when I visited home, she'd asked me if I would like to join her, and I had said that I would be too busy.

"But you don't have classes in the summer! Teachers get summer off!"

"I need summer to catch up on scholarly work, Ma. I need to read, write, and go to conferences."

I was thankful that she did not ask why I changed my mind.

"How long can you come? How much time will you be able to take off? When does school start in the fall?"

"Well, I don't need to worry about that at the moment."

"What's wrong?" She sounded worried.

"I'll tell you the whole story, Mom, when I see you."

In the weeks leading up to finals, I went out with various groups of friends and colleagues to say goodbye. I did not mention my firing in my classes, but some students found out and they started to show up at these parties, too. At some of the parties, too many people bought me drinks, and a couple of under-aged students were kicked out of the bars. I decided it was best to leave as soon as I could. I was sad to leave my colleagues, friends, and students, but I had never liked to linger around for a dragged-on farewell. Except for Harriton. I wrote to him to tell him I was fired. I told him that I was going to China. I wondered if he missed me, because I missed *him* terribly. There was no reply.

I sublet my apartment and flew to LA as soon as I turned in final grades.

"Oh Mei Mei, how thin you are! Your hair is like hay!" My mom hugged me tightly. "You still have not learned to take care of yourself! When are you going to move back here? I can't take care of you when you are so far away, in the middle of nowhere!"

She, on the other hand, looked great. She had always been a beautiful woman. I was worried, after my father passed away in 2012, that Mom would have a hard time adjusting. I thought about moving back to California, but that would have meant being further away from Harriton, who lived on the East Coast. It would not have made any difference since we didn't visit each other, yet where Harriton was concerned, I was all heart and no brain.

But Mom adjusted well. She went on many dates, always white men. I was secretly relieved that nothing turned out to be serious. She went on a cross-England hiking trip, a cruise to South America, snorkeling in Hawaii, and took yearly trips to China. One year she went on a cruise to Southeast Asia with my aunt Daisy, her older sister. Now she stood in front of me, a properly tanned, slim Californian woman with perfectly dyed hair. I didn't think people would believe that she just turned seventy. I believed that they would say she was my Jie Jie.

By the time I showered and sat down at the dinner table, my mom had laid out a full banquet of my favorite Sichuan food: hot boiled fish filet, Maopo tofu, garlic Chinese water spinach, and tomato soup with egg drops. She piled the dishes on my plate.

"You know, Mom, we have Chinatown in Chicago," I joked. "Lao Sze Chuan is almost as good as your cooking, and Ma Po in Naperville is pretty decent, too!"

"I don't think so! Otherwise, how can you be so thin?" she chided.

I didn't tell her that I hadn't paid attention to whatever food I was putting in my mouth, if I ate at all, since I learned I was fired in March. It was late May now.

Instead, I asked her about the trip.

"Ah, I bought tickets for us as soon as you called me. You know how prices of tickets jump up on June first. I managed to get us tickets to fly out on May thirtieth. Direct flight from LA to Chengdu. A new route."

"That sounds wonderful. No more hopping on another plane in Beijing or Shanghai."

"That's right. Hong-mei and her husband will pick us at the airport, and we'll drive to Three Rivers."

Three Rivers was my mom's hometown, where my aunt still lived. Hong-mei, Red Plum Blossom, was my cousin. The women in my mom's family were all named after flowers: my aunt Daisy, and my mom Lily. The exception was grandma Pearl. Pearl's mother, my great-grandmother, was Iris. Hong-mei had a color prefix because she was born in 1968, five years before me. Red was *the* color then, in the height of the Cultural Revolution.

"Tai hao la!" I said. I only see Hong-mei once every few years. Born and raised and still living in Three Rivers, she is outgoing, sweet, and bubbly. I was born and raised in LA, shy, and bookish. But somehow when I visit, we take to each other immediately, as if we met for coffee at the corner shop every day. We were connected by an invisible thread through time and space. We understood each other in some mysterious way. Her husband Shan—his name was the word for "mountain," which suited him perfectly, as he was reliable and steady as one—had the best Chinese jokes. Would they be surprised if I stayed longer this time? I was not ready to let them know I was fired. Two weeks were as long as I had stayed in the past.

After dinner, my mom and I stood next to each other in the kitchen, cleaning dishes as we always did: she cleaned and rinsed, and I dried and put dishes away. Halfway through, my mom asked me what I meant on the phone when I said I didn't need to worry about going back to school in the fall semester. I sensed that she had guessed, and she had waited for a time when I was relaxed to ask me.

"They let me go," I said. "The budget was tight, and they were trimming the faculty numbers. Thirteen were let go."

"What!" My mom stopped her gloved hands and turned to me. "Unbelievable! Even tenured faculty? I thought you couldn't fire tenured faculty."

"Yep." I shrugged. "I know. But this is considered workforce reduction due to budget cuts. I was low on the seniority rank."

"Well," she said, her hands still held up, as the suds started to drip. I was sure that she would hug me had she not donned those gloves. "That was their loss, but my gain. You deserve a long vacation. We'll have a great time in China, and after that, you can figure out what you want to do. Promise to look for something on the West Coast, will you?"

"Yes, Mom, I promise."

It was a good thing I had never mentioned Harriton to her. I'd been worried that she would scold me for having an affair with a married man. Now I was glad I didn't have to explain why Harriton didn't fight for me. I was sure she would say, "Why won't he leave his wife if he loves you as he says?" Things had always been more complicated for me than for her. As much as I love my mom, taking a *long* trip together would not have been something I chose had I not wanted to get away so desperately. I needed to be somewhere far from Chicago, from Harriton, and my ancestral country with its different time zone, language, and culture seemed the perfect place.

#

Several weeks passed. My mom was happy that she had "put some color" in my cheeks by stuffing me with food on a daily basis. It was finally the day to leave for Chengdu. Our luggage had been getting lighter each time as we visited China.

When I was younger, we brought various items that were hard to come by on the mainland: cameras, watches, electronic appliances, anything that was allowed on an airplane and could be stuffed into our suitcases. Now, everything is available there, and cheaper, except for designer brands that were not fake. I decided to bring Hong-mei a small plum-colored Kate Spade shoulder bag.

As soon as we finished the first meal on the plane, I tried to get some sleep. The cabin was dim. Most people, including my mom, next to me on the aisle seat, were already in their reclined positions, sleeping, or at least trying to. The teenagers had their headphones on and tablets in hand. The plane was filled to the brim. I was thankful that Mom paid extra for more legroom.

I put on my sleep mask and the noise-canceling headphone. I had learned from my past traveling experience that having as much sleep as possible was vital in reducing jet lag. Usually, I had no trouble sleeping on an airplane, good, dreamless sleep.

But this time, I had the strange sensation of being nowhere: suspended in mid-air, not able to go back where I came from, and yet not able to see where I was going.

And in the darkness and the muffled silence, everything that surfaced in my brain became amplified.

I saw Harriton and his wife walking down a flower-strewn path, he in a pale blue dress shirt and she a lovely flowy yellow dress. I was in the shadow of an enormous cypress tree, trying to hide. But Harriton turned and looked straight in my eyes. "Sorry, can't walk with you. You are fired," he said and poof, they were gone.

I started to run, humiliated. Then the running turned into flying. All of a sudden I was in front of a tall stone building, a place I had never been to before. It was Harriton's campus! I recognized the building because I had seen it in the pictures he sent me. But the grass, the trees, the flowers, they were from *my* campus. In my confusion, I heard someone calling from the top of a handsome, tall building, "R-o-s-e! H-e-r-e! I know you are coming. Wait for me!"

I waited, my heart thumping in my throat. That voice was clearly Harriton's, even though I could not see him.

But when that voice got close enough, I realized it was not Harriton. It was a huge, jet-black crow, its wings spreading wide, its eyes shining, its claws stretching out to grab me. I tried to run but could not move. I screamed, but no sound came out. I closed my eyes and was prepared to give myself to loss when I was plucked up and taken above the clouds.

It was my grandma Pearl who saved me. I last saw her in 1993, shortly before she passed away. "Grandma Pearl! Grandma Pearl! Where did you come from?" I asked.

"Oh, Meigui!" she called out my Chinese name. "My dear child, how I have missed you! Please, go to the temple and find my grandmother. She has been lonely and sad for too long!"

"What are you talking about, Grandma Pearl? Do you mean Great-Grandma Iris?" The wind was rushing by, and I was afraid I had not heard her correctly. I was afraid I could not understand her Chongqing dialect.

"No, not my mom. My grandma! Wode Waipo! My grandma! My grandma...!"

"What's her name? What does she look like?' I was getting desperate as I lowered to the ground.

"Don't drop me, Grandma Pearl!" I screamed.

26

#

"Rose, Rose!" Someone was shaking me and removing my mask and headphones. "Wake up, Mei Mei!"

The rumbling sound of the engine flooded my ears and the cabin lights went on, blinding me.

My mother was the one waking me up, and she looked worried. A couple of people stared at us. They quickly turned their heads when they saw me staring back.

I wiped the sweat from my forehead and caught my breath.

"I had a nightmare. I saw Grandma Pearl, and she told me to look for her grandmother."

My mom fixed a stunned gaze on me. Before she said anything, the loudspeaker announced that all passengers needed to have their seat belts fastened, their chairs in the upright position, and their tray tables stowed away. We were about to land in Chengdu.

Good, no more weird dreams, I thought. Then I heard my mom.

"Rose, now you, too, had the dream," she said, putting up her chair.

CHAPTER 4
THREE RIVERS AND CLOUD GATE, 1903,
PURE BRIGHTNESS

It had been five years since A-mei, Jasmine and Tiger came to Three Rivers. Jasmine grew from a little country child to a big-eyed city girl. She learned from Iris, whom she called Jie Jie, the ways of being a proper young lady raised in a well-to-do family. She was comforted by You-jun in her early days in the Han household, when she felt so unrefined, so clumsy, and so out of place, compared to the elegance and ease of Iris.

"Don't worry," You-jun often said to her. "Iris is your tutor, but I'm your protector. Nobody dares to say anything bad about you, as long as I'm here." This got Jasmine through all her worries. She did not know how she could be without You-jun. And You-jun did not know what he would do without Jasmine. Iris was good, but she was like a little grown-up, and she had no interest in anything he and Jian-da liked, such as firefly catching and cricket fighting. But Jasmine was different. She followed the boys around and loved everything they did.

Jasmine's baba visited during less busy times of his farming, bringing fresh sweet potatoes, corn, and sticky rice, but Jasmine, A-mei, and Little Tiger had not been back to Cloud Gate. Even in a place like the Three Rivers, far from Beijing and the province's capital of Chengdu, far from the Boxer uprising, one had to be very careful traveling those days, according to Master Han. The Boxers and their followers hated the Westerners, the foreign devils whom they called the "Old Hairs" because of the scandalously thick body hair that covered not only their heads, legs,

29

and arms, but also their chests and backs. The Chinese people who had converted to Christianity were called the "Second Hairs."

Master Han was no Second Hair, but it was well known that he had done business with the Old Hairs and Second Hairs. Therefore, just to be cautious, he had limited his travel in the past several years to the most essential business trips, which were still plenty. Sweeping the tombs of the ancestors and burning incense in Cloud Gate had all been done by Jasmine's baba and relatives who lived in the village.

But this year, Master Han announced after the New Year that the family would make a trip to their ancestral hometown to sweep the tombs. The Boxer Rebellion had ended two years ago. The wind had been calm and rain plenty after that. Master Han decided that society was peaceful and the family was prosperous. It was time to give praises where they were due: the blessings of their ancestors.

The household was busy for two months, preparing for the trip. Lady Han made a list of items to bring to all the relatives: silk for women, foreign tobacco for men, trinkets for children, and red envelopes with money inside for all. She bought the best incense she could find in the city to offer to the Guanyin Temple, the best-crafted paper houses and paper money to offer to the ancestors in the afterworld, and an entire roll of the best red silk to drape over the Guanyin statue in the temple.

The children were as excited as the adults. Every day they asked when it was time to go.

Finally, four days before the Pure Brightness Day, Master Han announced that the following day would be an auspicious day to travel to Cloud Gate. The family would set out as soon as breakfast was done. Old Lady Han, Master Han's mother had gone to the Diaoyu Temple in the city and planned to stay there for half a month. The family could leave town without worrying about taking care of the old lady. Jian-da wanted to go, too, but his mother was under the weather, and being a good filial son, even at his age, he knew he should stay home with her.

Jasmine could not fall asleep that night.

"Jie Jie," she whispered after the whole house was quiet. Her bed was on the opposite side of the room. The girls had shared a room since Jasmine's arrival five years ago. Lady Han proposed that they have separate rooms as they got older, but the girls chose to stay together. They liked to lie on their beds and talk.

Iris was just about to fall asleep when Jasmine called her. "What time is it? Are you still not sleeping?" she asked, half-awake.

"I just heard the watchmen beating their gong and clipper the second time. But I can't sleep. I'm thinking about Cloud Gate," Jasmine said.

"What about?" Iris whispered.

"I don't remember what it is like," Jasmine whispered back.

"That's all right. We'll find out soon enough. Mother said it was a fine village, a little too far from Three Rivers, but beautiful. She said the Guanyin Temple was her favorite temple in the whole world. Now go to sleep. We've got to get up early."

But Jasmine stared at the ceiling in the dark for a long time. Guanyin Temple, tombs, fields, and a large pond of fish and lotus flowers. . . she tried to picture them as she last saw them when she was a young child, before finally drifting off when the watchmen beat their instruments for the third time.

In the morning, Iris tried to wake up Jasmine. "Mei Mei!" She gently poked Jasmine. "It's time to get up!"

Jasmine mumbled something and turned to face the wall, still not awake.

Iris had finished braiding her hair into two long ropes that hung to the small of her back. She wore a simple lilac-colored jacket with lotus leaf trimming and matching pants. Unlike Jasmine, she couldn't sleep past the break of dawn.

Iris was about to shake Jasmine again when the door swung open with a loud bang. In came Iris'sbrother You-jun and Jasmine's brother Tiger, laughing and shouting, "The sun is way up on the bamboo tops now, sisters!"

Jasmine jumped up as if being stung by a bee. "Mother, Lady Han, I'm coming!" she cried.

Iris smiled. You-jun and Tiger burst into laughter. The boys were both ten. They were so rambunctious that they annoyed and amused the girls equally.

Iris, being the oldest, put on a straight face and said to the boys, "Okay, okay, boys, stop being so naughty. You-jun and Tiger, off you go. Jasmine and I will be there in a minute."

The boys stuck their tongues out and turned around. Jasmine was embarrassed. She hurried to put on her new outfit, similar to what Iris was wearing, but in an apple green color. Iris helped Jasmine braid her hair. They joined the family in the dining hall. They bowed to Master and Lady Han, trying to show their best manners. Even their brothers were behaving as perfect little gentlemen in front of the parents, especially Master Han. This was a rare occasion as Master Han was having a meal at the same table with them.

After breakfast, everyone went to the front courtyard. Two sedan chairs were waiting, one for Lady Han and A-mei, and one for Iris and Jasmine. But A-mei insisted on walking with the men.

"I don't have bound feet," she said, "and I can keep an eye on the boys.

It is not too far to the pier."

"I wish my feet were not bound either, just like Mama," Jasmine whispered to Iris.

"Don't say that," Iris scolded Jasmine, also whispering. "Your mama bound your feet so you are not just a country girl who has to do manual labor. She did this so you are now a proper city girl from a nice family."

The caravan walked down the winding steps to the river pier. The rising sun dispersed the morning fog. The river seemed to be shaking off a fine mist, like a beauty just waking from a leisurely nap. The silhouettes of houses, trees, and boats of various sizes were like a painting in the morning mist, accompanied by a symphony of the city sounds: shouting and yelling to get passengers on board, to sell freshly steamed sweet buns and eggs boiled in tea, and to call back children who had become excited and run away.

The luggage was loaded onto a rented passenger boat, bigger than a fishing boat. Then it was time to board. Iris and Jasmine held hands and kept up with Master Han. The boys were so rowdy that they had to be separated. Lady Han and A-mei each held the hand of her son.

It was a smooth sail on the river. Iris and Jasmine loved the songs the tow men sang. The tow men pulled the boats onshore when the vessels came to a stretch of the river that was too fast for the rowing oars alone. The British merchant Archibald Little had tried and successfully navigated parts of Yangtze river with his steamer Lee-Chuan in1898, the year Jasmine came to live in Three Rivers, but it would be another twenty years before there was a passenger steamer between Three Rivers and Cloud Gate.

By lunchtime, they arrived at Cloud Gate. As Lady Han had said, Cloud Gate was a fine village. It was a little far from Three Rivers, for sure, but it had the best Feng Shui. The village faced the river and was backed by the White Cloud Mountains. A majestic archway welcomed the visitors. The archway was carved out of white limestone and marble, with intricate patterns. A pair of dragons nested over clouds on the top, golden carps jumped over the dragon's gate, and boys and girls bearing various kinds of fruits sat on lotus flowers. The village had fertile soil and plenty of water to produce the best rice and other crops in the county. The village also attracted visitors to its famous Guanyin Temple, perching on a cliff at the top of White Cloud Mountain. As they got closer, the great excitement ignited Jasmine's memories, and she pointed out things she remembered to Iris, who marveled at the different kinds of beauty of the countryside and wanted to notice everything so she would never forget. Jasmine wanted to tell You-jun everything, too, but the mothers hung tight to their sons, and she did not get the chance.

There were no sedan chairs in the village, only huagan, a chair mounted on two bamboo poles carried by two men. Six men carried three huagans to take Lady Han and the girls to the Wang house. Master and A-mei with her big feet walked, two boys in tow.

The Wang House was a simple construction of bamboo, but it was clean and spacious. Old Wang had prepared a hearty lunch for the guests. "Nothing fancy here at our humble village," he said, "just some simple country eats. I must beg your forgiveness for such an unrefined, homely meal!"

"Aww, Brother Wang, you are too modest," said Master Han. "The dishes may not be so fancy, but the vegetables were freshly picked this morning, the rice was from the newest crop, the fish was still moving before being scaled, and the roosters and hens were feasting on worms and grains this morning! And I see you also have home-brewed rice wine! City people don't always have the good fortune to enjoy such freshness and such unadulterated flavors."

The two men held up their clay mugs, poured the wine down their throats, and slugged it down in one gulp. Then they picked up their chopsticks, each taking a piece of chicken and putting it on top of the rice in the other's bowl. With this as a signal for others to eat, the boys immediately started to shovel down what was in front of them. "You boys must be so hungry after such a long boat ride!" Lady Han and A-Mei laughed.

After lunch, Master and Lady Han retreated to the guest room for a mid-day nap. Master Han was a firm believer in the ancient Traditional Chinese Medicine and Taoism, which considered a quick nap after lunch in the middle of the day essential to restore and nourish one's Yin and Yang and sharpen one's mind. A-mei put the boys down, and after they fell asleep, she went to find her husband, and they too, retreated for some rest. Everyone hoped to have a refreshed face when visiting their ancestors.

Iris and Jasmine did not want to lie down. "I'll show you the lotus pond," said Jasmine.

"Are there lotus flowers now? So early in the spring?" asked Iris.

"I don't know," said Jasmine. "Let's go see."

The lotus pond was Jasmine's favorite place. There were water lilies, lotus flowers, carps, ducks, and geese. The rivers in the city were not the same.

The girls tiptoed out. It would be a challenge for them to walk that far, but the allure of the lotus pond was strong enough that they slowly trudged forward. The spring air was cool, even in the afternoon, but by the time they got to the pond, they both had tiny droplets of sweat on their foreheads and their noses. They sat down under a willow tree, on the edge of the pond, fanning themselves with their hands. There were no lotus flowers and no fish in sight, but the water was clear, like a mirror reflecting the white clouds. A mother goose floated around with her goslings.

"Goose, goose, goose, bend your necks, sing to the sky," Iris said, clapping her hands.

"White feather float on emerald water, red feet stir the wave clear!" Jasmine finished the poem, joining the clapping. They giggled.

"This really is the best place, Mei Mei! As if Luo Bing Wang himself had come here to write this poem!" Iris said.

"Let's ask Master Han and baba to bring us here in the summer to see the lotus flowers and water lilies. The entire pond will be covered."

"I can't wait," Iris said.

"I'm so glad you are here, Jie Jie," said Jasmine.

"Me too," said Iris, stroking Jasmine's hair.

They leaned on the willow tree, picking up pebbles around their feet and throwing them into the pond to watch the ripples spreading across the surface. Jasmine laid her head on Iris'sshoulder, and they went quiet.

"Ha! You are here!" A loud voice came from behind the willow tree, and the girls jumped.

"You-jun, is that you?" Iris turned around. "You scared us! What are you doing here? You are supposed to be napping!"

You-jun and Tiger emerged, face and hands dirty. They had been playing along the way. "Oh, that. What are *you* two doing here? We followed you girls as soon as you left the house. It's nice out here!"

Jasmine stood and took hold of Tiger's hand. "We probably should go back before Lady and Mother get mad. Come on, You-jun!"

"I'll just take a quick dip in the pond. I'm getting hot," You-jun said, starting to remove his jacket.

"You can't swim here, You-jun!" both girls said, alarmed.

"Oh yes I can! I'm a good swimmer!" You-jun smiled.

"You-jun!" Iris said again, "remember the stories of kids drowning? Baba says people who drown are always good swimmers! People who don't know how to swim will stay away from water in the first place. Baba says you can't go in the water unless he's with you!"

"Oh, just a little bit!" He stripped down to his underpants. "Kids drown in the rivers because the river water moves fast and there are underwater whirlpools that drag them in. This is different. It's just a little pond. Don't tell mother, Iris! By the time we get back, I will be dried. Are you coming or not, Tiger?"

"Coming, coming." Tiger had a big grin on his face. He had also stripped down to his underpants, while the girls stared at You-jun. The boys had planned this since Tiger told You-jun about the pond back in Three Rivers.

You-jun and Tiger ran towards the pond and jumped in like two cannonballs. The mother goose and her babies scattered, protesting with loud honking and flapping their wings.

Iris and Jasmine put their hands to their mouths so they wouldn't scream. They stared at the pond and saw only bubbles emerging from where the boys went in. They seemed to have vanished under the water.

Jasmine turned to Iris. "Oh, Jie Jie! What do we do now?"

Iris bit her lip. She cupped her mouth with her hands to make a trumpet and called out, in a trembling voice, "You-jun! Tiger! Get out, right this moment! I will tell Mother, and I will go to Father and tell him myself! Out! Now!"

After a stillness that seemed to last for an eternity, Tiger sprang up, followed by You-jun, both taking in deep gulps of fresh air. They were almost at the other side of the pond. They waved at the girls and started swimming back, this time with their heads above the water.

Iris sighed in relief. She turned to Jasmine and found her in tears. "It's all right now." Iris put her arm around Jasmine. "I'm sure they won't do it again."

When the boys came back to shore and dressed, Jasmine ran up to You-jun and said, emphasizing each word as if squeezing them out of her mouth, "If you did not come back, I would have jumped in to find you."

You-jun wiped the tears on Jasmine's face, looked her straight in the eye, and said in a similar fashion, "Jasmine, I will always come back to you."

Iris felt a shiver run through her spine. Their words. Their tones. She did not like those. This excursion to the pond had turned out to be too much. "Let's hurry back, everyone," she said.

The girls insisted on walking, but they were tired and worried that it was getting late. They finally relented and let their brothers carry them on their backs.

Lady Han and A-mei were not happy about the kids being gone. But when they returned there was no time to scold them. The right time to visit the ancestors' tombs was fast approaching. Everyone must be ready and go immediately.

They arrived at the adjacent Han and Wang family plots after a short walk from the Wang house. They laid out a banquet for the ancestors to enjoy: an abundance of pork, chicken, fish, rice, vegetables, fruits, and sweets. They burned incense and candles. They burned bundles of paper money as well; just because the ancestors didn't have that much to spend when they were alive didn't mean they should suffer the same fate in the afterworld. They burned paper houses and carriages so the ancestors could live and travel comfortably. Lastly, they burned notes on which their names were written to let the ancestors know who had made the pious offerings, to ask for blessing and protection. Each of them had been taught since an early age that filial piety was the most important of all virtues, which meant to always listen to one's parents and do what they said when they were alive, and to always provide the best offering one could afford when they were dead.

Iris lowered her forehead to kowtow. She knelt on her hands and knees, her head touching the cool slab of stone in front of the tombs. She again thought about the afternoon over the pond. The late afternoon wind made her shudder. She asked her ancestors for protection and for blessings.

She stayed like that for a long time, just like her mother a few steps away.

CHAPTER 5
CHENGDU AND THREE RIVERS, 2017

I had flown in and out of Chengdu Shuangliu Airport each time when I came to Sichuan province, my mother's homeland. It was like any mid-sized airport in the U.S., and it seemed to be getting more crowded each time. There were fewer international flights, compared to Beijing or Shanghai, however, so we breezed through customs.

The whole time I wanted to ask Mom what she meant when she said "Rose, now you, too, had the dream." But I could not seem to find the right moment.

As soon as we exited the terminal, I heard a familiar voice. "Auntie! Mei Mei!" It was the voice of my cousin Hong-mei, Red Plum. It was the warm and sweet voice that welcomed me back to my ancestral home.

Hong-mei was five years older, but you couldn't tell. Maybe it was her haircut. She had what I called mushroom hair: blunt, even bangs just above the eyebrows, and a round, short bob that covered the rest of her head like a mushroom. The first time I saw her with the haircut, I almost laughed at the childishness. But, as I got used to it, I had to say that the hair suited her well. Her wide and long eyes were full of sparkles, like a child, and her energy and enthusiasm were also like that of a child. Her youthful appearance might also have been due in part to her slender figure. Almost all the Chinese women I met were wonderfully slender, if a bit too pale for my taste.

We embraced each other. She squeezed me. Then she let me go and pulled my mother in for a tight hug.

"Auntie, Mei Mei, how was the trip? Did you get any rest? Such a long trip! Now let me and Shan take care of you! Just relax as soon as we get in the car." Hong-mei hooked her arms to our elbows so we walked as a three-person tandem.

"Hi Auntie, hi Rose, let me." Shan, Hong-mei's husband, pushed a luggage cart and insisted on taking our carry-on bags, which we piled into the cart.

"You both look so great! Thanks for coming all the way to pick us up," I said.

"Of course! Not worth mentioning at all! You came all the way here. Of course we will take care of you," Shan said. Good old Shan. I pushed Harriton's face out of my head.

While we waited for the checked luggage to arrive, Hong-mei took both my hands and sized me up. "Aya, Mei Mei, how come you lost so much weight since I last saw you? Was it five years ago? How have you been? Working too much? We all like to be thin, but you are way too skinny now! We'll have to feed you some good food here! Right, Auntie?"

My mom nodded. "Yes, yes! That's what I've been telling Rose. This will be a nice vacation for her."

I smiled. I was glad the topic quickly went to how to feed me instead of what was troubling me. Instead of my needing someone like Shan to "take care" of me.

Until I started high school, I thought all mothers were like my mother. My mother loved me to death, and she would not hesitate to give me her liver or her kidney to save me if needed. But she was also ruthless in her comments about my appearance and my weight.

In high school, I became friends with a couple of white girls and visited their houses frequently. I was stunned to see how affectionate white mothers were. I could not imagine that any one of them would have said, "Your face is so round! It's almost flat," or "You have a thick waist naturally, and dieting won't do anything to it." I asked my friends, and my suspicion was confirmed.

I was resentful and could not understand why my mother would be so cruel in her words, but so loving in her action. Then I met my families in China.

They were all like my mother, at least the older ones.

The tailor lady who sewed my qipao that my mom and aunt insisted I have, which I dutifully brought with me on this trip so I might wear it if we went somewhere fancy, commented on my "big bosom," which she said was "fat for a girl your size." She had to make an unusual cut just for me.

My aunt usually wondered why I was so dark. "A pale skin covers all the flaws a girl has," she said. "At least that is what the Chinese idiom says." I told her I had a tan, and I had intentionally gone sunbathing to achieve that color. Then she said, "But your undertone is yellow, not pink, and a tan only makes you look old, as if you have been doing hard labor your whole life!"

My cousin did not make as many blunt comments. She was close to my age, a newer generation. But even she sometimes would tell me, point-blank, whether I was too fat or too skinny.

I began to know that these comments were like the way we talked about weather in the Midwest, only a bit more intimate and only to show one cared about a person.

"Definitely, my mouth waters just thinking about the hot pot!" I said. I was relieved, once again, that she didn't ask why I had time to visit after five years.

We got in their car, a brand-new BMW equipped with GPS and a dashboard camera. "Nice ride! It's a different car than last time," I said.

"Oh, we still have the other one. I drive that one in town. Shan drives this one since he's a better driver!" Hong-mei said sheepishly.

Shan suggested that we stop and have lunch before heading to Three Rivers.

"It's lunch hour now, and the three-ring road will be jammed like the parking lot of a supermarket before Chinese New Year. If we eat lunch now, we will avoid the traffic jam and have an easier time getting to G43 and G93." These were the interstate highways from Chengdu to Three Rivers, Hong-mei explained.

Hong-mei asked Mom and me what kinds of food we would like. "Dandan noodle," I said without thinking. Dandan noodle was my go-to meal when I arrived in Chengdu. The spiciness of hot chili and Sichuan peppercorn, combined with the richness of stir-fried ground pork and the freshness of thinly sliced scallion and cucumber, all poured over a bowl of freshly made thin noodles, was the flavor that woke up my American taste buds dulled by the blandness of Midwestern meat and potatoes.

"That sounds great! I know just the place to go." Shan started the engine.

I didn't know that a quick lunch place could be so fancy: white linen table cloth, high-back chairs covered by the same fabric, and young women in qipao uniforms attending the table.

"This is a renovated shop of one of the most famous Small Eats restaurants," Hong-mei said. "In addition to Dandan noodle, we could also sample a couple of other famous dishes: dumplings of the Zhong Family, wonton of the Long Family, and sticky rice ball with sesame pastes and sugar filling from the Nai Family."

While we waited for the food, my mother told the story she told every time we came to visit.

I was three or four at the time of my first visit to China. China was poor then and there were hungry people everywhere. My aunt, my mother, and I had gone into some roadside noodle shop for a bowl of noodles.

We sat down at a small table and the server brought three bowls of steaming noodles in pork broth. As soon as he set the bowls down on the wobbly wooden table, a beggar who had been lingering around the door rushed over and put his hands in the bowl in front of me.

"Rose screamed," my mom said. "We knew the beggar did that so we had no choice but to give him the whole bowl of noodles. He was willing to burn his fingers in hot broth, just so that he could have something to eat, probably for the first time in a few days. I wanted to buy him another bowl, but my sister said if I started that, there would be a mob of them all wanting me to buy them noodles, and we would never get out of there. Plus, Rose continued to scream and refused to stay in that place and eat anything afterward. So we hurried out. We were lucky that at least nobody tried to run with our suitcases. We gave our other two bowls of noodles to the beggars as well—yes, more of them had come. Word had traveled fast on the streets." She paused and sipped her green tea.

"You had to open the pack of Danish cookies you brought home for relatives because I was so hungry and frightened, I couldn't stop crying," I finished her story. I used to feel a bit embarrassed by the story and my mom's re-telling of it. But strangely this time they both felt like comforts. I suddenly became aware of how far I was from Chicago. And I would be here for a while. That was space and time. There was nothing that couldn't be changed and erased by space and time.

"Things are so different now!" Hong-mei said. "I remember it was such a trek from Chengdu to Three Rivers. We would sit on a train all night from Chengdu to Chongqing, and then it took a bus a couple of hours to get to Three Rivers. The train and bus were always crowded, so we carried small plastic folding stools with us. I remember sitting on the folding stool in the middle of an aisle of a crowded bus, feeling so sick. Now the car ride from Chengdu to Three Rivers is only about four hours, and it's even quicker on the speed train, about two hours! It's amazing. I keep telling Elsie she's so lucky." Elsie was Hong-mei and Shan's daughter.

"How's Elsie? She likes London?" my mom asked. "It's so amazing she goes to school there now!"

"She loves it there. Very busy and stressed out but loves it. She asked me to say hi, and she's hoping to come back later in the summer. She's wondering if you are still around when she comes back."

"Oh, we're not in a hurry to go back, unless you guys are tired of us!"

My mom laughed, and I thought she glanced at me. I turned around to pretend to look at the paintings on the wall. It occurred to me that the longer I stayed, the more likely I had to answer all the questions why I could stay for so long. Maybe I ought to get back to the States, or maybe just go somewhere else, Cambodia, Laos. Somewhere, before too long. Luckily, the food came just then.

After lunch, as Shan drove us out of Chengdu, we passed a high-rise with the advertisement of a smiling LeBron James taking up its entire sidewall. He was dribbling a ball and selling Nike shoes to the masses. Another advertisement on the side of another tall building depicted Leonardo DiCaprio selling used cars! Yes, I thought, things had changed. Chengdu was a big city and reminded me of Chicago. Three Rivers was much smaller. I couldn't wait to go there.

I was just about to drift into a nap—it was about midnight LA time—when my mom said, "Rose had the dream. On the airplane."

Hong-mei, who was sitting in the front passenger seat, turned around to face me in the backseat, while Shan made the car sway.

"Did you, Rose?" Hong-mei asked.

"I had a dream, yes, a weird one, you might say."

"What was in the dream? Was it Grandma Pearl?" Hong-mei asked.

This chased away the sleepiness I had started to feel.

"How in the world...how did you know?" I hoped she didn't know the other part of the dream, the part with Harriton. "Mom, did you..." But how could she have told Hong-mei? We were in each other's company the entire time.

"Rose, I know because I had the same dream. Or at least we think it's the same dream," Hong-mei said.

"And I had one a few years ago," said Mom.

"And my mom, too," said Hong-mei.

"So the women in the family all had the same dream?" I was incredulous. This had to be one of those tall tales my mother and Aunt Daisy made up. But I trusted Hong-mei.

As if reading my mind, Hong-mei said, "I couldn't believe it myself when I first heard about it. But mom told me her dream before I told her mine, and they were almost identical: our grandmas asking us to go look for someone the family doesn't remember! I think in my dream Grandma Pearl asked for her own grandmother. But who was she? Grandma Pearl never mentioned her when she was alive. It was very confusing."

"In the dreams we had," my mom said, "me and Daisy, it was our grandmother, your great-grandma Iris. Before Iris passed away, she tried to sit Daisy and me down and tell us something. But that was during the Cultural Revolution—1967 or 68. I think. Ah yes, it must be 1967 because

41

Hong-mei was born in 1968, and it was the year before that—and we were afraid the old stories would get us in trouble. We were too young to know better. I was 22, and Daisy was 24."

"So you didn't listen?" I asked.

"Well, I don't remember. We might have pretended to listen but only let the words go in one ear and out the other."

"So Grandma Pearl asked us to look for her grandmother," I said, trying to figure out whom we should be looking for, "and, that would be…Iris's mother."

I looked over to my mom, and she nodded.

"But why? And how? And where? And why does no one remember her?" I continued. "Did anyone try to figure it out?"

"Well, dreams are just dreams. Even if by coincidence we all had similar ones. We are from the same family, and might have heard the same stories," my mom said.

But I was not convinced, and my sleep was gone.

Looking for an ancestor nobody knew? Was this why I got dumped and fired, so I could be here for that?

Something churned in my head. Yes, this is probably what I should do. Find out who this ancestor was. Solve a family mystery. Nothing would bring me out of my haze better than a good detective project that kept me busy. That is, if I didn't have to flee from questions about my job and boyfriend. If I didn't have to rush back to the States for a new job…or an email from Harriton…

CHAPTER 6
THREE RIVERS, 1905

The Beginning of Summer: the twentieth day of the fifth month and the seventh solar term of the twenty-four seasons. Summer begins.

It had been two years since the Han household visited the village of Cloud Gate, their ancestral hometown, to sweep the tombs of their ancestors and to visit the Guanyin Temple. Master Han decided that the family should make a yearly trip, as they could not have had such good fortune if not for the blessings of the ancestors and Guanyin, the Goddess of Mercy.

But they could not make the trip last year. The older Lady Han, Old Ancestor as she was called, was getting frail, and she died soon after the New Year. It was a good death: she was eighty-years old and died in her sleep. She had lived a good life, never having to worry about where her food would come from or whether she had proper clothing for different seasons. Her husband had been kind to her, and after he died, her son was respectful and always showed filial piety, most of all giving her a grandson, the strong, mischievous and smart You-jun, who grew bigger every day. Oh, how that old woman loved You-jun! She had been very devoted to the Buddha and the Huguo Temple, next to the Diaoyu Fortress, especially in her later years. All the incense and candles she had burned, all the sutras she had chanted, and all the money she had donated would surely carry her to Nirvana.

Such a blessed person in her old age had died in the best possible way, and this was something to celebrate, not to mourn. Yet Master Han did his best to show his grief. He ordered that for forty-nine days, no grandchildren, including the servants who were of the same generation as the grandchildren, could have haircuts. He wore black mourning clothes for one hundred days, and after that, did not wear anything red for six months. Because he had to attend his business, he could not stay near his mother's grave for a year as he would have liked—she was carried back to Cloud Gate to be buried in the family cemetery—but he did have a hut built next to the grave, and Old Wang went there regularly to burn incense and paper money.

Master Han also wrote notes when he was away. "My Dear Mother, Your Excellency," he wrote, "I beg your forgiveness for not being in the hut to keep you company. I make up for this by working diligently to provide for my family, your descendants, and I promise I will donate in your name to the temple." He signed the note "Your humble, grieving, and unworthy son," and asked Old Wang to burn the notes with the paper money. True to his word, Master Han made yearly donations to the Huguo Temple for the rest of his life. He also made donations to the Guanyin Temple in Cloud Gate, where his wife frequented. His mother and his wife, both devoted lay Buddhists, visited different temples, places they found their separate comforts.

Lady Han did what was expected of a good daughter-in-law. She and Iris wore white mourning clothes and white sackcloth hoods on their heads. She wailed during the wake and the funeral, and no one who heard that wailing could be spared tears. "What a good daughter-in-law! Not only did she give a grandson to her mother-in-law, but she loved her so much as well!" said the people in Three Rivers.

No one other than Lady Han and A-mei knew the truth. Only they remembered the years when the old woman had cast unpleasant looks on her daughter-in-law. The first grandchild was a girl. Even though the Han family had enough to feed the household, it was still a waste to feed a girl, who would not bear the family name. Not only that, when marrying her off later, the family had to pay for a dowry. And a married daughter was like a dumped bucket of water, spilled, gone, of no more value to the family. Then Lady Han was pregnant again, and everyone had hoped that this time it was a boy. It was a girl again. The baby died at birth, and Lady Han had the good sense to dispose of it before anyone could see it.

In the years after the baby died, the old woman made numerous innuendoes about the fact that her daughter-in-law had not given her a grandson.

"The old hen is getting more useless each day! Look at all the good rice we feed her; not even a single good egg she can give us!" This was a typical remark by the old woman. She hinted a couple of times to her son for him to take in a concubine so she could have a grandson. He always nodded but was too busy with his business to actually do it. Or at least that was what he told his mother. Lady Han was grateful to her husband's devotion, but she felt the urgency of having a son. How long could Master Han hold off his mother's request before he gave in? Oh how much she, as his wife, wanted to please him by giving him a son!

The old woman did not like Iris. From an early age, Iris learned that she needed to be as quiet as a mouse when her grandmother was in the vicinity, or better yet, she should simply stay in her room, so she wouldn't cause her grandmother a headache by appearing in front of her.

Lady Han kept her head down and her hands busy with needlework and other household work. She set up a small altar for Guanyin in her room. She draped a small table with red velvet cloth and carefully put a small Guanyin statue, about three inches tall and made of white porcelain, on the table. The statue was a gift from her husband when he came home from one of his trips. In front of the statue, she laid a small bronze incense burner.

And she prayed and prayed. She burned bundles upon bundles of incense. She saved and donated her allowance to the Guanyin Temple in Cloud Gate and to the Huguo Temple near Diaoyu Fortress.

And finally, Guanyin heard her prayers and You-jun was born. All was good, and all was forgiven.

This first year without her mother-in-law, Lady Han went to the village of Cloud Gate as the new lady of the house and there was no one above her anymore. But her nature was gentle, and she had been taught the Confucian moral code for women since she was a young girl: the three obeys—obey her father before getting married, her husband after getting married, and her son if her husband died—and the four virtues, morality, physical charm, propriety in speech, and efficiency in needlework. All these made her retain her calmness during times of difficulty and her humbleness now. She was the same lady to all, even though she ascended to be the head of the internal affairs of the household. Her reputation in Three Rivers, Cloud Gate, and beyond was impeccable. All mothers-in-law wanted a daughter-in-law like her, and all young women wanted to be her.

The trip was uneventful until the visit to the temple. The adults kept the children on tight leashes this time, so there was no spontaneous trip to the Lotus Pond. Iris was scolded by her grandmother last time when the old woman heard what happened at the lotus pond, as if it were Iris'sfault that You-jun could have drowned, even though she was not the one who came up with the idea of visiting the pond and even though You-jun could swim well and he was not swimming in the rivers where the undercurrents could be dangerous for even skilled swimmers. Lady Han thought it was unfair but kept this opinion to herself.

To Lady Han's delight, it seemed that Iris was determined to stay out of any trouble this time. Iris was getting to the age when matchmakers started to show up at their doorstep, which she disliked intensely. Lady Han began to scrutinize everything about her: how loud she talked—too loud; how demure she was when she was presented to the matchmakers—not enough, as Iris tended to stare at those old women who had too much rouge on their cheeks, which made them look like clowns in an opera show. Nor was she modest enough either, as she would argue with You-jun and Jian-da, for she failed to see why she could not when she read the same books they did and was taught by the same teacher. Wasn't it she who had to help the boys when they failed to recite whatever difficult passages from the Analects or the Book of Songs the teacher assigned them? In fact, the old teacher had praised Iris and Jasmine for their sharp wits, "despite being female."

Lady Han was determined to find a good husband for Iris. So far no one suggested by the matchmakers had been able to live up to her standards. There was also the small problem of not being able to find any young men whose eight characters of birth time, Ba Zi, or Four Pillars of Destiny, matched with Iris. Ba Zi, calculated by the year, month, day, and hour of one's birth, gave insights to the interactions of the five basic elements of metal, wood, water, fire, and earth and their relationships with time and space, and thus illuminated one's personality, strength and weakness, fortune and luck, and for a girl, most important of all, whom to marry. What Lady Han didn't realize was that Iris was relieved that no match had been made for her. She did not like the thought of leaving home, leaving Jasmine. But still, she knew she was at the age that she could not go about freely as she did two years ago.

The day before they returned to Three Rivers, Lady Han, Iris, A-mei and Jasmine went to the Guanyin Temple on White Cloud Mountain. It was always a difficult trip. They climbed using their hands and bound feet to scale the narrow steps, slowly and carefully. After offering incense, putting money in the donation box, and kowtowing to the statue of Guanyin, they drew their lots.

They each took their turn. They bowed their heads and held their hands in prayer in front of their hearts. They prayed three times in silence, "Dear Guanyin, Goddess of Mercy, save me from suffering!" Then they told Guanyin, still in silence, their names, birth dates and times, ages, current addresses, and the questions they were asking for advice. Lastly, with their faith planted firmly in Her mercy, they held the thick bamboo tubes with the lots in their hands and shook them. Bamboo slips fell out of the tube, which they picked up with trembling hands and hearts.

They brought their bamboo slips to the nun sitting in the side chamber.

The room was very simple; a short desk was the only furniture. The nun sat behind the desk, cross-legged, on a straw mat. Eyes closed, she beat the wooden fish on the desk, "da, da, da," chanting a sutra. The women stood by the door and waited. After a few minutes, the nun opened her eyes. She was middle-aged, had a shaved head, and wore a simple brown linen kasaya.

"Amitabaha," the nun said, hands together at the heart, head bowing slightly. "Welcome, Benefactress Han."

"Amitabaha, Master Wise and Bright!" Lady Han returned the honor by repeating the gesture. Standing behind Lady Han, A-mei, Iris, and Jasmine did the same.

"We are here to seek wisdom and blessing from Guanyin. We would be so grateful if Your Excellency could enlighten us."

"This old and humble nun will do her best," Master Wise and Bright replied.

Lady Han bowed again and presented her bamboo slip to the nun with both hands.

The nun examined the slip carefully. Then she said, with a gentle smile, "Congratulations, Benefactress Han! This is one of the best draws. Not only are you blessed with a prosperous life, but also you have a special connection with the Buddha. You have the five spiritual faculties: faith, perseverance, mindfulness, stillness of mind, and wisdom. Amitabaha."

Hands together, Lady Han bowed again and backed out. Once outside, she put a silver coin in the donation box next to the door.

A-mei went in next. The nun studied the bamboo slip carefully. "Benefactress A-mei," she said, "you might have started humble, but your kindness, generosity, and loyalty will bring you utmost prosperity, not of money and status, but of a long, peaceful, and simple life."

A-mei bowed and came out. She, too, put a silver coin in the donation box.

It was Iris's turn. She looked at her mother, and Lady Han smiled and nodded. Iris walked in and handed her slip to the nun. This was her first drawing, and she wanted to ask if her future husband would be kind to her, whoever he might be.

Master Wise and Bright took a little longer this time. Iris's heart pounded. She thought everyone could hear her heartbeat and they all knew what she asked.

Finally, the nun said, "Young lady, your drawing is very interesting. You will have a good married life, but inform your parents that they should not rush into anything. Let your predestination happen naturally, like water running through a forest on its own course."

Iris did not have to tell her parents, for Lady Han heard every word. She put a silver coin in Iris's hand so Iris could put it in the donation box.

Jasmine's turn finally came, and she could barely wait. She almost ran before she remembered the proper way of walking as a lady. She couldn't run very fast anyway, with her bound feet. She handed her slip to the nun and was eager to hear what she had to say. She asked the Buddha to tell her about her future, about the outcome of the secret that she had not shared even with Iris.

But she waited and waited and grew worried in the waiting. Color slowly drained from Lady Han's face, and her leg wobbled lightly. Standing to her left, A-Mei extended her right hand to steady Lady Han's left elbow.

Finally, the nun spoke.

"You had the most unusual beginning," she almost whispered, but they all heard her. "That will affect your whole life. But a benefactor, someone who would take you under the wing and protect you, may be able to direct you to the good path. Amitabaha, my child." She closed her eyes again and started to beat the wooden fish.

Jasmine was not sure what the nun meant. "Mother," she asked A-mei, "does it mean good luck or bad luck? Who's the benefactor?"

Before A-mei answered, Lady Han came over to hold Jasmine's hands. "Jasmine, your mother, and I will make sure it is good luck that you have. I'm your benefactor."

Iris nodded in agreement. "Is a benefactor like a sister? Can I be one, too?"

Lady Han took both girls in for a hug. "Yes," she said.

#

They caught the cargo barge to Three Rivers since the passenger boat had already left. After they got back to Three Rivers, Lady Han said that the trips to the village and the temple had made her extra tired and she asked sedan chairs to be sent, insisting A-mei keep her company. Iris and Jasmine got in the other chair. Master Han had gone back to attend business the day before, when the women were visiting the Guanyin Temple.

"Peony," A-mei said to Lady Han, once they were alone in the sedan chair, calling her by the name she had called her since they were children in Cloud Gate. "We heard Master Wise and Bright. Now that Old Ancestor is gone, do you think—"

"Yes," Lady Han said, "It should be much easier now. But A-mei, I don't want you to be sad…"

"How can I be? Anything to make Jasmine a lucky child will make me happy."

"Oh, A-mei!" Lady Han said, her eyes moist. "How blessed for me to have you, my friend! What have I done to deserve all you have done for me?"

"Peony!" A-mei said, eyes also wet, "You know I would do everything for you, and I know you will for me, too. You have done a lot for us! For Tiger to be educated and for my old Wang to have land to farm. Jasmine

FLOWING WATER, FALLING FLOWERS

X.H. COLLINS

is my daughter too, remember, and I want her to have the family status so she can be matched to a proper gentleman. My Old Wang is wonderful, but it's better Jasmine doesn't end up a countrywoman like me."

"Oh, you are not, A-mei!" Lady Han said, and they both smiled through their tears.

When they got home, Master Han was still out on business. They went to the master bedroom, closed the door, and talked about their plan.

CHAPTER 7
THREE RIVERS, 2017

I glanced at my mom next to me and saw that she had closed her eyes, her head supported by a travel pillow. I looked at Hong-mei in front of me and saw that she had leaned back on her seat. She must have closed her eyes, too. Shan put on some soft background music, which I recognized as a collection of the Korean pianist Yiruma, called "River Flows in You."

This was the collection I would put on when I used to write to Harriton. Its soothing and calming melody put me in a perfect mood to write to my love. But now, every note that flew in me was drenched in the river of heartache.

I had never thought that Harriton should choose between me and his wife. But when he chose her, he rejected me, and it hurt. Of course I knew she came first. I knew from the beginning when Harriton and I started to correspond to each other. But I also thought there was something special between us. Or was there? How much had we known each other? Did I love him because he was an excellent scholar? But there were many excellent scholars in the world! I admired them but didn't fall in love with them.

I was ashamed of feeling lovesick like a teenage girl. I was forty-four years-old! Some of my age had already had grandchildren. I could be the mother of all those who died young with broken hearts: Werther was in his early twenties or even younger, as Goethe wrote the semiautobiographical book when he was just twenty-four. Juliette was sixteen in the original story, and Shakespeare made her thirteen when she died. Du Li-niang in the Peony Pavilion, the classic Chinese opera from the Ming Dynasty, was sixteen. At least Li-niang had revived from death to be with her true love. I didn't even know what true love was.

Although I couldn't get Harriton out of my head, especially since I didn't have anything better to do, I told myself that I was trying my best. I was so far from him in space now, and all I needed was to wait for time to do its trick.

An ache pulsated across the back of my head. That was my tension headache. It visited me whenever I was physically exhausted, lacked sleep, or worked too hard.

I took my travel pillow from my backpack, put it around my neck, and closed my eyes. I let Yiruma float me through time and space.

When I opened my eyes again, I saw that we were traveling on a bridge. It was long: we were already on it when I woke up, and it took another five minutes to clear it.

"Where are we now?" I mumbled, rubbing my eyes.

"Only about ten minutes away. We just passed the Jialing River Bridge." Shan said.

"Oh, that was the Jialing River Bridge? No wonder it was so long."

"Watch for the dinosaur!" Hong-mei pointed out the window.

"What?" I turned my head into the direction she was pointing. Shan slowed the car for us to have a better look.

There it was, a huge dinosaur sculpture, standing right next to the river.

"It's China's largest Sauropod dinosaur and the longest dinosaur ever discovered in Asia, called Mamenchisaurus," Shan explained. "It was unearthed in Three Rivers in 1957. The giant beast was between sixteen and thirty meters long, its neck accounting for half of its full body length. It weighed about twenty to thirty tons. It was an herbivore and walked the earth during the Late Jurassic Period."

There were so many things I didn't know about Three Rivers.

Thirty miles northwest of Chongqing, Three Rivers was the meeting point of the Jialing, Fu, and Qu Rivers. Flowing across the city, Jialing, one of the largest tributary waterways to the Yangtze River, was in the middle, flanked by Fu, coming from the west, and Qu, from the northeast.

The city had a recorded history of more than 1,500 years. Before the construction of highways and high-speed railways, Three Rivers had been a major commercial port, and its population at one point was second only to the capital city of Sichuan Province, Chengdu.

I had only been to Three Rivers a handful of times when I was younger. Besides the long, uncomfortable train rides and bus rides, what I remembered most vividly were two things: eating fresh fish from the rivers and the summer nights when everybody slept outside, on cots on the street.

Three Rivers was where I discovered that fish had bones! In California, I ate fish fingers or filets my mom bought me from the supermarket, while my parents might have gone to the Asian market and gotten fish completed with the head, scales, and bones for themselves. I forgot what real fish looked like, on a dinner plate anyway. What a surprise when I had fish at Three Rivers! I would chew a piece and then spit it out, a mush of chewed flesh and bones, and my relatives would laugh at this American girl who did not know how to eat fish.

If not eating fish properly made me embarrassed, I forgot it quickly when we got to sleep outside. It is so hot and humid in Three Rivers that the city is nicknamed "Three Steamers." The only bedding in the summertime was a bamboo sheet, bamboo pillow, and a towel. Even so, it was still impossible to sleep on the hottest nights of July and August. We sprinkled cold well water on the bamboo sheet and wiped it to cool it down. But when we got up, we could see that our sweat left the shape of a person on the bamboo sheet. So on those hottest nights, we moved outdoors. It seemed that the entire neighborhood was outside. Circles upon circles of mosquito-repelling incense was burning. Older people sat or reclined on their bamboo loungers, each with a huge round fan made of cattail that brought them some cool breeze and kept the mosquitos away. Kids played until they were exhausted. All these were so interesting to me, I didn't mind getting bug bites by being outside so much. My legs were covered with scabs by the time we returned to Los Angeles.

As I got older, we had less frequent visits to Three Rivers. We had visits to see potential colleges after I entered high school. Then I had internships, backpacking in Europe; something always kept me away. My parents continued their visits but I lost touch with Three Rivers. In recent years I led groups of students to China for study abroad trips, which included bigger and more famous cities, not a place like Three Rivers.

There were too many places like it in China: beautiful, ancient, full of history, but not big or spectacular enough to be on an average tourist's travel map.

I pressed my face to the car window, trying to take in the view. There were so many cars on the street it reminded me of New York City, in a strange way: cars honking, pedestrians everywhere. But I knew it was a different place when I saw the bicycles and mopeds that carried heavy loads haphazardly stacked on the passenger seats. The old courtyards like the one where my aunt used to live in were nowhere to be seen; all I saw were high-rise apartment buildings. The orange glow of the sun faded, replaced by the lights of the high rises, reflecting on the water surrounding the city. It was a beautiful sight. A strange sensation went through my body. I was home. I wanted to know more about Three Rivers. I wanted to know more about my cousin, my mom, my aunt, my grandma, my great-grandma, and my great-great-grandma. Being fired and breaking up with Harriton forced me to think what I should do going forward, and to do that maybe I should first find out where I came from. Did Chinese love stories like the Peony Pavilion all have happy endings, even though the middle could be sad? Was I a Chinese in heart, or only Chinese in face?

#

My aunt and uncle lived in one of those high-rise buildings on the fifth floor. They were downstairs waiting for us when Shan slowly pulled the car up in front of the building. He dropped the passengers and the luggage off and pulled away to park the car in the underground garage.

Aunt Daisy took me in her arms. She had the same hug as my mom, a little hesitant as if she were afraid of getting so close to someone, yet somehow still managing to pass an undeniable signal of love. I gave her a tight squeeze.

"You lost a lot of weight, Mei Mei!" She touched my cheeks with both of her hands. "Too much work?"

"Not really, Auntie Daisy." I smiled. She, like her daughter, did not seem to age very much. Her face was smooth and radiant, and her hair, nearly all white, was permed and neatly styled. She was two years older than my mom.

"Anyway, we'll need to feed you and your mom well while you are here. She always complains there is nothing to eat in the U.S.! After all these years!" Aunt Daisy gave my mom a hug as well.

54

I went to hug my uncle De-chen. He was the one who always brought fish home, and he was a great cook. "Rose, I made you and your mom's favorite dish, hot boiled fish! And fresh vegetables, all from Cloud Gate. You must be hungry now. Everything is ready. Let's go."

We walked into the elevator.

"Uncle, you didn't ride your moped to Cloud Gate to get the fresh food, did you?" I asked Uncle De-chen in my best Mandarin, which I had been brushing up on since I decided to join my mom on the trip.

"I wish I had! Your aunt won't let me anymore. One of the nephews from Cloud Gate brought the food. They knew you were coming and they invited all of us to visit them."

"I would love to." I had never been to Cloud Gate. There were always comings and goings between the families in Three Rivers and Cloud Gate, and I understood that there were significant connections between our family and the village, but I was not sure what they were. Small villages usually did not make it into my itineraries.

The elevator came to a stop and we got out. But instead of the fifth floor as I had been expecting, we entered a large, well-lit courtyard with trees, bushes, flowers, and two concrete ping pong tables. This was the fourth floor on the elevator. We then climbed some stairs to the fifth floor. Three Rivers and Chongqing were built on mountains, and people used to climb hundreds of steps to get around. But in recent years elevators did the work. When you stepped out of an elevator, you could be on a floor of a tall building, or on a busy street. Out-of-towners were always surprised by this, as I was.

Uncle De-chen and Aunt Daisy presented us with a welcoming feast. Of course, once again everyone talked about the story of "the little American girl who doesn't know how to eat real fish!" We all laughed. I didn't feel embarrassed anymore. Maybe because I did know how to pick bones out of fish now, or maybe the joke made me feel I belonged to the family. You only had jokes like this for your own people.

When sliced oranges were brought up as dessert, everyone moved to the couches in the living room.

"What is this?' I saw a photo album on the coffee table and picked it up. It was filled with black and white photos. Some had turned yellow, others had colors painted on them.

"Ah, I asked your aunt to dig the old photos out of her trunk. I had not looked at them for a long time, and I want to," my mom said. "I want you to look at them, too."

"Even I had not looked at them for a long time," Aunt Daisy said. "It was at the bottom of my trunk, and I hadn't thought about bringing them out until your mom asked."

The four of us squeezed onto the couch, Hong-mei and I in the middle, our mothers flanking us. My mom and Daisy were little girls in some of the photos, no more than ten years old. They wore long dresses, tunics or boxy jackets with wide sleeves, and long or short pants. Most of the photos seemed to be taken in a garden, as a pavilion, a pond, trees, bamboo, various flowers, and landscape rocks stood in the background.

"I didn't know there were so many pictures of you as young girls," I said.

"Well, there would not have been had our family not owned the Three Rivers Photo Studio. Look, that was our garden. It was on Number One Cypress Street. I don't think you and Hong-mei had ever been there," Aunt Daisy said.

One photo caught my eye. It was about the size of a 3.5 x 5 picture by today's standards. My mom and aunt Daisy were two little girls, between them was an older woman I didn't know. In the back row stood Grandma Pearl, whom I had met a couple of times, and a man I assumed to be my grandfather Ching-yu, whom I had never met.

Aunt Daisy noticed my gaze and took the picture out of the album. "Look, Lily, this is probably the only picture of our family left."

My mom took the picture in her hand.

"Who's this?" Hong-mei pointed at the woman in the middle.

"That was our Grandma Iris," Mom and Daisy said in unison.

Iris had her arms around the girls' shoulders. She had big, deep-set eyes and a high forehead. The corner of her mouth curled slightly upwards, a barely-there smile.

"Mom, Aunt Daisy, I want to hear more about Grandma Pearl and Great-grandma Iris." I was thinking about the dream I had, the dream we all had.

"Certainly!" Aunt Daisy said. "But it's almost midnight now. You and your mom are tired, I'm sure, after the travel. Hong-mei and Shan have to work tomorrow. Let's call it a night."

Hong-mei and Shan left. I took a shower and lay down on the soft cotton sheet over the spring mattress, not a bamboo sheet on a wooden bed. It was the end of May, but Three Rivers was already hot. The air conditioner was on, and it was familiarly comfortable, as if I were back in the U.S. But I wished we were outside sleeping on bamboo futons. If we had, maybe time could turn around, and my life would be back on its old path, the path before I met Harriton. The path I had been happily walking with a job I loved and a heart unbroken.

I took two gummies of melatonin and fell asleep quickly.

CHAPTER 8
THREE RIVERS, 1905

The Beginning of Autumn: the eighth day of the seventh month and the thirteenth solar term of the twenty-four seasons. Autumn begins.

Number One Cypress Street was bathed in excitement. Starting at dawn, various groups of people bustled in and out of the house nonstop. Butchers delivering fresh pork arrived first, followed by nearby villagers who brought several feisty roosters, fat hens, and vegetables freshly plucked from their gardens that morning. Fishermen brought fresh carp that were still jumping, trying to escape the wooden buckets that held them.

Hired hands also arrived. Some helped slaughter the fowl. They cut a slit in the bird's neck and carefully drained the blood into a bowl of salted water. They dunked the roosters and the hens into buckets of boiling hot water set out in the courtyard. The large stove in the kitchen had two parts: the front part, the main cooking stove, was only lit up during the actual cooking time, but the smaller stove on the back had embers that never went out. A kettle with water sat on top of the second stove so there was always hot water for tea and everything else.

The hired hands swiftly plucked feathers, saving the tail feathers of the roosters to make shuttlecocks for the children later. Then they took out the innards and cleaned them. The innards were not to be thrown away; instead, they were fried in chili oil with pickled vegetables, a tasty dish that went especially well with white rice. The cook and his helpers made the rest of the birds into various dishes. The rooster was made into cold cuts mixed with plenty of chili oil, sesame oil, and seeds, good soy sauce, and topped with thinly sliced green onions. Hens were simmered all day with herbs, the water kettle on the back fire replaced by a clay soup pot.

Women from the neighborhood were in the kitchen helping the family cook, a short, squat man who had fine sweat beads on his forehead and was busy giving orders: who was to keep an eye on the fire, who was to chop, to slice, and to peel. The women didn't mind the busy work. They considered it an honor to help the Hans, who always remembered favors the neighbors did for them and returned the favor in double the dose. It was also a perfect time to gossip.

"So Lady Han decided to take A-mei's daughter as a gan nü'er? Why, though?" one woman asked.

Another woman said, "Lady Han had A-mei as her maid back in her village. She treated A-mei more like a sister than a maid though, don't you all think? When Lady Han was married to the Master and came to Three Rivers from Cloud Gate, she insisted in bringing A-mei, not as part of a dowry but as her own helper, so A-mei really didn't have to answer to anyone but her. It's only natural that Lady Han wants to take Jasmine as a gan nü'er. What a lucky girl."

"Now Jasmine will be treated as Miss Iris, with a good dowry and good prospect of a proper husband," a third woman said.

A fourth woman continued, "From what I can tell, she's already treated the girl like her own daughter. Today's ceremony is just to make it official, so when match-makers come over, they will be serving another Han daughter and not a peasant girl and a poor relation."

The women all nodded and continued their work and talk, admiring the benevolence and generosity of Lady Han, the enviable friendship between Lady Han and A-mei, and the good fortune of Jasmine.

Meanwhile, several tables and many chairs were set up under the two one-hundred-year-old magnolia trees on each side of the courtyard. The summer heatwave had receded, but it was still scorching in the afternoon sun. The trees provided a welcoming respite in the yard.

Occasionally, A-mei came to the workers to give instructions or hand out tips to the delivery people. She had tied her hair into a neat bun at her nape as usual but added a jade hairpin to hold the bun in place. She had on a new green silk tunic with delicate blue trim and matching green capri pants. She wore a radiant smile. "Auntie A-mei," the women said to her, "Congratulations! Look at you! This happy occasion has made you look years younger!"

A-mei held her hands at her heart and bowed to them. "Yes, thank you! Thank you! With your blessings!"

When she was not attending household chores, A-mei went to Lady Han's room, lending a hand to her old friend in preparing Jasmine for the special occasion. Iris was also there helping her mother, along with Mrs. Fang, a friend of the Han family and Jian-da's mother. There were no lessons for the children today, but the old teacher took You-jun, Tiger, and Jian-da out for a stroll and instructed them to write a poem about the beauty of the beginning of a new season. You-jun complained about this mistreatment: why should they stay away when there was so much action going on in the house?

"So you boys won't be getting in the way," his mother said to them. "Everyone is so busy today, and I don't have time to deal with you boys if you get in trouble. When you come back in the afternoon, the ceremony and banquet will be ready. That's when the fun begins, anyway."

A-mei bathed Jasmine with rose petal-scented water and washed her long black hair with the oil from honey locust pods mixed with grapefruit peel. Jasmine's fourteen-year-old body was a tender bud, not yet blossoming, but the waiting could be over in the blink of an eye. Iris and the grown-ups worked in silence to get Jasmine ready. They put her in a silk red tunic with a wide golden trim, high Mandarin collar, and ample sleeves. She wore matching pants with golden trim at the bottom of the legs. The buttons of the tunic were shaped like a phoenix.

Iris braided Jasmine's hair and the thick braid hung all the way down to her slim waist. She had bangs just above her eyebrows, naturally dark and perfectly shaped like a new moon. Lady Han took a jade hair-pin from her black and red lacquered jewel box and Iris carefully put it in Jasmine's hair, just behind her left ear. Last, Iris put a new pair of silk slippers on Jasmine, embroidered by Lady Han. Mrs. Fang gave Jasmine an amber pendant attached to a red silk string.

"Mei Mei." Iris held Jasmine's hands and sighed. "You are so

61

beautiful."

The three women all dabbed their eyes. "You are so beautiful!" they echoed.

"But Jie Jie," said Jasmine, "you are more beautiful! The yellow color of a baby goose suits your porcelain skin so well!"

The grown-ups laughed.

"Look," Mrs. Fang said, "how they like and complement each other! They are such good sisters. No one will believe they are gan sisters. Even sisters who grew up together from the first day will not have gotten along so well!"

"That's what we hope," said Lady Han. "We hope they will confide in each other and help each other. Like A-mei and I. We are not blood sisters but I can't imagine what I would be without A-mei."

They all smiled and nodded. Lady Han looked at Iris and Jasmine, her beautiful daughters. Iris was like a white gardenia on a hot summer night: she brought grace, calm, and beauty. Jasmine, on the other hand, was like a red rose in a summer garden: she was beautiful, but in a more untamed way. Lady Han thought, *I named them for the wrong flowers*! And she smiled at that. Then she took her daughters' hands, one in each of hers, and led them to the courtyard. She said her silent prayer to Guanyin and made a promise to the Goddess of Mercy that she would go back to Cloud Gate to offer incense once everything was done.

When they reached the covered front porch, A-mei said to Jasmine, "Wait here." Jasmine nodded and sat on the bench. Her heart fluttered wildly in her chest. Green Jade, the maid, stood next to Jasmine, holding her hand.

Lady Han, Mrs. Fang, A-mei, and Iris continued into the courtyard. Guests had taken their seats. The cook and his helpers brought out the banquet. Master Han and Old Wang sat at the head table, and Lady Han, Mrs. Fang, and A-mei joined them, A-mei with great reluctance. Earlier, Master Han had taken Old Wang for a tour of his rice shops around town. Business had been good, and Master Han thanked Old Wang for taking care of the affairs at Cloud Gate. The men only got to know each other because of their wives, but both were quiet, easy-going, hard-working types, and they liked each other.

Iris sat at the children's table where You-jun, Tiger, Jian-da, and other children were sitting, supervised by the teacher.

"How are your poems coming along?" Iris whispered to her brother.

"Who wants to work on poems today?" You-jun whispered back. "Teacher just tried to keep us away as long as possible. We didn't want to miss anything!"

"You didn't miss anything," Iris said. The teacher shushed them.

They stopped talking, stuck their tongues out, then sat up straight and turned to the head table.

Old Wang stood, cleared his throat, and began. "Dear relatives and friends, welcome to the banquet! My wife and I, with the kind permission of Master and Lady Han, have chosen today as the auspicious day to present our little daughter Jasmine to the Han family as their gan nü'er. Jasmine is blessed to gain the favor of Lady Han. As their gan nü'er, Jasmine will have a bright future, better than what we can provide her in our little village. According to tradition, we should have held the banquet in Cloud Gate, and invited Jasmine's honored Gan father and Mother to the banquet to present our daughter. But Cloud Gate is far and tiresome to travel to, so Master and Lady Han have been so generous as to allow us to hold the ceremony in their esteemed home." He paused and picked up the goblet in front of him with both hands. Turning to face the Hans, he said, "This first toast is for you, Master and Lady Han! Thank you for sharing your good fortune and life with my daughter!"

Master and Lady Han stood up, goblets in their hands as well. "Thank you for sharing your daughter with us. We shall treat her as our own!" Master Han said. They drank the rice wine in a gulp.

Old Wang put down his goblet and motioned for his cousins from the village to come forward. The two men brought forth a wooden box. Two servants brought out the high-backed nanmu chairs from the front hall.

Then Old Wang turned to the Hans again and said, "Now, honored Master and Lady, please take your esteemed seats."

Master and Lady Han went and sat on the chairs. They both wore their best clothes: she a fine dress of red silk with golden trim and matching pants, he a jacket of the same color and material and black silk pants.

Old Wang called to Jasmine, "Come here, lucky daughter!"

Green Jade brought Jasmine and handed her to her parents. They took her hands and brought her in front of Master and Lady Han. Jasmine kneeled on a mat laid in front of them, put her hands on the ground, and kowtowed to her gan father and mother three times. Then A-mei took something from the wooden box and handed it to Jasmine. Jasmine tilted her head to the ground and held the item over her head with both hands as she presented it to Master Han

"Dear father," she said in a small, trembling voice, "please accept this hat from your daughter, for from now on you are my master, and I will obey you like obeying my own father."

Master Han took the hat from her hands and laughed. "Good daughter, good daughter!"

A-mei took something else from the box and handed it to Jasmine. Jasmine presented this to Lady Han. "Dear mother," she said, "please accept this pair of embroidered slippers that your daughter made herself. From now on you are just like my own mother, and I will learn to be a good wife and daughter-in-law from you."

She lifted her head and saw Lady Han looking at her. Lady Han had a gentle smile that made Jasmine feel calm.

Lady Han took the slippers and put them on the table. Then she held her hands out to Jasmine. "That was enough kneeling, dear daughter!"

She then gave Jasmine her own gifts. She put a jade amulet over Jasmine's neck. "This will lock you in the Han family." She handed Jasmine a gilded wooden bowl and a pair of gilded iron chopsticks, both of which would never break, and said, "You will always have something to eat as long as the Hans have." And finally, she gave Jasmine a set of red silk tunic and pants. "You will always have the nice clothes that we have."

After Jasmine went to the front hall, kowtowed, and offered incense to the ancestors, Lady Han asked Jasmine to sit next to her.

Old Wang stood up again, holding his goblet. This time, he toasted the crowd. "Thank you all for coming to witness the ceremony! We are honored. Please eat and drink to your hearts' content!" Then he downed his own rice wine.

In the evening, after the last guest had left, Lady Han gathered Iris, Jasmine, and You-jun in her room.

"Are you all tired from this big day?" She smiled at her children.

"Not at all!" You-jun jumped in.

"That's good," Lady Han said. "You are always a bit naughty. Make sure you respect your older sisters! They may be girls, but they know just as much, if not more, of all the lessons the teacher has taught you children."

"That's true," Iris said. "Just today, You-jun did not write the poem like the teacher asked!"

"But I did!" You-jun said. "I didn't write what the teacher had asked, but I wrote something for Jasmine."

"You did?" His mother and older sister and new gan sister were surprised. "Show us!"

"It's for Jasmine only." He turned to her. "I'll only give it to you, and you can't share with anyone else!"

"Oh, just like I said, being naughty again!" Lady Han said and laughed.

Jasmine went bright red and lowered her head. She wished for a crack in the floor so she could disappear into it, like that day when she first met You-jun when she was seven. Inside, however, happiness blossomed in her heart like a peach tree after a spring shower. Jasmine would not hear You-jun's poem for her until years later, when they sat under a full harvest moon, the brightest in the entire year, reciting the Water Song by Shu Shi.

"I have something for Jasmine, too!" Iris said, taking something out, carefully, from the inside pocket of her tunic.

"I embroidered this silk handkerchief for you. It has two flowers on the same stem—sister flowers. The light yellow one is you, Jasmine, and the light mauve one is me."

She handed the handkerchief to Jasmine, still warm from being so close to her heart.

CHAPTER 9
THREE RIVERS, 1910

Mid-Autumn Festival: the fifteenth day of the eighth month. A celebration to enjoy the harvest, family, and the brightest moon of the year.

Five years had passed since Master and Lady Han took in Jasmine as their gan daughter. In later years, the three families, the Hans, Wangs, and Fangs, considered these the happiest years of their lives. Children grew into young adults; adults turned older but still had good health. In those five years, the wind had been calm and the rain plentiful. There had been great a harvest each year, and no shortage of food and clothes.

On the day of the Mid-Autumn Festival, one of the most important holidays and second only to the Chinese New Year, the three families gathered in Three Rivers to celebrate. Old Wang and Tiger came from Cloud Gate after finishing farm work. Master Han rented a showboat so everyone could be on the water, under the brightest full moon of the year, and enjoy the good food, wine, scenery, and each other's company.

The cook and his helpers worked all day to prepare the feast: moon cakes, roasted duck, pumpkin soup, steamed marbled pork belly with taro, and the must-have delicacy of the occasion, fresh river hairy crab steamed with thinly sliced ginger, garlic, and scallion. Old Wang brought wine made from osmanthus flowers. Everything was packed into baskets and brought on board.

The wind was calm. The water was smooth like glass. The full moon hung low in the sky, white as silver, its shadows of Chang'e and the Jade

Rabbit dark as spilled ink, as if reachable if they kept rowing the boat just a little further. The osmanthus trees were in full bloom throughout the city and their pleasant fragrance permeated the air. Other showboats and tour boats crowded the river and laughter and lively conversations floated around them.

Master Han held his glass of osmanthus wine and made a toast to the Moon. "In ancient times, poets and scholars and monks often experienced a sense of melancholy on this day, when the moon was full. That is, if one was alone and without good company. But we are here today and we only have happiness and gratitude because of our families." Everyone agreed and held their glasses up to echo the toast.

"But still, Mid-Autumn Festival is not complete without reciting Su Dongpo's *Water Song*," Lady Han said. "I'll start and let's see how the children remember the verses."

Old Wang, Tiger, and A-mei declined to be part of the game. "We are country bumpkins," they said with a laugh, "and we would rather just enjoy listening to it!"

So Lady Han began.
> *How rare the moon, so round and clear!*
> *With cup in hand, I ask of the blue sky*

Master Han continued,
> *I do not know in the celestial sphere*
> *What name this festive night goes by?*

Mrs. Fang added:
> *I want to fly home, riding the air,*
> *But fear the ethereal cold up there*

You-jun chimed in,
> *The jade and crystal mansions are so high!*
> *Dancing to my shadow,*
> *I feel no longer the mortal tie.*

Jian-da thought for a moment, then exclaimed,
> *She rounds the vermilion tower,*
> *Stoops to silk-pad doors,*
> *Shines on those who sleepless lie.*

Iris said, quietly but proudly,
> *Why does she, bearing us no grudge,*
> *Shine upon our parting, reunion deny?*
> *But rare is perfect happiness--*
> *The moon does wax, the moon does wane*

Jasmine finished the poem:
> *And so men meet and say goodbye.*
> *I only pray our life be long,*

And our souls together heavenward fly!

Everyone clapped and cheered. Iris, being the little scholar among the children, felt a sense of melancholy as she contemplated what her father just said. What an eloquent poem that fits the occasion! How often did people have to be reminded that beautiful things like this full moon were fleeting, and nothing lasted forever? All we could hope was to be together like this as long we could.

They would have liked to linger, but the gentle evening breeze in mid-autumn was chilly. The parents decided that it was time to retreat, though the children begged to stay longer. They rowed the boat back to the pier. Everybody disembarked, but Master Han, in a jubilant mood, allowed the children to stay on the river bank and play, and Green Jade stayed with them. Jian-da needed to escort his mother home, so he left reluctantly. The rest threw pebbles in the water and tried to catch some frogs without any success. Soon Iris grew tired.

"Go on then," You-jun said. "Green Jade, take Iris and Tiger home. Jasmine and I are not tired yet, and we'll come home soon enough."

"Oh no, young master, can't do that," Green Jade said.

"It's okay," You-jun said. "If Master complains, tell him I made you do it. I promise we'll be home before anyone finds out. Just ten more minutes, okay? We are not kids anymore." He was seventeen, and Jasmine was nineteen.

Green Jade hesitated, but she had been the one who raised You-jun along with Lady Han and she could never say no to him.

"Just hurry home soon then," she said. "I don't want any scolding from Master and Lady."

After watching the three of them disappeared at the top of the steps, Jasmine said to You-jun, "Why did you say I was not tired?"

"Jie Jie," You-jun said, "because reciting the Water Song made me think about the poem I wrote for you on the day when Father and Mother took you as their gan nü'er. I want to recite *that* poem to you now that everyone is gone. Let's sit down."

They sat under a large willow tree with their backs against the trunk.

"I can't believe you still remember it," Jasmine said, her face hot.

You-jun whispered, "Never will I forget."

Then he said,

When you first walked in
  I knew somewhere in Heaven
  A fairy had given up her celestial being.
Since then your laughter scattered around me
  Like petals of spring flowers, shining pearls.
  They made me smile, cry, and sigh.

69

Now you are here to stay
I knew Heaven's gates will open again.
For you to enter, and for me to follow.

"It's a beautiful poem," Jasmine said, "but it did not fit the occasion. No moon, no autumn. And it sounds like you were making fun of me."

"Jie Jie," You-jun turned to face Jasmine and took her hands. Jasmine trembled but did not pull her hands away.

"You know what I mean, don't you?" You-jun said. "You are like a fairy from Heaven to me. I would follow you if you turned out to be like Chang'e and fly to the moon!"

Jasmine said, "I'd rather stay here on Earth, in the Han household!"

She smiled in the dark, and You-jun sensed her smile.

CHAPTER 10
THREE RIVERS, 2017

It had been about a week since we came to Three Rivers. I always enjoyed summer: no papers to grade, no lectures to prep, no committee meetings to attend, no grades to agonize over, and no work e-mails to answer, or only occasionally. But this summer, knowing such a void of duties would persist into fall made me panic at times. I had one or two dreams in which I misplaced students' papers or lost my voice in the middle of talking and half of the class left before I could find my paper or my voice.

I checked my e-mails out of habit, hoping to catch job postings from various listservs I belonged to, and hoping for an email from Harriton, even though I did not want to admit it. But there was only spam. Most of my friends were on Facebook and Instagram or Twitter, but access to Facebook in China was tricky. In starred hotels where foreigners stayed, it could be accessed, but otherwise, it was blocked by the Great Firewall. I could have climbed the firewall with help from Shan, but this gave me a perfect excuse to go off all the social media sites I was on. Under Hong-mei's tutelage, I downloaded WeChat, a social media platform like Facebook, only better, in my opinion, since there were no ads and all my "friends" were relatives: aunt Daisy, uncle De-chen, Hong-mei and Shan, and my mom. I loved their postings—yes, like everyone else in the world today, they were posting on social media even when we were in the same room!

Uncle De-Chen and Aunt Daisy kept mom and me busy, as if we were going to leave the next week. We went to a new restaurant almost every day because Uncle and Aunt thought we must sample all the cuisine, old staples like hot pot and new inventions that nobody knew what they were, with their poetic names. One dish was called "A green dragon crossing white water," which I ordered out of curiosity, only to discover it was nothing more than a perfect stem of green onion on top of a bowl of broth. I wondered if the wait-staff and cooks were laughing in the kitchen. We followed that routine until all three of them thought they needed a break from the greasiness. Even though we ate out a lot, usually for dinner, we still went to the market every morning to buy fresh vegetables and meats and fruits, since lunch could not be just so-so fare. My uncle was a fantastic cook and enjoyed showing off his skills.

I loved going to the market. It provided me with much-needed distraction. Instead of dwelling on my miseries, I focused on the important task of picking and preparing one's food. The most Chinese part of me, I had long thought, was my love of authentic Chinese food. I relished having all my senses assaulted from every possible angle: the colors of freshly picked cabbage, cucumbers, carrots, lettuces of many varieties, onions of every color, and blooming Chinese chives; the smell of noodles, steamed buns, and fried donuts, all of which were cooked right in front of your eyes on the street; the sounds of the singing voices of vendors peddling their goodies, as if they were pleading to potential lovers. Sometimes I couldn't understand all the words because of the dialects, but I imagined they said, "Oh, please, my dear! You must see how good my stuff is, better than anything else your money could buy!"

The market place was shielded like a carport but was the size of a football field. My uncle and aunt were regulars at this market and they knew which vendor had the best pork belly, which had the freshest produce, and they stopped multiple times to chat with vendors and other shoppers. Buying ingredients for Dandan noodle could easily be a two-hour trip, but I loved it.

All the good food we ate had to be digested properly through exercise! We did this twice a day: early morning before breakfast and in the evening after supper. Or I should say the three of them did, and I walked with them and watched. I did not feel comfortable running by myself. There was exercise equipment along the streets and in small spaces, what I called mini-parks. On the equipment they pedaled, twisted, swung, and ran.

The first morning I overslept because no one woke me up. But Mom said to me later, "You should come with us, Mei Mei! You'll love to see what people do!"

I did. In the light mist of early morning, on the sidewalks next to the river, under the gently swaying willow trees, groups of what I guessed were retirees practiced Tai Chi in unison as if commanded by a master, even though there was no obvious leader. They firmly anchored in their horse stances, gently parted the wild horses' mane, and gracefully spread their white crane wings. I was not surprised that Uncle and Aunt could do it so well; I guess they did this every day since they retired, Aunt as a school teacher and Uncle...I guess I never knew what he did! But my mom surprised me. I didn't know how she was keeping up with her twenty-four forms of the Yang style Tai Chi when she was so busy with so many other adventures.

I sat on a park bench, watching the energetic old people, following their moves with my eyes and my heart. I did not join in, even though people invited me. I had neither the spirit nor the physical grace for it.

Evenings were different. We strolled along the river, passing by the vendors who sold everything from used books and socks to undergarments and snacks. My aunt told me not to look at any of their goods in case I would be forced to buy something, which reminded me of the warning I got from friends who were locals when I walked in Time Square. No matter where you were, you could always tell the difference between natives and visitors: in New York, the locals forged ahead with a frown on their forehead and a pair of plugs in their ears. The visitors looked around, their eyes wide and mouths slightly agape. Here, locals did not stop to look at the vendor whom they saw every day in passing. So I followed the three of them, and if any vendors came up to show me something, I said, *bu, bu*, no, no.

Back in the States people sometimes came up to me, talking very loudly and very slowly, in a sing-song voice, as if I could not comprehend them. They asked me, "Where are you from?" and were not satisfied when I said, "Torres, California." "But where are you *really* from?" they pressed. On the streets in China, no one ever asked me where I was from, and people talked to me in rapidly firing dialects, which actually were foreign languages to me. So the word I used most often was "*bu*," no, which made me sound like a naughty small toddler, back at the age of the "terrible twos."

On those evening walks, we also passed by women who were dancing, choreographed group dancing, to music from a boom box.

"Your aunt loves this stuff!" Uncle De-chen laughed.

"Really?" I looked at Aunt Daisy and said, "Then go dancing! I want to see it, Aunt Daisy! Please!"

"Oh, but I'm terrible at it. I just do it sometimes for exercise!" Aunt all of a sudden became a shy young girl, and she would not go up to join the dancing women no matter how I prodded her.

One evening we walked a little further along the river. My aunt, who was walking with Uncle De-chen ahead of Mom and me, stopped and turned around to face us.

"Lily, do you know what street this is?" she asked.

My mom was not sure. "It doesn't look familiar to me." She hesitated. "The buildings...some look old, but I can't tell what they are. Wait." She paused and looked down the street. "There's a large cypress tree across from the pier. Is it...Cypress Street?"

"Cypress Street?" I asked. "Isn't it the street where your old family house was?"

"Yes!" said Aunt Daisy. "It looks nothing like when we were kids, but it *is* Cypress Street."

"Where is Number One?" My mom asked, and she started to walk across the street, away from the river, towards the cypress tree.

"This way, Sister!" Aunt Daisy caught up with Mom. Holding hands, they went further down the street.

Uncle De-chen and I followed.

"Number One Cypress Street was the address of your mom and aunt's home, a long time ago," he said.

"Yes, I heard Mom mentioning that, and I've seen pictures of it, too. One was of Mom and Aunt in front of the front door. The others had them and other people in the garden, standing in front of the rockery, sitting in the pavilion and by the pond."

"Ah yes, I remember those. I think it was your mom and aunt and several cousins." He nodded. "That was when Number One Cypress Street was also Three Rivers Photo Studio. Your aunt said that the front hall in the house was used as the studio to take portraits of clients, and the garden in the back was a popular location for an outdoor setting. There was a water lily pond, with carp and a pair of Mandarin ducks in it, a rockery, a pagoda, a patch of bamboo, and many different kinds of flowers and trees. The family lived in the rooms on the west side, and the rooms on the east side were turned into storage and dark rooms. Your grandpa was quite a photographer. They had hired help but he usually did the darkroom work himself," my uncle said.

"How did he become a photographer? Wasn't that strange, in the 1930s and 40s? Here in Three Rivers?" I asked.

"That's true. Three Rivers was not Shanghai or Beijing, or even Chengdu and Chongqing. It was such a small city. Your grandpa was a school teacher, but he was very curious about new things. The family on your grandma's side had been very prominent in Three Rivers, and I think your grandfather got a camera from some old family friend as a wedding present."

We reached the end of Cypress Street where the cypress tree was, surrounded by a low barbered wire fence. There was no old-style family mansion. The last building on the street was a tall, luxurious apartment building.

"This is Number One now," my aunt said.

We walked around. A young man came to us from the building. He was the security guard. They were at all the apartment buildings I visited. They were not policemen, but they wore uniforms and might carry Tasers or batons or long staffs. No guns though. Even policemen rarely carried guns in China.

"You don't live here," he said.

"No, we don't," my aunt replied.

"Are you looking for someone?" the security guard asked.

"No," my aunt said, "we are just taking a walk."

The guy shrugged and was about to walk away. This was when I was glad I had a Chinese face. As long as I didn't open my mouth, no one would bother me. There were not that many blue eyes and blonde heads in Three Rivers.

"But we used to live here," my aunt added.

"Oh yeah? Which unit? You must have sold it for a lot of money. The price now is about five thousand yuan per square meter." The guard sounded impressed.

"Is that so?" my aunt said. "Well, we didn't make that much money. We lived here when this place was just a home, long before the apartments were built."

The guard arched his eyebrows. "Before the apartment building? When was that? What was this place then?" he asked.

"Three Rivers Photo Studio. Also our home. The cypress tree was in front of the house. The tree is nearly two hundred years old now," my aunt said.

"Hmm, never heard of the house, but the tree, yeah, it's real old. It's a relic protected by the city. Builders must take care to not damage it when they work on projects around here," the guard said.

On the way home, I asked Aunt Daisy, "What happened to Three Rivers Photo Studio?"

"It's a long story. The government purchased shares of it in the 1950s, so it became a state-private joint venture. We still lived there. Then came the Great Leap Forward, and everyone tried to manufacture steel in their backyard furnace, and no one was interested in having pictures taken. Then our dad, your grandpa, died during the Three-Year Famine Period and grandma couldn't maintain the studio anymore, so she sold all the shares to the government and became an employee in the studio," Aunt Daisy said.

"Well, 'sold' was an overstatement. It was not fair market price," my mom said.

"True," Aunt Daisy said. "But that was all Mom could manage. We were able to avoid being labeled as Exploiting Class because we didn't own properties anymore. She was able to get a job at the studio to support us, and I was able to get a job there when I came back from Cloud Gate, after going to the countryside to be reeducated."

"Wait," I said, "I thought you were a school teacher."

"I was. I was helping in the studio after high school, but I went to the countryside as soon as the Cultural Revolution began in 1966. I listened to the call by Chairman Mao and volunteered to go there to be re-educated by the farmers, to let the hard, dirty, smelly farm work clean off all the dregs I carried over from the old feudalistic past. Sounds crazy, doesn't it?" Aunt Daisy laughed. "After I came back from the countryside, I worked at the photo studio again for a while. Then I went to Teacher's College. I could not have gone if we were considered Exploiting Class," she said.

"Your aunt is very smart! So is your mom and so are you! And Hong-mei and now Elsie! Hong-mei is the first licensed school counselor in Three Rivers. Elsie is attending London School of Economics and Political Science on a full scholarship. All the women in the family are so bright!" my uncle said proudly. He put his arm around his wife and looked at her with affection. "I'm glad you came to Cloud Gate, even though I knew you suffered for that, the hard farm labor you had to do. Had you not come, I would not have met you."

As if reading my mind, he turned to me and said, "I know, I don't sound like I'm from Cloud Gate. I'm not. I was in the army stationed near Cloud Gate. I'm a Northerner!" He laughed heartily.

"Uncle De-chen gave up his political career to marry Aunt Daisy," my mom said.

"Oh, wow." I was amazed. All the family affairs that I didn't know!

"Did mom go to Cloud Gate to be reeducated? When did they take down the mansion and build the apartment building?" I asked.

"Your mom was not as crazy as I." My aunt laughed. "And our mother, your grandma, wanted someone to stay with her, so Lily stayed."

"As for the apartment building, that happened in the 1990s," Daisy continued. "I can't even remember which year that was, but it was after your grandma Pearl passed away. The city had plans to develop the area, the busiest commercial area, so they negotiated with me to buy the mansion, which we still owned after the state-private joint venture started. So we made the deal."

"It was not a fair deal!" my mom said again.

"But that's all we could manage. And you were not there, Lily!" Aunt Daisy said.

"What was the deal?" I asked.

"We got a four-bedroom apartment, and some cash, about ten thousand yuan, and that was a lot of money then. Later we were able to sell the apartment to buy two smaller ones, one for us and one for Hong-mei. So maybe it was not a good deal, but we had comfortable living, compared to a lot of people. We owned our apartments when most people still rented."

My aunt sounded calm, not a hint of sadness or bitterness.

"You wouldn't leave because you had De-chen. I didn't have anyone, so I went. That's why I wasn't here!" My mom's voice trailed off. She turned her head to the side. I had heard before that thanks to Nixon's visit in China, my mom was able to go to America, sponsored by an old family friend of our parents, Mr. Liang Fei, in 1972.

"That was a good decision that I made," Aunt Daisy said, holding hands with her husband, and they smiled at each other. I almost wept at the sight.

"And you met Alvin," Aunt Daisy said to my mom. Alvin was my dad.

"Yes, thank goodness!" My mom smiled at the mention of my dad's name. "The kitchen work was so hard, but Alvin helped me to get through. The only fun thing we did was going to the YMCA for a swim once in a while. Until finally we saved enough to open a small grocery store."

"We all turned out to have a good life," my aunt agreed.

I knew the story of my parents, a typical hard-working first-generation immigrant story. But hearing what happened before they came, which they seldom mentioned, made me appreciate that much more the life they built for themselves, and for me, in a foreign land. It was time for me to know more.

On the way home, my mom walked with Daisy ahead of us. My uncle whispered to me, "The only time I ever saw your mom and aunt argue was about selling their family home. It's best to steer clear of the topic." He winked at me, and then said, "Okay then! Tomorrow morning we all leave early to go to Cloud Gate. We are going to a relative's birthday banquet. She's a riot and you'll love to meet her, Rose"

I couldn't wait. I sensed there were a lot more stories waiting for me. For the first time since I came, I was not thinking about merely finding distractions to occupy my mind. I truly looked forward to what I had to discover.

CHAPTER 11
THREE RIVERS, 1911

The fifteenth day of the fifth month. It was not a special day, but the moon was full.

The full moon dangled up in the sky, shining like a well-polished silver plate. The rivers reflected the silver rays of light, moving as a thousand fish scales.

You-jun sat under a willow tree on the bank, facing the river. He had caught quite a few fireflies, which he dropped into a fine-gauze cloth sack. He held the sack up to look at the faint light that came through. Then he carefully suspended it on a low branch. He picked up pebbles around him and threw them into the river one after another. He had heard the watchmen earlier, striking their bamboo clapper and beating their gongs, "dung, dung! dung, dung!" and he knew it was late. Would she come tonight?

As if hearing his thought, a small voice whispered, "Here you are!"

He turned around and saw the girl from his dream emerge from behind the willow tree. Dressed in a light summer linen tunic and wide-legged pants, a long braid reaching the small of her back, she bathed in the silver moonlight like a celestial being.

You-jun's heart ran fast. It did whenever she was near. He stood up and said, "I thought you would not come tonight!"

"Oh, but you know I would, You-jun! It's a full moon! But Iris was awake for a long time. After she finally did sleep, I waited for the watchman to pass before coming out."

You-jun helped Jasmine sit down, under the willow tree. He took the sack from the branch and handed it to her.

"This is for you," he said. "It's hard to catch them in the moonlight, but under the shade of the tree, it was easy. I just had to use a branch to sweep the grass and they all flew up like a cloud."

"Thank you, You-jun!" Jasmine held it up at eye level to enjoy the faint light that flickered through the sack. Then she said, "Are you ready?"

You-jun nodded.

Jasmine loosened the string that tied the sack and gave it a gentle shake.

They watched as the fireflies rushed out of the sac and flew away, as if awakened from a dream.

Jasmine took something out of her pocket. "This is for you," she said.

You-jun opened the neatly folded silk handkerchief and held it up to see what it was like. The moonlight illuminated the shapes of the embroidery.

"Is it our willow tree? And two mandarin ducks under it?" he asked.

"Yes. I hope you will like it." Jasmine said. She was glad that even though the moonlight was bright, it was not enough to reveal her burning cheeks.

"It is beautiful. I shall take it with me wherever I go." You-jun folded the handkerchief and carefully tucked it in the pocket of his inner shirt.

He reached for Jasmine's hands and held them. Her hands were small, soft, and warm.

"Where do you intend to go? Like Master?" Jasmine said.

"Yes, Jasmine," You-jun said. "And more than that. Father has mentioned a friend of his who's been to America! Think about how far it is! I want to go and see faraway places like that."

"Will Master, Father, allow you? He wants you to take over his business," Jasmine said, "And Lady, she'll be heartbroken."

"I'll be back, of course," You-jun said.

After a moment of silence, Jasmine sighed, "I wish I were a man sometimes. I wish I could go, too. Or maybe just pretend to be a man, like Zhu Ying-tai. Zhu Ying-tai and Liang Shan-bo were classmates just like we were."

"Jasmine." You-jun squeezed her hands gently. "When I come back, I'll tell you about everything I see. I'll write to you while I'm on the road. If the outside world is peaceful, I'll come back and take you, and then we can both go again."

"You will?" Jasmin turned to face him, her eyes widening.

"Jie Jie," You-jun said, "the full moon today is our witness: I promise you that no matter where I go, I will only think about you, and I'll come back to you. Will you promise the same?"

Jasmine's eyes started to well. "Yes, I will. I will only think about you, and I'll be here waiting for you to come back. But..." Her voice trailed. "What if Master and Lady marry me to someone else when you are gone?"

"They won't," You-jun said. "Mother loves you as much as she loves Iris, and she will not let you suffer. You are her gan nü'er. I shall talk to Father and Mother soon and ask them to send a betrothal gift to Cloud Gate. I hope your father and mother will agree for me to have your hand."

He let go of her hands, gently stroked her hair, and wrapped his arm around her shoulder. "Are you cold?" he said.

"No, I'm happy," Jasmine said. She tilted her head to let it rest on his shoulder. And like that they sat for a long time.

After they heard the watchmen beating the third hour, "dung-, dung, dung," one slow two fast, they knew they had to return to the house. You-jun quickly scouted the route. When he saw everything was clear, he let Jasmine go first, and he followed a few paces behind.

Jasmine went through the side door silently, followed by You-jun. She knew the way well because she had accompanied her mother to receive deliveries at the side door. Only after she was formally taken in by the Hans as a gan daughter did she stop doing that, as A-mei had pointed out to her that she had become a miss of the family, not just a servant's daughter, and she must learn to behave appropriately.

Jasmine turned, waved at You-jun, and then tiptoed across the porch and corridor into the room she and Iris shared. She was relieved that no one saw them. It was always an adventure to go and meet You-jun during those full-moon nights. Yes, they were sister and brother, but she was only a gan daughter. If anyone saw them, her reputation would be ruined, the family would be scandalized, and Master and Lady and her mama and baba would all be furious with her. Every time when she went, she thought that she would tell You-jun that it would be her last time. But every time she went, she knew she wanted to go back, and she did not want to say what she ought to say. Sighing in her heart, she carefully sat down on her bed and began to remove her shoes. But in the dark, something stared at her, shining like a pair of small lanterns. She almost jumped up.

"Jie Jie!" she exclaimed and covered her mouth. "You scared me!"

Iris sat cross-legged on her bed, across from Jasmine's. The moonlight spilled through the open window, making Iris look like a looming phantom.

"Where have you been?" Iris asked in a hushed voice. Her tone did not tell Jasmine what she thought about her coming in at this hour or if she knew where Jasmine had been to.

"I...I..." Jasmine stammered. She did not know what to say. She should have been prepared for this, but Iris caught her by surprise.

"It's past the third hour. You have been gone for the whole time between the second and the third hour," Iris said.

"I..." Jasmin hesitated. She couldn't see Iris's face very well, except for the piercing stare of Iris's huge eyes. "You were not sleeping?"

Iris did not answer.

"Jie Jie, please don't tell anyone. I didn't do anything inappropriate. I just went to...went to..." She struggled to find her words. All of a sudden, saying what she did seemed to confirm what a terrible act it was.

"Went to meet You-jun?" Iris finished the sentence for her.

"You knew?"

"And the other nights when the moon was full," Iris continued.

Silence fell over the room.

"You-jun is our brother, Jasmine!" Iris spoke, with slightly raised voice, though still only a whisper.

"But, Jie Jie, you know even before Father and Mother took me as their gan nü'er, I, I liked him!" Jasmine's voice trembled. She did not want to upset Iris. Iris was her sister, her protector. And how shameful for a girl to admit that she liked a boy!

"What about Jian-da?" Iris asked.

"What about him?" Jasmin was confused.

"Couldn't you tell? Jian-da likes you, too. And I overheard Mother and Mrs. Fang talking about betrothing you to Jian-da," Iris said.

82

"No! That can't be true! Jian-da is kind to everybody. Mrs. Fang wants you to be her daughter-in-law. I can tell," Jasmine said.

"Well, whatever happens, we don't have much to say, do we?" Iris said. "I'm worried about you. If someone finds out that you are meeting You-jun, it'll be a scandal for the family. Even if you two are engaged, you should still not be out by yourselves, especially this late in the night!"

"I won't go see him like this anymore, Jie Jie," Jasmine said. "You-jun said that he would talk to Father and Mother and send betrothal gifts to Cloud Gate for me…"

"Are you happy?"

"Yes," Jasmine murmured, her face hot.

Iris sighed. "The two of you, what can I say. Two idiots."

Jasmine was relieved. "You are not mad at me?"

"Why should I be? I would rather keep you in the family. You would be a good daughter-in-law for Mother. And I don't have to learn to get used to a different girl as my sister-in-law. I just don't want any gossip about us," Iris said. "Now it's really getting late. Let's sleep."

"Will you…tell anyone?" Jasmine asked.

"Your secret is safe with me," Iris said. Jasmine sensed her smile.

"Oh, Jie Jie, I know you are my best friend!" Jasmin came over and put her arms around Iris. "I know you will always be on my side!"

Then she nudged Iris. "Can I lie with you? If we both can't sleep, we can talk all night!"

Iris sighed again and made room for Iris. "I really don't know what to do with you sometimes!" And she squeezed Jasmine's cheek gently.

They giggled and lay down, facing each other, their arms around each other's neck, as they had done many times before.

After a while, Jasmine said, "Too bad you will be married out, even if I get to stay."

"I'm not sure about that. Maybe Father and Mother will let me stay. Why does a girl have to marry out?" Iris whispered as she stroked Jasmine's hair.

"Jie Jie," Jasmine whispered back, "I know what to do. You should marry Jian-da. Yes, I know Mother and Mrs. Fang will love the idea! Jian-da will be a great husband to you."

"Naughty girl." Iris squeezed Jasmine's cheek again. "If you say that again, I'll tell Mother about you and You-jun. Poor Jian-da. He likes you.

His mother has to find him a fairy maiden so he can forget you."

"Okay, okay," Jasmine said, "I won't say it again. But Jian-da likes me because I'm almost like a boy, a good buddy for him. His temperament is perfect for you, can't you see?"

Iris didn't answer this time. Instead, she stuck her hands under Jasmine's armpits and tickled her. Jasmine giggled and almost fell off the bed.

Soon, Jasmine faded into sleep. She was relieved that Iris was on her side. She did not know that Iris stayed awake, listening to her soft, even breath, thinking about their conversation, hoping everything would go as they had wished, and worrying it would not.

CHAPTER 12
THREE RIVERS, MORNING, 1911

Summer Solstice: the twenty-sixth day of the fifth month and the tenth of the twenty-four solar terms. It has the longest day and the shortest night of the year.

The blazing sun and gentle summer breeze made it perfect for the Day of Drying out Clothes. On Number One Cypress Street, everything was brought out to the sun: winter garments, bedsheets, and covers, pillows, and cushions. They were hung on ropes that had been fastened between the branches of the large magnolia trees in the courtyard or laid flat out on bamboo mats in the yard.

Under A-mei's orders, Green Jade and several other women used long bamboo poles to beat the dust out of everything. Fine particles danced around in the sunlight, making the women turn their heads and cover their noses and mouths. Then they moved to the other side of the hanging sheets and garments, turned over the pillows and cushions, and beat everything some more. This process continued throughout the day, until finally there was no more dust left to fly. The linens and cottons would soon smell crisp and warm, the scent of the sun, and the bed covers, pillows, and cushions became soft and fluffy.

Another activity that kept the women in the household busy was the preparation of the Summer Solstice dinner. The dinner would be held as a garden party. Only the Fangs and a special friend of Master Han's were invited, so the dinner would not be an extravagant event, but simple and elegant with seasonal food.

After checking on the kitchen to make sure everything was in proper order, Lady Han joined Iris and Jasmine on the covered porch under the eaves. Iris was making a pair of embroidered shoes, and Jasmine was doing cross-stitch work on a pillowcase.

Iris was twenty-two and Jasmin was twenty. They were almost too old to still be living at home. Some girls at their ages already had children. Matchmakers had been coming steadily, but both girls had refused to accept any of the proposals, and Lady Han indulged them.

"That one sounded so dumb. I probably had read more books than he did," Iris would say about one of the prospective husbands.

"This one, if he looked like his father, who came to our house to do business with Father, would just be repulsive," Jasmin would say of another.

And then they would giggle.

Lady Han knew it was her job to find good families to marry her daughters into, but, though she was anxious, she did not want to hurry. There was no mother-in-law to whisper in her ear about her failure as a mother or give her icy looks of disapproval. There was enough food on the table to feed everyone and enough clothes to dress them all, and she did not need to rush them out of the door. She did not want to deliver the girls to unsympathetic, harsh mothers-in-law, either, so she checked the background of the families proposed by the match-makers discreetly, and none had satisfied her entirely.

And she was lucky that her husband still doted on her. He might have had "wild flowers," the occasional lovers, out somewhere during all his business trips—he probably spent more time on the road than at home—but he never brought anyone home or married a concubine. He never touched opium. He let Lady Han be the mistress of their home, inside of the walls of this house, and he the master to face the outside world and to provide for his family.

The only thing he interfered with regarding the girls was to stop them from being in the same classroom with You-jun and Jian-da Fang. Tiger,

Jasmine's brother, A-mei, and Old Wang's son, who dreaded the reading and studying imposed on all the kids by the family teacher, had long ago returned to Cloud Gate to learn farming from his father.

One day several years ago, Master Han returned home after a long trip. He changed into comfortable linen shirt and pants, washed his face, had a cup of green tea his wife brewed herself, and strolled into the garden at the back of the house.

What a surprise he got there!

The classroom was on the east side of the house, its door opening to the garden. The pupils had snuck out of the classroom and were having fun outside. You-jun and Jian-da were imitating the "husband" and "wife" of the Sichuanese opera comedy *Rolling Lamp*. The children saw the show at You-jun's grandmother's last grand birthday party, and it had since become their favorite make-believe pastime.

In the opera, the husband loved to play mahjong and gamble, but he always lost at the table. When he got home, the wife would pull him around by his ears and make him hold a burning oil lamp on his head. The husband had to do all kinds of tricks—crawling under a table, doing somersaults, walking backwards—without putting off the lamp and spilling the oil.

Thank goodness that You-jun, the "husband," did not have a flaming oil lamp on his head, but this did not prevent him from trying hard to pretend: he gasped, grimaced, and wobbled while holding his neck stiff and his head still. Jian-da, with his naturally delicate features—his skin was pale and his eyes dark—made a fine "wife," who was the tigress to You-jun's "Soft Ears," what obedient husbands were called in Sichuan. The girls were laughing to the point they had to hold their stomachs and fan themselves while saying, "Enough, enough, stop!"

You-jun, walking backwards, almost backed right into his father. The other three saw Master Han, and they froze. You-jun turned around to see what the matter was and his father grabbed him by both of his ears.

Master Han marched the kids into the classroom, where the senile teacher, with his glasses drooping on the tip of his nose, was taking a nap in the rocking chair behind his desk. When Master Han knocked on his desk, he jumped up and grabbed his ruler, probably thinking that his pupils were playing a prank on him. He was ready to dole out punishment by hitting their palms with his ruler before he realized who did the knocking. He was embarrassed and apologetic to the master and said that he had assigned his pupils to memorize certain passages of Confucius' Analects and would check on them soon.

Needless to say, none of the kids could recite the so-called passage that was assigned them. Iris did the best but still missed some important words. They all received a good beating on their palms by a wooden ruler from Master Han himself.

After this episode, the old teacher was relieved of his teaching duty. But "once your teacher, always your teacher." Master Han could not bring himself to kick him out of the house. After all, this was his first teacher that his own father had arranged for him. A teacher was like a parent. So the teacher was given duties helping Lady Han calculate household numbers, write couplets for Chinese New Year's, and write letters for servants if they needed to have one sent home.

As for the kids, Master Han said to Lady Han, "The kids are old enough now, and you must teach them that men and women should keep proper distance from each other. They should not be in the same classroom anymore. For You-jun and Jian-da, I'll look for a different tutor, and teach them myself when I'm around. The Civil Service Examination has been abolished for three years now, and they don't need to focus on writing eight-legged essays. You-jun should learn some business trade now. I have been thinking about taking them to Chongqing and Chengdu, to see the world.

"As for the girls, I don't mind them learning how to read and write because a truly learned husband would appreciate being able to talk about poetry and classics with his wife." Here he stopped for a moment, looking at his wife, who sat on the opposite of the big table, her hands folded on it. He reached across, put his right hand on her hands, and continued, with a smile, "I remembered how much fun we had when we first married!" Lady Han nodded, smiling back. "But I think Iris and Jasmine have learned enough about how to read and write. If they want more, you or I can teach them in private. How are their household skills coming along? You need to teach them more about those things. My daughters, even the gan daughter, do not need to be rushed out of the door to be married, but when they do, I don't want their mothers-in-law to be unhappy with them, and I don't want them to be topics of gossip."

"Yes, Husband," Lady said. "The girls are doing very well in learning household chores. They have good needlework, have followed Green Jade to learn how to do laundry, and have learned basic cooking from the cook. I will teach the girls so they will be proper wives. I hope they are lucky like me and find someone who dotes upon them as you do with me." She smiled again.

On this summer solstice day, the longest day of the year, Lady Han thought about this conversation with her husband as she sat down with the girls. She looked at both girls' needlework and admired how tight and neat the stitches were. Both girls had grown into beautiful young women. They were about a head taller than Lady Han, with a similar slim build. They both had big eyes framed by thick eyelashes, striking features that drew the attention of anyone looking at them. Jasmine had a perfect oval-shaped face and Iris had a more baby-looking full-moon face. On this day, they wore short-sleeved linen tunics and matching short pants that stopped just below their knees. *My beautiful daughters*! Lady Han sighed in her heart. Flowers were beautiful but they needed to be shielded from rain and wind. Before too long she would have to relinquish her beautiful flowers from the greenhouse she took such care to build and hand them to husbands and mothers-in-law, and pray that *they* would cherish her flowers as much as she did. She would do all she could, but she needed a higher power beyond herself to ensure her success. Guanyin was the higher power. She would not fail if she relied on Guanyin's benevolence.

Lady Han called out to A-mei, "Come sit with us and rest a little bit! I'll ask the kitchen to bring some plum tea to rid us of some heat."

As they were sipping plum tea, they saw You-jun and Jian-da coming from outside. The boys had gone to the pier to see if Master Han's rice shipment had arrived. Lady Han asked them to join the ladies for some plum tea and they happily sat down. Thin beads of sweat ran down their noses and foreheads, so Lady Han sent for fresh towels to wipe their faces.

The boys were both eighteen that summer. You-jun had a handsome face with a square jaw that gave him a look of determination. Unlike his sister, his eyes were slender, and when he laughed, his eyes became slivers of new moon, making him look like a little kid, softening his grown-up determination.

Jian-da was taller than You-jun. He was handsome in a different way, almost as beautiful as a girl, with pale skin, deep, dark eyes, and an air of melancholy. He and You-jun had grown up as brothers, but they had very different personalities, like the sun and the moon. You-jun was outgoing, easy to laugh, quick to act, and quick to forget. Jian-da was an introvert, sensitive, more careful, and calculating. The personality difference could come from their parents, but it could also be attributed to their family circumstances. You-jun had never had a hard day since he was born. His parents and his sister adored him. His grandmother, before she passed away, had spoiled him. She would not so much as acknowledge the presence of Iris, but she loved her grandson, the one who would bear their family name. She played with him, saved the best food for him, and gave him money so he could buy treats from street vendors.

Jian-da's father passed away when he was a toddler, leaving behind him some money, a house, and small plots of land in the country to be rented out, and so Jian-da and his mother managed to get by. Mr. Fang was a good friend of Master Han, who had promised to look after his friend's widow and son. Jian-da had been taught by the same teacher as You-jun, and Mrs. Fang became a close friend of Lady Han. Both mother and son understood their situation and Mrs. Fang had taught Jian-da to be cautious: careful in what he said or did, and sensitive not only to the words of others, but also the tone of their voices and the look on their faces when they spoke. Over time, Jian-da took the motto "Silence is Golden" to his heart and learned what to say, and when to say it. Master Han and Lady Han treated him like another son. Master Han sometimes lamented to his wife that he wished You-jun were more reserved and acted more mature like Jian-da.

Now they all sat under the shade of the eaves, enjoying the breeze created by hand-held cattail fans and the soothing taste of cool plum tea. The morning was turning into afternoon and the early summer heat was slowly rising, but the air was still bearable. The young people paid particular attention to their manners. Iris and Jasmine did not say much, and they covered their mouths when they laughed. You-jun and Jian-da resisted the urge to take off their outer shirts even though that would make it much cooler for them.

"What are you working on?" Jian-da asked the girls. He was good at being sweet to them. He wished he had a sister like Iris, and his heart fluttered at the sight of Jasmine.

"Jie Jie is working on making a pair of embroidered shoes. I'm making a pillowcase. Just some boring stuff."

"Not boring stuff." Lady Han smiled. "You are doing lady's work and that's important."

"That's right," A-mei agreed. "Your future mothers-in-law will look at your work and judge how good a wife and daughter-in-law you would be."

Hearing this, both girls' cheeks flushed much redder than what a hot summer morning could have brought.

"Why do they have to marry out? Go to serve some snobbish mothers-in-law who will treat them poorly, and some filthy, unworthy husbands," You-jun said loudly. With his eyes wide open, he looked angry at the thought of the gloomy future of Iris and Jasmine.

"Don't be such a silly boy." Lady Han smiled fondly at her son. "I don't like the fact that you are all grown now. But that is what happens when kids grow up. You and Jian-da will find your brides, and Iris and Jasmine will marry out. That's something we can't change."

"But maybe we can!" You-jun stood up abruptly. "I know we can! Tomorrow I'll ask father about it." He shot a look at Jasmine, who lowered her head, her hands turning the tambour over and over.

Jian-da reached over to pull his friend to sit down. "Hey, calm down my friend," he said. "Master and Lady know best." He patted You-jun's shoulder, and his delicate face was overshadowed by sorrow, if only for a moment.

Lady Han took all this in, and her heart skipped a beat. Slowly, she swayed her fan. *I don't want to hurry*, she thought, *but I may not have a choice.*

Just then, sounds came from the front gate.

CHAPTER 13
THREE RIVERS, 1911, SUMMER SOLSTICE, AFTERNOON AND EVENING

"Master and his friends are here," Lady Han said. "The wind must have been blowing the right direction. I think the barge is early today." She put down her fan, stood up, and said, "A-mei, ask Green Jade and the girls to collect everything in the yard. I will need to apologize to our guest about this. Iris and Jasmine, you go back to your room, come out when I send A-mei for you. You-jun, you come with me to greet your father and the guest. And Jian-da, do you want to come with us or go home and escort your mother when she comes later today?"

Jian-da went home. Everyone else did as told. Lady Han smoothed her hair, let her son take her elbow, and went to the front gate. They stood there as Master Han and a young man walked across the street towards them.

The young man stood out by not having a long queue. He had a short haircut under a Western-style gray fedora. Instead of a long tunic, he wore a Western-style white button-down shirt, which was tucked inside a pair of cream-colored pants. On his feet, he wore shiny brown leather loafers. He held a cane, but he was obviously young and healthy and in no need of a cane to help him walk. Several children came to stare at this strange-looking young man. He smiled and said hi, which stunned the kids and they scattered like a bunch of sparrows hit by a rock before gathering up again.

Lady Han greeted her husband and the guest by putting her hands together, bowing her head, and bending her knees slightly. She waited for the men to speak first.

You-jun also bowed his head, and said, "Father, you are home!"

"You-jun, Wife," Master Han said. "This is Mr. Liang Fei, my new young friend that I have told you about. He has made this special trip from Chengdu to Three Rivers to visit our family."

"What an honor! Welcome!" Lady Han said and bowed again.

"Hope it's not too much trouble for your household." The young man named Liang Fei took off his hat, held it in front of his chest, and bowed to Lady Han.

Then he put his hat back on and turned to You-jun, holding his left hand over his right fist at the chest to greet him. "And so you are You-jun! Your father has talked so much about you. I can't wait to get to know you more. And your friend…"

"Jian-da," You-jun said. "He'll come soon. Father has talked a lot about you, too! I can't wait to hear your stories about your study in America!"

"All right then, let's go in and have some plum tea to cool off," Master Han said. "We'll have lots of time to talk and chat."

They went around the shadow wall and walked across the yard. Half of the sheets that had been hung out to dry had been collected but the other half still swayed in the breeze like many flags. Lady Han apologized for the untidiness of the yard. "Mr. Liang, you must excuse us for all the hanging sheets! The sun was so bright and the servants wanted to hang out all the sheets as long as they can!"

"The yard is actually quite beautiful this way!" said Liang Fei. "Nothing is more beautiful than people doing their household work, going about their daily business peacefully. I missed the beauty of domesticity while away in America, so you mustn't apologize, Lady Han. This is like homecoming for me!"

They sat under one of the magnolia trees. There were a stone table and several bamboo chairs. A-mei brought a tray with plum tea, sliced watermelons, fresh towels, and several cattail fans. She greeted Master Han and retreated to the kitchen. After making sure the men had everything they needed to sit and relax in comfort, Lady Han excused herself as well, saying that she needed to check on progress in the kitchen.

"Please make yourself home, Mr. Liang," Lady Han said before she went away.

The men wiped their faces with the fresh towels, had a few sips of the plum tea, and fanned themselves. You-jun began, "Mr. Liang..."

"Just call me Fei," Liang Fei said, "No need to be too polite and formal!"

"Okay, Older Brother Fei," You-jun continued. "How did you go to America? Were you awarded a Boxer Indemnity Scholarship?"

"Yes, I was very lucky," Liang Fei said.

"Well, it was not just luck," Master Han said. "Fei would have passed the Civil Examination had it not been abolished, and he would have had a bright future. His family is one of the most esteemed families in Chengdu. I heard him giving an invited speech in Chengdu at the Sichuan Provincial Assembly and I was so impressed that I used all my network of relations to find a way to be introduced to him. I'm honored that he accepted my invitation to visit Three Rivers. You-jun, I want you and Jian-da to learn as much as possible from Fei!"

"Ahh, Mr. Han, you are too generous in your kind words," Fei said. "My father has always spoken very highly of you as well. He says that even though you are immensely successful as a businessman, you are a scholar in your heart."

"Your father knows mine?' You-jun was very curious.

"Oh yes," Master Han said. "Older Mr. Liang and I were childhood friends. But he left Three Rivers when he was still young, when his father, Fei's grandfather took a government position in Chengdu."

"So You-jun, what have you been studying? Mr. Han said that you and your friend and sisters were taught by a tutor at home," Fei said.

You-jun detected a heat wave rising to his cheeks that had nothing to do with the early summer warm weather. "Nothing special, just the Four Books and Five Classics. And...I ...I have not been as diligent as I should have in my studying..."

"That's true!" Master Han laughed, which made You-jun feel relieved. "Once I caught him and Jian-da making fool of themselves, pretending to be the buffoons in *Rolling Lamps* when the teacher napped. They made my daughters laugh but earned themselves a good beating on their palms!"

The men laughed, even You-jun. He did feel like a fool when his father recounted the story in front of Fei.

"That's all right," Fei said. "It is important that young people study Four Books and Five Classics. But what I see and learn in America makes me think that we have to learn other things to make China a strong nation. Like science and engineering. The Western forces are strong because they have science and technology that we do not have. They have steamboats and trains! We use gun powder for firecrackers; they make guns and cannons!"

You-jun widened his eyes. He was fascinated by the new terms Fei spoke of. "Science! Technology!" He repeated the words. He had heard about steamboats but had not seen one. These boats were propelled by an engine and not pulled by tow men. When he went down to the rivers with Jian-da, he sometimes thought what it would be like if steamboats sailed on the rivers.

"Tell us more," he asked Fei, full of admiration.

"The Western nations are strong because they have advanced science and technology. China, on the other hand, is very backwards. We laugh at them, call them barbarians, and think we are the center of the world, but we cannot stop their guns and cannons, like the Boxers believed. The Four Books and Five Classics will not save us. We need to study math and science. We need engineers like Zhan Tianyou to build roads and railways. I'm fortunate enough to have followed Mr. Zhan's footsteps and gone to Sheffield Scientific School of Yale University in America," Fei said.

"The Sichuan-Hankou Railway Company hired Mr. Zhan last year to be the chief engineer, didn't they? There was also a great effort in raising funds to build the railway. I remain hopeful that the twelve hundred kilometers of railway from Chengdu to Wuhan will soon be built," Master Han said.

"We can hope, Mr. Han," said Fei, "as long as the company is not as corrupted and mismanaged as before."

"That's true," Mr. Han said. "Some people believe the government should nationalize the construction of railways because of all the problems of inefficient local management. What's your take on this?"

"I do think we need a better way to raise and manage the funds needed. Many people bought shares on paper but never paid the money. Only ten percent of the promised money was raised. As a result, only about ninety kilometers out of the planned thirty-five hundred kilometers were built so far! At this snail's pace, it'll take a hundred years to build the Sichuan-Hankou railway! None of us will see it in our lifetime!" Liang Fei said.

"Well, I hope not!" You-jun chimed in. "This railway project sounds fascinating."

Master Han nodded. "Because of this, those who advocate nationalization of the railways also think that the only way to raise enough money is to borrow from foreign banks," he said.

"That's true," Liang Fei said. "Great Britain, Germany, France, and the United States have formally requested to provide loans to the railway projects. We need to be careful, however, so we don't end up losing autonomy of these railways."

He paused for a moment, and added, "No matter what, at least I get to apprentice with Mr. Zhan, and that's more than I can ask! I'm an engineer and building a railway is what I want to do. I hope one day I will be able to do just that."

"How I wish to be a part of it, too!" You-jun said. He was so absorbed by their conversation, he didn't realize Jian-da had come in and stood quietly by him, not wanting to interrupt the conversation.

But Master Han saw Jian-da. He always liked the boy, sometimes even more so than You-jun because Jian-da was more quiet and obedient. Since Jian-da lost his father at a young age, Master Han, an old friend of Jian-da's father, had taken it upon himself to care for the widow and the boy, and he was like a father to Jian-da.

"Come here and sit down, Jian-da!" Master Han said, affectionately.

Jian-da went over and bowed his head. "Master Han, you are home!"

"Jian-da, you are taller than You-jun now! How is your mother?" Master Han asked.

"Mother has gone to the kitchen to help. She asked me to pay respects to you on her behalf." Jian-da bowed again, still standing.

"Jian-da, this is Mr. Liang Fei. We are talking about his study in America and the future railway between Chengdu and Wuhan. Sit down and join us!"

The four of them continued their conversation as afternoon turned into evening, during which time Green Jade refilled their teacups several times, until Lady Han came to invite them to join the Summer Solstice dinner.

The special sweet summer fragrances of roses, jasmine, and gardenias as evening closed in saturated the air. The day was so long that when the moon rose in the west, it only painted a faint impression of a waning crescent on the cerulean sky.

A long table was set out in the courtyard. Summer foods were served: roast pork ribs, cucumber salad, and spicy cold noodles with bean sprouts. Various squashes were always main players in a summer feast: there was soup made from loofah squash, bitter melon stir-fried with red chili peppers, and freshly squeezed watermelon juice. There was also rice wine made and brought to Three Rivers by Old Wang during one of his visits.

Iris and Jasmine stood by the table as the men approached. Lady Han had told them that since they were old enough and since the only guests were the Fangs and Mr. Liang, it was okay for them to join the table. The women would sit at one side and the men on the other.

Lady Han did not need to remind the girls about good manners. Iris and Jasmine put their hands together, bowed their heads, and lightly bent their knees. They sat down after the men did. They started eating after the men had started, and they kept their heads slightly bowed, their mouths closed as they chewed. They did not speak other than nodding their heads in agreement with what the men said, and they covered their mouths while laughing at their jokes.

Lady Han was proud of her daughters. It was not very often that they dined with their father and his esteemed friends, and her daughters, even Jasmine, carried themselves elegantly and flawlessly.

Mrs. Fang observed the girls with great admiration as well. She wished that Jian-da could marry one of the Han daughters, preferably Iris. While she liked both girls, she preferred the older girl, who was calmer than the younger one. Besides, she was the real Han daughter. But as a widow, who was she to decide? Fortunately the Hans did not seem to be in a hurry to marry the daughters out. She would need to inquire carefully with Lady Han, soon.

The men continued their conversation at the dinner table. Occasionally, Master Han would stop and explain to the ladies about the railways, the steamboats, and the Westerners. The ladies were particularly interested in the latter.

"There were a few I saw in Chengdu. Funny looking fellows! Their hair can be red or yellow or brown or black. Their eye colors vary a great deal, too. Some look like those of cats. They are hairy. They have big, high noses. Men don't wear a queue, of course," Master Han said, to the subdued laughter of the ladies. "The only thing I admire is their height! I wish I could be tall like them!"

"That's true. I like many things Western, except for their food! I suppose the Westerners are so strong and tall because they eat cheese, drink milk, and eat lots of meat. I can bring myself to eat the steak and potatoes, but not cheese. So pungent!" said Fei. Everyone at the table was thinking about this pungent flavor of something called *chee-shi*.

"Was it like stinky tofu?" Jasmine, forgetting her manners, asked in a loud voice. Lady Han and A-mei, who was also invited to sit at the table, gave her a reproachful glance. Jasmine turned red and lowered her head.

"That's exactly the same question I have!" You-jun said and smiled at Jasmine as if to say, "Don't worry about silly rules!"

Liang Fei did not seem to mind at all. "Yes, Jasmine." He turned his body slightly to face her. "Something like that, only worse in certain cases!"

Everybody shook their heads and marveled about the strange Western food.

Liang Fei said to Lady Han, "Thank you for such a nice dinner! It's such a treat to have a fine meal. The meal is perfect in its color, its texture, its flavor, and its taste. And above all, it's made with what's in season. Confucius would have approved!"

Not used to being praised in front of everybody, Lady Han felt a bit awkward. "Ahh, Mr. Liang! You are too kind. Please don't laugh at our simple country meal. You have seen the world and I'm afraid what we have in Three Rivers is not worthy of your taste!"

"But what the world has is stinky *chee-shi*!" You-jun said. Everyone laughed.

"That's so true!" Fei caught his breath after laughing heartily. "You shouldn't be so modest, Lady Han. Western women would say thank-you if they were praised. They are free-thinking almost like men. There were no women in my engineering class, but I have seen them on college campuses. They became teachers and nurses. They have large feet, not very beautiful, but they can walk and hike like men do. And I personally think it is nice for them to be able to walk like men."

The three older women giggled and shook their heads, as if they didn't know what to make of this piece of information. But both Iris and Jasmine were fascinated, though not showing it outright. They remembered their manners and did not ask any questions or make any comments, but their minds had taken on a wild flight of imagination. Be like a man! This idea was exciting, yet dangerous and frightening.

"The reformists have promoted natural feet, too," Master Han said.

"Indeed," Fei said. "I read 'On Natural Feet' by Liang Qichao. He made a compelling argument why women should have natural feet." He stopped, as if just becoming aware of the fact that other than A-mei, the women sitting at the table had bound feet. In his article, Liang Qichao had argued that only women with natural feet can nurture healthy offspring and become good workers rather than parasites to the family and society.

You-jun said, "Older Brother Liang, so many fascinating things you have enlightened us! I wish I could go to see the world like you someday!"

"So you could find yourself a large-footed woman?" Jian-da said and winked at his friend. This surprised everyone, coming from the quiet and reserved Jian-da, who had said nothing until now.

"No, not that!" You-jun hastily added.

"I don't think our Han family will be able to live up to a big-footed Western daughter-in-law, son!" Master Han joked.

"Never, Father!" You-jun said through the roaring laughter. "I give you my word on that!"

The conversation and laughter continued. The food and wine disappeared. The sun was finally starting to set in the west in this longest day of the year. The waning crescent moon was now visible on the indigo sky. Number One Cypress Street was enveloped in a soft glowing rosy light of a perfect summer sunset.

The lives of everyone sitting at that table became entwined afterwards, beginning on that beautiful evening.

That night, You-jun couldn't sleep. He played Liang Fei's words in his head over and over again. He saw Jasmine's smile when he closed his eyes. By the time he finally started dreaming, he had made up his mind.

CHAPTER 14
THREE RIVERS AND CLOUD GATE, 2017

When we came downstairs in the morning, Hong-mei and Shan were waiting for us in a shining brown Wuling Hongguang seven-passenger minivan.

Shan lifted the middle seats so Hong-mei and I could get in the third row. My mom and Aunt Daisy sat in the middle row, and Uncle De-chen sat in the front passenger seat.

As if reading my mind, Shan turned around and said, "I borrowed this minivan from my company. It's nice to have the whole family in the same car." He was an engineer for a construction company.

"Thank you, Shan. This is so nice," I said.

"I hope it's as comfortable as the American cars you and Aunt Lily are used to."

I told him that I didn't have a car. Everybody other than my mom seemed to be surprised.

"How come?" Aunt Daisy asked.

"I live close to work, so I bike or walk most of the time," I explained.

"What about shopping? Or going to places further than going to work?" my aunt asked.

"I take the city transit. And the buses. Or cab, now Uber."

"We were like that just a few years ago," Hong-mei said. "Biking to work and taking buses. But now almost everyone has a car, unless you are really old, or really poor."

"Isn't that interesting," Aunt Daisy said.

"It is," I said. "Like the Chinese and Americans try to be each other." Everyone laughed.

As we chatted, Shan drove us out of the narrow backstreet where my aunt and uncle's apartment was to the main thoroughfare of the city. We left early to avoid morning traffic, and soon we were out of Three Rivers and on the highway to Cloud Gate.

"So whose birthday party is this that we are going to?" I asked. "Is there a place we can stop before getting there? I think I should bring some gifts. Maybe a fruit basket?" I spoke from my limited experiences visiting elder relatives in China: always bring some gifts. The best would be American Ginseng from Wisconsin, and if you neglected getting that in Chinatown before leaving, then a fruit basket or a crate of imported milk—organic, from Australia or New Zealand—would do. I figured there would not be a fancy enough grocery store on the way to buy imported milk.

"It's nice of you to think that, Rose!" Aunt Daisy said. "When we go to the countryside, most of the time, we just bring a red envelope. People in the countryside have nice fresh fruits and vegetables. Cash usually will be very useful."

"Oh, I thought red envelopes are only given to children and unmarried adults in the family at Chinese New Year's!" I said.

They laughed again.

"Clearly, I have not taught you enough," my mom said.

"Don't worry, you'll learn it soon!" Hong-mei smiled at me.

"And the birthday banquet is for Auntie Wang. You won't know who she is, Rose," Aunt Daisy said. "Hong-mei is always confused about who the relatives are in Cloud Gate."

"Even me," my mother said. "Sometimes."

"I understand that Cloud Gate is our ancestral home," I said.

"That's right." Aunt Daisy said. "Auntie Wang married the youngest cousin of our mom, your Grandma Pearl. I do believe that she is the last one left of that generation."

"How old is she going to be?" I was curious.

"One hundred years!" Aunt Daisy said.

"Wow," Hong-mei and I said together.

"Yep, and still sharp as a tack. She always wants to go for big when playing mahjong. I always go, Auntie, five jiao are good enough for a round! And she'll laugh at me and say, well, why should I take the money to my grave? Let's do two yuan! And she ends up winning most of the time!"

More laughter.

"Aunt Daisy," I began, "do you think this Auntie Wang will by any chance know anything about Grandma Pearl's grandmother?"

"Are you thinking about your dream?" Mom said.

"Yes. In the dream, she asked me to…"

"I know. We all had the same dream," Mom said.

"Ahh, the Dream of the Fang women!" Uncle De-chen said. "I thought your aunt was joking when she said that your mom and she had the same dream, about their grandma Iris asking them to look for somebody in the family. But one day when Hong-mei was in college, I happened to be in Chengdu and was visiting her. She told me a dream she had the night before that bothered her. Hong-mei did not know about her mom and aunt's dreams. I admit that I had a shiver running down my spine when I heard the story. In Hong-mei's dream, it was Grandma Pearl who visited, but she asked for the same thing. I have no reason to doubt that the Fang ladies all had the same dream on this matter."

"So strange," Shan agreed. "It sounds like superstition. If it's not you ladies who were telling this, I would definitely have thought it a hoax."

"It is just coincidence. Dreams are just that, dreams," Aunt Daisy said.

"Is that why nobody followed up on the dreams?" I said. "But I still want to hear what you all had, if you don't mind."

"I never heard anyone do something because of a dream. But okay then, I'll go first," said Aunt Daisy. "I had the dream on the day when we took Grandma Iris's body to be buried in Cloud Gate. So it was in the spring of 1967. I was already in Cloud Gate for my reeducation and to be honest I was embarrassed about having to take the time off from farm work for the funeral."

My mom nodded. "Yes, Grandma visited her cousin Uncle Tiger often and she made arrangements for her funeral. Sometimes she went there for a day or two, and sometimes she stayed longer. Mom went with her sometimes, but mostly someone from the village came to visit Three Rivers for something, and they would take her back and forth. She would bring home fresh produce from the village. Our favorite was new sweet potatoes. They were so sweet after being roasted. Just thinking about them makes my mouth water, even today."

Aunt Daisy continued, "When I was a kid I asked her what she did there in Cloud Gate. She said that she liked to visit Uncle Tiger and his family and the family's tombs. She would have liked to visit the Guanyin Temple, but nobody did or dared during those years of the Cultural Revolution.

"I was alarmed by the fact that she mentioned the temple. Temples were something from the feudalistic past, and most of them had been destroyed. I was surprised to hear that the temple was still standing in Cloud Gate. But I didn't say anything, because I already got in big trouble with Grandma Iris by burning my family genealogy book the year before. It was the beginning of the Cultural Revolution, right before I left for Cloud Gate. I was afraid that the history of my unfortunate, petty bourgeoisie family might fall into the hands of the Red Guards.

"I can't forget the look on her face when she caught me in the middle of action. The book was on full blaze in the stove, the same one she used to roast sweet potatoes for us. She stared at the fire and then me, with her eyes that seemed to sink deeper as she aged, her color almost transparent. And she whispered, with her bony hands folded in front her, 'What have you done, Daisy?'

Daisy turned to look out the window, as if avoiding her grandma's eyes. We were quiet. Then she took a breath and continued.

"So when Grandma Iris died, they took her body on a barge arranged by Uncle Tiger, and she was buried in Cloud Gate. For the first time, I saw headstones of her family.

"There was no funeral procession or ceremony for Grandma Iris, except that my mom insisted on burning incense and some paper money, and who knew where she got hold of those. They were remnants of feudalism and nobody used them anymore. I rolled my eyes and sneered at all the superstitious rituals that poisoned people's minds. After the funeral, Mom said that we needed to go to the temple and offer our respects, just this once. I refused. I said I had to get back to farm work. I told her that temples should have been destroyed, and I couldn't believe there was still one in Cloud Gate and she was even going to visit it.

"My mom looked at me the same way as Grandma looked at me when I burned the family book. Her face was pale, and her eyes were dark. She walked away, saying nothing. She never did mention it again, but I thought she had never forgiven me for that."

Aunt Daisy sighed and looked out the window again. We all waited.

After a while, she continued, "Anyway, Mom and Lily went to the temple, and I turned around towards the village. It was a long walk from the graveyard. So I sat down under a willow tree when I came upon a pond. It was springtime and the hanging branches of the willow tree had just started to turn a soft yellow-green color. I didn't know why I would fall asleep in the middle of the day, and that was when I had the dream.

"In the dream, Grandma Iris spoke to me. I was so happy to see her. The moment I saw her, I realized how much I had missed her, even during the short time she was gone. I missed having her waiting at the front door when I got back from wherever I was. I missed the short visits we had in the past year when she came to Cloud Gate. I missed her smile, her voice, her white hair that was always neatly put in a bun. I missed holding her small and bony hands and rubbing her bound and deformed feet with warm water on cold winter nights.

"*Grandma!* I cried out to her, *you are back! Oh I missed you so much! You are not really gone, are you?*

"She sat down facing me, and her right hand held my hands, her fingers cold and thin, and her left hand stroked my hair gently. Through her beautiful smile, she said, *my dear, I may be gone, but I'm always with you whenever you want me to be.*

"I told her how sorry I was for burning our family book and for not visiting the temple. When she was alive, I never apologized for burning the book. Now Grandma said to me, *You did what you had to do. But don't forget your family. Come back to Cloud Gate often. Sweep our tombs and trim the weeds that will cover all our headstones. Look for my mother. She has been forgotten. I did that. I let her be forgotten. When you are ready, visit the temple.*

"I promised her I would. Grandma laid my head down in her lap and started a lullaby, like she had done so many times before when Lily and I were little kids:

Rolling, rolling, rolling.
Roll the boat to the bridge of my maternal grandma
She always praises me, a perfect little baby

"I didn't know how long I had slept. By the time Uncle Wang's sons came out looking for me, it was dusk."

The only sound in the car after Aunt Daisy finished her story, was that of the engine and the noise of the wind rushing in. My mom had cracked open the window on her side to get some fresh air.

"That's incredible," I said finally.

Then my mom broke the silence and we heard her story.

"I remember Grandma Iris's funeral in Cloud Gate. It was a cloudy and unusually windy day. I remember the sounds: trees blowing in the wind as if they were weeping, and my mom's sobbing. I couldn't believe that Daisy would hurt Mom like that, on the day when Grandma had to be put in the cold ground." She reached over to take Aunt Daisy's hand, as if to say, "But that was in the past; I have forgiven you."

"Anyway, I went to the temple with Mom. The temple was in the opposite direction of the village, on White Cloud Mountain, on a high cliff. I didn't know how people managed to build it so high up. There were narrow stone steps leading up to it, but it was very hard to walk on those steps: it would be too wide if you tried to scale two steps at a time, but too narrow if you took only one.

"Grand-uncle Tiger led the way. He was very old. He was Grandma Iris's cousin. You could tell Grandma's death had taken a toll on him. *Now they are all gone, only I'm left*, he said, as he wiped tears from his eyes turbid with cataracts. But he had lived in Cloud Gate all his life, and he knew the way. And he was still strong for his age. Mom followed him a few steps behind. I followed Mom, worrying that she might slip and fall, walking on those narrow steps. She had 'liberated feet.' Grandma started binding mom's feet, but abandoned the effort halfway, urged by our grandfather, so mom's feet were not completely deformed but they were not made to walk on steps like these. The wind had made it worse. I thought several times that we would all be blown away. Grand-uncle Tiger's three sons and daughters-in-law followed me. The only one from that party left today is this Auntie Wang, wife of the youngest son, whose birthday party we are going to.

"Finally we got to the top of the cliff. The temple perched on it; when I looked through the windows, I didn't see any edges.

"We walked through a small courtyard leading to the temple. Calling it a temple may be exaggerating a bit. The vermilion painting on the door, the walls, and pillars were mottled. There was a small pavilion with a bell under it. It was a small and tidy place, but there had been few visitors; you could tell by the incense burner which contained barely any ash or incense ends.

"The main hall had a Guanyin statue. Guanyin sat cross-legged on a lotus seat, her right hand in prayer in front of her chest, and her left hand rested on her thigh. She sat there, looking forlorn, with no other paintings or statues to keep her company.

"On both sides of the main hall, there were several small wing rooms. They were locked. I peeked inside and saw that the ones on the west seemed to be living quarters for the nuns, and the east ones seemed to be storage rooms. Of course, there were no nuns present. There might not have been any Red Guards in Cloud Gate to destroy the temple, but the nuns had all scattered. Some got married, willingly or forced.

"Grand-uncle Tiger's daughters-in-law took out matches, incense, and offerings from their bamboo rucksacks: rice balls, oranges, and some hard candies. My mom laid all the offerings on a tray in front of Guanyin. We took turns to light up incense sticks, using both of our hands to hold the incense over our heads, and bowed three times before sticking them in the sand inside of the burner. And then we knelt on a cushion that was so old you could not even tell what color it used to be, and we kowtowed three times.

"I didn't know what others prayed for. I asked for Grandma Iris to be ferried peacefully to the West Pure Land, for Mom to not miss her mother too much, and for something good to happen to Daisy and me."

Both Aunt Daisy and Mom dabbed their eyes. Silence fell over the car again.

"What about your dream, Aunt Lily?" Hong-mei asked, her voice gentle. "Did you have the dream then, too?"

"Oh, no," my mom said. "I didn't have the dream until about 1980, when I came back to Three Rivers from America for the first time, about eight years after I left. I was so excited about coming back, I couldn't sleep well for days before the trip. So when we finally got on the airplane, I fell asleep quickly, and that was when I had the dream."

"On the airplane!" Hong-mei and I said together.

"Yes, I know, just like Rose did," Mom said. "In the dream, I was back at the temple, which had been repainted and it was beautiful: vermillion pillars, gilded panels, and a pure white Guanyin. Grandma Iris, Mom,

Daisy, and I were all there and we were having a picnic in the courtyard. It was sunny, the sky was blue, and it felt like we were floating on clouds. Then Grandma said to us, it's time I tell you more about my mother and my family. Promise you will look her up. She's in the temple."

This time, Shan broke the silence. "Look," he said, "we are here. You can see the gate."

I wished the car trip had continued. On the other hand, I was excited to actually be in Cloud Gate. Perhaps Auntie Wang would tell more stories. Perhaps I could find out whom we were supposed to look for.

CHAPTER 15
THREE RIVERS, 1911,
THE DAY AFTER SUMMER SOLSTICE

Lady Han got up before dawn to make sure a proper breakfast was ready for her husband and their guest. The men were going to visit the Diaoyu Fortress in the morning, before Liang Fei left.

It was early, so she decided to go through the garden in the back of the house to enjoy the crisp morning air, smell the roses, and listen to the birds chirping. She passed by the room shared by Iris and Jasmine. Their door was still closed. She smiled and shook her head. The girls were at the age of getting married, but they still behaved like children. It was not their fault. She spoiled them. Iris was her first child. The first child changed a girl to a mother, and no matter how many children a mother had in her life, no one would be a match to the firstborn for the joy, the excitement, the worry, and the wonder.

But Jasmine…Her heart ached a little every time when she thought about her. How could she be blamed if all she wanted was to keep Jasmine by her side, as long as she could, and treat Jasmine as if she were still a little child?

But they grew, no matter what she thought. She and A-mei had been teaching them needlework and both girls were getting good at it. They also learned how to cook. They didn't necessarily have to cook at home, but when they got married, they must know how to do it to please their mothers-in-law. Even if they were fortunate enough to have a cook at their married home, they still needed to know what food should be served at different seasons and what food was good for certain types of ailments. They also learned how to launder and how to hang out everything under the summer sun. Again a skill they might not need if they would be fortunate enough to have someone else doing it for them, but they must still know it, just in case. No one could tell what the future would hold.

And she as their mother needed to find them good families to marry. Jian-da and Jasmine would be a good match; she had secretly had their birth dates and times and their eight characters examined by Master Hui-Ming, Wise and Bright, at the Guanyin Temple in Cloud Gate earlier that year. She was careful with Jasmine's birth date, and she was satisfied with the results. Jian-da seemed to really like Jasmine, and that was a plus. Mrs. Fang might need a little persuasion, as she had hinted that she would prefer Iris. But the matching characters of Jian-da and Jasmine should settle the matter. Mrs. Fang would not be so ungrateful for all the help the Hans had given her over the years. And she would have to give face to Lady Han. Lady Han would just need to make sure that Jasmine's dowry would be equal in value to, if not more than what she would provide for Iris.

For Iris, she had made contact with a prominent family in Chongqing through the most expensive, but also the best matchmaker in town, and things were looking promising.

If things would work out as she had planned, both daughters would be married to good families, and more importantly, they would both still live nearby. She would still be able to watch over them, like a hen over her chicks. For this, she was diligent in her prayers, frequent in her offering of incense and candles to Guanyin, and generous in her financial support of the temple in Cloud Gate. And she had been practicing being a vegetarian on the first and fifteenth day of each month.

A-mei was already in the kitchen. She did not need to do much here in Three Rivers, but she had done household work her whole life. She was happiest when she was busy working with something, and she still felt most at home in the kitchen.

The breakfast would be millet congee, steamed white flour bun with shredded pork fillings, and pickled cabbage. Lady Han was happy with the preparation. A-mei offered to go and wake the girls. They should be dressed and washed, and they needed to be at the dining table waiting when the men came in.

A-mei knocked on the door and said in a slightly raised voice, "It's A-mei, I'm coming in." She opened the door a crack and squeezed herself in.

Both girls were still asleep, jammed into Iris's bed. They'd kicked off the bed cover, each wearing only a pair of short pants and belly covers. Jasmine had one arm draped over Iris's shoulder.

"It's time to get up, "A-mei whispered. When they didn't stir, she nudged them both. The girls sat up, half-awake, asking what time it was. "It's time to get up!" A-mei repeated, smiling. "You need to be in the dining room before your father and his guest are there." She helped Jasmine put on her shirt. "You girls need to sleep on your own bed and keep the covers on. You will catch a cold and have belly aches if you sleep without covers on."

"Yes, Mama!" said Jasmine in a sassy tone. "Brush my hair, Mama!" She loved Lady Han but she was always worried about doing something wrong or having poor manners, even though Lady Han, her gan mother, was never critical of her. With A-mei, she could be a silly little girl.

"Okay, okay, Miss!" A-mei said, and she started to brush Jasmine's hair using a comb made from a bull's horn.

Iris sensed the intimacy between A-mei and Jasmine as mother and daughter, and her heart twitched a little, like it had been pricked lightly. Her mother was very loving, but she had rarely had such a moment with her. Lady Han was calm and reserved, not prone to frolicking with her children. Iris played mostly with Green Jade growing up. She was glad A-mei and Jasmine came to live with them.

Lady Han had Green Jade brought in a washbasin and the girls washed their faces. Both looked fresh and dewy.

The ladies were sitting at the dining table when the men appeared. Liang Fei walked in first. He was not wearing his Western clothes today. Instead, he dressed like a local man in a summer linen jacket, pants, and black cloth shoes. Master Han and You-jun followed. You-jun smiled at the girls.

After everyone sat down, Lady Han inquired about the guest's sleep the night before.

"Very well!" Liang Fei said. "It was a refreshing rest. I do love the cool touch of bamboo sheets and bamboo pillowcases."

He was appreciative of the delicious breakfast as well. "Lady Han, with your hospitality and the wonderful food, I could stay here at Three Rivers, and never want to go back to Chengdu!"

"You are too kind and generous with your words, Mr. Liang." Lady Han bowed her head slightly.

"Three Rivers is too small for you, Fei!" Master Han laughed. "I'm hoping you will take You-jun and Jian-da with you and show them what the world is like outside Three Rivers. I'm too old and I'm content to make an occasional trip to Chengdu, but You-jun and Jian-da are different."

"I'll be delighted," said Fei. "They should come with me to Chengdu, help at the firm, learn about railway building, and go to the Christian school. Once they learn some English, I shall see if I can ask my mentors in the U.S. to make arrangements so they can go overseas and study. We need young people who have bright ideas and who are scientifically-minded to help make China strong."

Everyone at the table nodded in agreement.

"I can only imagine how wonderful that world will be!" You-jun sounded excited. "I can't wait!"

"Master," Lady Han said with a small pout, "you are trying to send away my only son! Aye!" She sighed.

"Mother," You-jun said quickly, "you know I will be back! When I establish myself, I'll come back to bring you and Father with me." He glanced at Jasmine when he said that. Jasmine turned red and lowered her gaze. Nobody but Iris noticed the exchange.

"Then we can count on you when we get old," Lady Han said.

"Of course you can, Mother!" You-jun said.

Jian-da arrived as they were finishing breakfast. He greeted everyone but declined to eat, saying that he had had a big breakfast at home. Then the hired sedan chairs arrived. Fei wanted to walk, but Master Han insisted that it was too far.

"Once we are at the foot of the mountain, we will climb to the top and then back down, and that will be a lot of walking," he said.

The girls were sad watching the men take off. They wanted to go, but alas their bound feet would make it impossible to enjoy the outing. They should stay home and do chores anyway.

As they started up on the long steps leading to the main gate, the Huguo Gate—there were eight gates in total—Fei said to Master Han, "Thank you for arranging this excursion. I had wanted to come to the site where Möngke Khan died. The only Mongol Khan who was killed. Defeated by the Song army."

"It's my pleasure," said Master Han. "Of course you must visit Diaoyu Fortress, no matter how busy your schedule is. This is one place everyone must visit when they come to Three Rivers. We are very proud of this place."

"It's justifiable to say that this little fortress changed the course of history," Fei said.

You-jun and Jian-da followed, and the four traced the steps of ancient soldiers from more than four hundred years earlier. They were amazed by the beauty of the place: a fortress situated on the hill and surrounded by water on three sides. They admired the old stone walls, the wide horse tracks, the old arsenals and training camps, and the numerous stone carvings and sculptures of Buddha: sleeping and sitting Buddhas and the bodhisattva with a thousand hands. They watched the three rivers, the white pagoda tower on the shore, and the mountains near and far, and they admired the scenery of the city. On the way down, they stopped at the Huguo Temple and offered incense and candles. Master Han explained to Fei that his late mother was a loyal patron of this temple and they carried on her tradition of donating to the temple each month and visiting whenever they came to the fortress.

In the afternoon, Liang Fei took the passenger boat to Chongqing where he would visit friends before going back to Chengdu. The plan was for Master Han to take You-jun and Jian-da to Chengdu at the beginning of autumn, after the summer heat died down, making travel easier.

They said farewell and Master Han, You-jun, and Jian-da watched the boat sail down the river.

At home, Lady Han didn't supervise the preparations for dinner. She knew that her husband's favorite dish, braised pork seasoned with soy sauce, was already made, so she told the cook that they could make do with whatever else was available. Entertaining guests was something she knew she was obliged to do, and she enjoyed it if the guests were pleasant enough like Liang Fei. But still, such events exhausted her. She needed quiet time to do needlework, pray, burn incense, and chant, inaudibly, her sutras.

Iris and Jasmine sat on the porch, each working on her own creation.

They didn't say much, other than to occasionally look at and appreciate each other's patterns. What they heard about the world at the dinner party the day before stirred something deep inside them. Iris, who was usually content, thought for the first time what it might mean if she, a woman, could do things like a man. Jasmine imagined that one day with You-jun she would go places far from Three Rivers. They were both burdened by their own dreams, hopes, and worries.

#

The waning crescent moon shone even brighter the night after the summer solstice. Night watchmen announced that it was approaching midnight. The air was cooled by the breeze from the rivers. After the night watchmen passed, the only sound was that of the river, the occasional barking of a dog or croaking of a frog.

Lady Han and Master Han lay in bed in their room. Neither could fall sleep. Finally, Lady Han sat up and said, "Turn and lay on your side, Yu-wen, and I'll rub your shoulders and back. The moon is waning but it seems so bright. It's hard to fall asleep. Tell me something fun from your trips."

Master Han turned to his side, his back facing Lady Han. "Sounds lovely. Let's see…oh, about Liang Fei. Wherever he went, kids followed him around because of the way he dressed and his lack of a queue. So he wears a hat. But now the bold ones want to climb him and see what's underneath. They think he hides his queue under the hat!"

They both laughed. They liked and admired Liang Fei.

"Well, even with all his foreign ways, he does seem to be a nice fellow," Lady Han said.

"He really is. That's why I'm eager for him to mentor You-jun. I agree with him. China needs science and technology to become strong. Old scholars like me are useless but we have hopes for our sons. The younger generation is our future," Master Han said. "Were you really upset about You-jun leaving someday, or were you just making a party conversation?"

"You know me." Lady Han sighed, her hands busy kneading her husband's neck and back. "I know that You-jun is a young man now, but still, I'm a mother."

"This will cheer you up," Master Han said.

"What will that be?' Lady Han asked.

"On the way home after sending off Fei, You-jun asked me to tell you not to worry about him leaving. He said someone here will hold him like a kite; no matter how far he goes, he'll come back for her," Master Han said.

"Oh, I didn't know he fancies any girls in Three Rivers. Is it the girl from the Li family? Truth be told, it is time to ask the matchmaker to look for a wife for him. I'm only worried about the girls and never thought I should be thinking about him, too!" Lady Han said.

"Well, this one you don't need any matchmaker for," Master Han said. "She's right under this roof."

Lady Han stopped her hands. "What do you mean?"

"Can't you tell? You-jun is in love with Jasmine. I only feel bad for Jian-da because his face looked ashy when You-jun confided this on our way home." Master Han said.

There was a silence. Then Lady Han said, "They can't. They are brother and sister."

"But You-jun said, and I agree, that Jasmine is just our gan nü'er. Yes, she has been living with us, almost like a child bride. Of course we didn't treat her like a child bride. We treated her like a daughter. And we made a big deal in officially taking her as our gan nü'er," Master Han said. "All we have to do is to take her back to her home and send a matchmaker and betrothal gifts to Old Wang's house in Cloud Gate and make an official proposal and engagement. I think Old Wang and A-mei will be very glad."

When his wife didn't say anything and didn't resume rubbing his back, Master Han turned. In the dim light, he saw that his wife's face was white as the moonlight itself.

"What's wrong?" He sat up and tried to take his wife in his arms. "I thought you'd be happy."

"No, they can't," Lady Han said, grinding the words out of her teeth. "I won't let them."

CHAPTER 16
CLOUD GATE, 2017

"Is that the famous Gate? The Cloud Gate?" I pointed to the half-crumpled arch on the left side of the road.

"That's the old, original Cloud Gate, made of limestones and marble," Aunt Daisy said. "It stood intact all the years until the Cultural Revolution. The Red Guards from Chongqing came and smashed it down. Local people wouldn't do it, because they believed that destroying the gate would bring bad luck. The Red Guards also went to destroy the Guanyin Temple. Without the help of the locals, they climbed halfway but several of them fell and broke a few bones. They gave up. The students who came to Cloud Gate to be reeducated were too tired and too busy with the dirty farm work they had to do and no one seemed to have thought about doing any damage to the arch or the temple."

"A few local people did try to haul the marble away for sale or to build their houses," Uncle De-chen said.

"And all seemed to end up badly," Shan said.

"Like what?" I was curious.

"The usual stuff, like not being able to bear a son, or children, at all. One or two died in bizarre accidents."

Then Hong-mei pointed. "Look, Rose, that's the new Cloud Gate."

The new structure was impressive, if a bit gaudy. It was a tall archway, with five-colored clouds and dragons carved all the way from the two pillars that a grownup could barely wrap arms around to the top. Red ink carved out the words "Cloud Gate" on the arch.

"A top local politician wrote the words," Hong-mei said. "Not the best calligraphy if you ask me!"

"It's an impressive structure," I said.

"Sure, even though I'm not certain that's money well spent." Hong-mei shrugged.

Along the road, there were rice paddies on one side and yellow rapeseed blossoms on the other side. The plots were scattered and small, smaller than the backyards of my friends' suburban houses back in the States. It was a picturesque drive, much like I thought the countryside would be.

One more turn and we reached Auntie Wang's house, our destination for the birthday party. Auntie Wang's house was a nice three-story building with a neat fenced-in courtyard. In the crowded city, there were only apartments, but in the countryside, people built houses on their farmland if the family had the money. Looking around, I saw several other houses as well. It seemed like Cloud Gate was a rich village.

Shan parked the car on the side of the house. We got out and walked into the courtyard. Several hens, prodding around for worms, scattered as we walked. A lanky young man with glasses and a middle-aged woman came to greet us. The young man said with a huge smile, "Welcome! Welcome! You must be tired after such a long trip! Grandma is taking her nap and she'll be up soon. She is really looking forward to seeing you all."

The woman was his mother, one of Auntie Wang's daughters-in-law. "Make yourself at home! I'm finishing up with making dinner in the kitchen so I won't be keeping you company now. Wu Er will help if you need anything." She then excused herself.

We decided that instead of going into the living room with the air conditioner, we would sit under the locust tree and get some fresh country air.

Wu Er, or Number Five grandson, brought freshly brewed green tea and roasted sunflower seeds and peanuts.

"Wu Er," Aunt Daisy said, "how's school?"

"Going well, going well. I signed an internship contract with a company in Chongqing and will report to them next week."

"Excellent!" Aunt Daisy and Uncle De-chen both said. Wu Er just graduated from college.

We drank tea, cracked sunflower seeds, and shelled peanuts. I was calm and happy, sitting under the giant locust tree. I was flooded by a sensation that could only be described as…being home. The air smelled familiar. The rustling of the tree sounded familiar. My mind was at peace, I was keenly aware of the pounding of my heart. As if something would happen soon. Whatever it was, I would be okay with it, because I was where I should be.

A couple of women arrived while we were chatting. They carried various pots, bowls, and baskets. After saying hello, they headed towards the kitchen. "They are relatives, aunts, and cousins," Aunt Daisy said. "To be honest, other than the one with a ponytail—I know she's the wife of one of the grandsons—myself am not sure exactly how they are related to Auntie Wang, but in Cloud Gate, everyone is somehow related."

As Wu Er refilled our teacups for the second time, I looked across the courtyard and saw a tiny woman in front of the house.

"Auntie Wang, you are up!" Aunt Daisy went over to greet Auntie Wang.

"I can walk, I can walk!" Auntie Wang let Aunt Daisy hold her hand instead of supporting her by the elbow. "Have you been here long? I thought I was just going to doze off for a minute, but you know, that didn't happen. Things are like that, at this old age!"

"We were having a good time, Auntie Wang. Wu Er was keeping us entertained," Aunt Daisy said.

"That's good, that's good," Auntie Wang said.

My mom also walked over to greet Auntie Wang.

"Auntie Wang!" my mom said. "It's been several years since I last saw you, but you are getting younger each year!"

"Ah, Lily, you are still so sweet!" Auntie Wang smiled, her wrinkles spreading over her entire face like a blooming chrysanthemum. "It is not true, but I like to hear it just the same!"

The three of them walked and talked, Auntie Wang in the middle, my mom and aunt Daisy holding each of her hands.

I stood and waited until they were right in front of us. "Ni Hao, Auntie Wang!"

Auntie Wang stopped. She looked at me as if she knew me, but was stunned by the sight of me.

"Iris?" she whispered, but I heard the name clearly, as a sound of fleeting thunder in a cloudless afternoon.

"Auntie Wang." My mom let go of Auntie Wang's hand, grabbed my shoulder, and nudged me forward, as if to present me to Auntie Wang. "This is my daughter, Rose. This is her first time visiting Cloud Gate."

"Rose, Rose," Auntie Wang mumbled. She kept staring at me, as if she were somewhere else and saw someone else. Then she snapped out of it.

"Look at me. I'm losing my sight and my memory at this age! I thought you were someone else." She sat down and said, "Come over here, child, let me take a good look at you. Yes, Daisy mentioned you many times, I remember now. I'm so glad you came."

We sat under the large locust tree, talking until dinnertime. Auntie Wang made me sit by her side. She held my hand the whole time. Her hand was small, rough, cool and bony, but strong. Once in a while she turned her head and looked at me again, not so much staring as studying, as if to say, *I know this face.*

Several long tables were set up on the courtyard, and chairs were brought out. Plates and bowls magically appeared on the tables. People started to file in, and they all came to the locust tree to pay respect to the birthday lady. Finally, Wu Er's mom came over. She had changed from her kitchen outfit to a nice flowery blouse and I noticed how young she seemed.

"Ma," she said to Auntie Wang, "all is ready. The men are back." I figured she was talking about her husband, his brothers, and nephews. I heard that two of Auntie Wang's sons were back from Chongqing and Guangzhou recently for her birthday.

"Yan, you worked so hard on this!" Auntie Wang stood and patted the arm of her daughter-in-law fondly. They walked to the banquet table, and we followed.

Auntie Wang's sons all stood to toast their mother's good health, followed by nephews, grandsons, other relatives. They all said, "It's an honor for the entire village to have a party for a one-hundred-year-birthday!" The toasting seemed to go on forever, until Auntie Wang laughed and said, "Okay, okay, that's more than enough 'life longer than the South Mountain, and good fortune deeper than the East Sea!' I'm glad you are all here for the time I'm still around. Eat up and drink up, please!" We all obliged. The food was simple, homemade country fare presented in unrefined crockery, but it was fresh and scrumptious.

The eating and drinking lasted into the dusky hours, long after Auntie Wang had excused herself. "Old people! Early to bed, early to rise. Make sure you young people enjoy yourself!" she said to the crowd.

Then she took both of my hands, her gaze fixed on me. In the fading afternoon light, something from her eyes burned into my soul. I shivered, even though it was an early summer day.

"I'm glad you came," Auntie Wang said.

"Me too, Auntie Wang!" I said whole-heartedly. "Happy birthday! I hope to come and celebrate more of your birthdays!" I squeezed her hands back.

"We'll see, we'll see." She smiled. "But I'm glad you came."

Then she let go of my hands, turned around, and her tiny body disappeared from sight.

I stood there, trying to understand the sensation that went through my body. All of a sudden I thought about Harriton. I had kept him out of mind for days. Did the festivity make me realize some innate loneliness in me? We were in such different places and times, but I longed from my bones to reach out and connect with him.

Hong-mei appeared behind me. "She really likes you," she said.

"She took me for Iris. Do you think that's strange?"

"You probably look like her. Auntie Wang would be the one person who knew what Grandma Iris looked like when she was young."

"I suppose so," I agreed. "In the pictures, we saw the other day, Great Grandma Iris was older. I can only imagine what she would be like when she was a young lady. Maybe I will ask Auntie Wang about this."

"Hey, do you want a little adventure?" Hong-mei hooked her left arm into my right, and we were walking side by side now.

"What would that be?" I asked.

"I'm taking you to my favorite spot in the village, the Lotus Pond," she said, eyes twinkling. "It's been a long time since I went there. I hope it stayed the same. Everything is changing so much so fast."

"I didn't realize you knew the village so well." I was surprised.

"I grew up here until I was about ten, before Mom and Dad finally got permission to move back to Three Rivers," Hong-mei said.

"Ahh, yes," I remembered.

We walked out of the front gate of the courtyard.

"Hong-mei, where are you going?" Aunt Daisy called.

"Just taking Rose for a quick stroll. Don't worry, we'll be back soon! The day is long in the summer!" Hong-mei called back.

Soon we were out of the main part of the village and in the middle of rice paddies. But the walk took only a few minutes before a pond appeared in front of us, its water shimmering in the orange glow of the setting sun. Ducks and geese were frolicking. Several kids were swimming and diving. And yes, there were lotus flowers.

"It's beautiful," I said.

"Isn't it? I loved coming here. But Mom was always afraid of me drowning. She did not like me to go near any water for that matter, and think about this: we live in Three Rivers! She said that she heard when she was a child that somebody in the family had drowned. So I had to sneak out." Hong-mei laughed.

We sat down under a willow tree, our backs against the trunk. I had a strange sensation again, as if I'd known this place all along. As if I had been here, had sat under the very same willow tree, had heard the sounds of children playing, and smelled the summer air.

"Now Hong-mei," I said, "tell me your dream. When did you have it?"

"It was my last year in college as an undergraduate, in 1989. I was doing my senior honor's research in my biology professor's lab. It was early June. Actually, June fourth," Hong-mei began.

"The day of the Tian An Men Massacre?" I was astonished. "Did you march?"

"Well, yes. Once we marched from our university to People's Square and we sat for a hunger strike. Just for a couple of hours. I was a book-worm and didn't pay much attention to politics, but this was for democracy. And also for the boy I had a crush on."

"Shan?"

"No, not him. It was my first crush." Hong-mei smiled. Her face was exquisite in the twilight.

"We met when we were freshmen, so by then we'd known each other for four years. I had been admitted to graduate school in our senior year, and the entrance exam requirement had been waived because of my high GPA. He was still preparing for graduate school entrance exams so I went to study halls with him all the time, to help him prepare. Sometimes I even sharpened his pencils for him."

"No, you did not, Hong-mei!" I exclaimed.

"Yes, I did." Hong-mei smiled. "I just wanted to be with him. So when he went marching I went along so I could march with him.

"But I was also a good student. A nerd, you Americans would say? June fourth was a Sunday, and I spent the whole day in the lab for an important experiment, so I didn't go with him. When I came out of the lab that night, I heard that something went wrong. I knew he was out that day in the march. He was the student leader of our university and he had direct contact with the students in Beijing.

"I rushed to his dorm room. I would not have been able to go to a boy's dorm so easily, since our university had a night curfew, but the curfew had been lifted for a few weeks because of the student protests. But he wasn't there. His roommates didn't know where he was.

"I decided to wait in his room. I lay down on his bed—the top one of a bunk bed—and waited. I buried my face in his blanket, trying to inhale his scent, and I fell asleep. And that was when I had the dream.

"Just like in your dream, Grandma Pearl asked me to look for her grandma. I didn't know what that meant, so I tried to follow her. I said, Grandma, who is she? Why do you want me to look for her? Does Mom know her? She wouldn't answer. She just looked at me with her sad eyes.

"Then somebody was shaking me and trying to wake me up. It was a roommate of his.

"Get up, Hong-mei! You can't stay here! The university has just issued new curfews!" he said. "All students have to be in their dorms if they are not in class. No lingering around on campus. Curfew time has moved up from 10 pm to 8 pm. The dorm director is checking names. Hurry back to the girl's dorm, before you get into any trouble!"

Hong-mei stopped. A goose flew up and slid right back onto the water. I didn't want to break the silence.

Finally, Hong-mei sighed. "Let's go back," she said. She stood and pulled me up.

On the way back, I couldn't help but ask, "What happened to him? Did you find him?"

"Oh, yes and no. I heard that he had already prepared to leave. Some students died, but some others had plans to leave. They knew the crackdown would happen. So he left on June fourth, with his girlfriend, whom he met while coordinating the student movements. She was the student leader from another university in Chengdu. They had American visas and everything and claimed asylum in the U.S. Last time I heard, he was in Florida. But I've never seen him since that day."

"Oh, Hong-mei!" I wrapped my arm around her shoulder. I almost told her about Harriton right then and there.

Instead, I asked, "Do you find it interesting that in all the dreams it was the grandma who visited her granddaughters?"

"You are right." She said, "Iris visited Mom and Aunty Lily, and Pearl visited you and me."

"Why, do you wonder?"

She thought for a moment, and said, "Perhaps it was that special bond between a grandma and her granddaughter? When I was a kid, a lot of times I thought Mom was too stern, too harsh. I worried I couldn't live up to her expectations. But with Grandma Pearl, I was carefree. I could just be her little girl."

I nodded. I had so many questions. Why did Auntie Wang think I was Iris? What could she tell me about these dreams? I came here to escape from my heartbreaks, and I had planned to stay for a short time. But, now something in me told me to stay longer and find out answers.

CHAPTER 17
CLOUD GATE, 2017

It was raining. The sky was dark like the bottom of a well-used wok. A June morning was surprised to be bright. Hong-mei was not in the guestroom we shared, a spacious room on the second floor of Auntie's Wang's house, with two beds, comfortable couches, a coffee table, two dressers, and a TV.

I left the room and went downstairs, looking for Hong-mei. She was nowhere to be seen, nor was anyone else. Was there a plan to do something this morning that I missed? I stepped into the courtyard.

The rain looked like a drizzle but drenched me immediately, as if it were a downpour.

Before I could call out, "Hong-mei, where are you?" a thin but strong arm grabbed me and pulled me under the eaves.

"You'll catch a cold if you get soaked," Auntie Wang said. "Come with me."

I followed her as if drawn by an invisible thread. The surprising strength that pulled me out of the rain carried me along.

"Where is everyone?" I asked, in a daze.

She didn't answer.

We entered what I assumed was her room, at the back of the first floor. In the dim light of a bedside lamp, I saw that the room was sparsely furnished: a narrow bed, a nightstand, a small desk, two chairs, and an old-fashioned wooden trunk.

"Sit down," Auntie Wang said, and she sat on one of the chairs. I sat on the bed. It was hard, not at all like the beds with mattresses upstairs in the guest bedroom.

"I have been waiting for you, my dear," she whispered, slowly, in her Cloud Gate dialect. But I had no trouble hearing and understanding her. "I didn't know it would be you until I saw you. You came to me yesterday, and I thought Iris was back. Your great-grandma, she was. It was like the first time I saw her when I was only a little girl in the village. Everything about you, your face, your voice, the way you walked, reminded me of her. I knew right away you were the one I had been waiting for."

I didn't know how to respond to that. But somehow I knew that she wasn't expecting a response, either. I remained silent.

"Iris was the only one left of her siblings at the time I met her. She and my father-in-law, the old Tiger, were the only ones left of that generation. Tiger was not her brother, but they both told us, me and my husband, that they were like brother and sister, and that the Han and the Wang families were one family and we must always look after each other. We went all the way back to Iris's mother, your great-great-grandma Peony, and Tiger's mother A-mei. When Peony left Cloud Gate and married into the Han Family in Three Rivers, A-mei went with her. Later they each lost a child."

The room was so quiet; I could hear our breathing and the muffled sounds of rain. *This is it*, I said to myself. *Don't. Make. Any. Sound. You are about to be led into the world you are looking for. Don't interrupt.*

Auntie's small frame was right in front of me, but her voice seemed to drift in from a faraway place.

"I have no memory of Peony or A-mei, but I remember Iris vividly. When Iris came to the village, she often had her daughter, your grandma Pearl, with her. Pearl and I played together and became best friends. I think that was the reason Iris wanted me to be married into the Wang family: she liked me a lot. My parents were poor, and they were more than happy for me to be married to a son of the Wangs. Everyone knew how the Wang family was connected to the Han family, and how both families were kind despite their wealth and fortune. My parents knew that I would never have to worry about putting food on the table and having clothes on my back.

"Now everyone else is long gone. I might have taken all of the memories with me to the grave, too. But you are here, I can go now."

After a long silence, I whispered, "Auntie Wang, Grandma Pearl appeared in my dream and asked me to look for her grandma."

Auntie Wang nodded. "Pearl told me that Iris made her promise that the children of the Han family would never forget Peony. On her death bed, Iris said that she had forgiven her mother for abandoning her family.

"It's too late for me, Iris said to Pearl. *I visited the temple when Mother entered it, but never again. I'm grateful to Tiger, who kept going in my place all these years. But the Han family needs to know about my mother. When it's time to visit, you go, and tell Daisy and Lily and their children so."*

Auntie Wang fixed her gaze on me. "Now you are here, like Iris herself is here. You will all go and find her mother. The key is in my sewing basket." Then the lights in her eyes flickered, like that of a candle, and she closed her eyes.

"What? Why do we have to find Peony? And where? What happened between her and Iris?"

She shook her head, eyes still closed.

I sat there, trying to remember everything she said and decipher the meaning of it all. Then I, too, drifted into sleep.

#

"Rose! Rose! Wake up!" Hong-mei was shaking me. "You are soaked! You are not used to this weather, so hot and humid. The electricity went out last night, and so did the air conditioner. I hope you won't catch a cold. A summer cold is a lot worse than a winter cold."

"I got caught in the rain…"

"Rain? What rain?" Hong-mei wiped my forehead with a towel.

"Did the rain stop? What time is it?" I sat up. My head felt heavy and I had trouble opening my eyes.

"It's eight in the morning. We need to get going. Shan has a meeting this afternoon."

I opened my eyes, then closed them immediately. The room was flooded with the bright June morning sunlight. Hong-mei had rolled up the blinds.

"Sorry, had to do it. You wouldn't wake up. I have never seen anyone sleep so deeply." she said. "But I knew you were alive, since you were making noises." She smiled at me. "Come on, let's go."

Aunt Daisy, Uncle De-chen, my mom, and Shan already had breakfast and they were ready to leave. Wu Er and his mother were there, too, and had packed me a sack breakfast. There were baskets of freshly picked vegetables in the trunk.

"Where is Auntie Wang? Should we say goodbye?" I asked.

"Oh, Wu Er went to knock on her door earlier, and she said she was very tired from yesterday and wanted to sleep in. We told Wu Er to let her know that we would be back soon to visit her again and asked her to visit us," Aunt Daisy said.

We thanked Wu Er and his mom one more time and packed into the car.

I was fully awake by then. I saw that ground was dry and it did not seem to have rained at all, like Hong-mei said. Then I knew the rain, Auntie Wang, me soaked, were all a dream. They had to be. But everything felt so real. I could recall every detail of it, the dimness of the room, the shape of the furniture, the sound of the rain, Auntie Wang's words, and the wrinkles carved on her face.

I decided that I would talk to Hong-mei about it later.

I wished we had stayed longer. But when I asked my mom about it, she said it was best we went back to Three Rivers so we would not be a burden on Auntie Wang's family. They did perceive us as Americans and were worried that their living conditions were not "up to American standards."

The smell of the pork-and-vegetable-stuffed steamed buns suddenly made me hungry. I ate two and washed them down with freshly brewed green tea.

The trip was quiet. Everyone seemed to be in his or her own world. I could not stop thinking about what Auntie Wang said to me in the dream. Could I find Iris's mother? She entered the temple? What did that mean? She abandoned her family, according to Iris, but why? And why were Iris and Tiger the only two left? Who were the children lost?

#

In Three Rivers, Shan dropped us off and went straight to work. Hong-mei went out for some errands. Aunt Daisy, Uncle De-chen, and Mom sat down at the big kitchen table to sort out the fresh vegetables that were plucked from Auntie Wang's gardens that morning: Chinese water spinach, cucumbers, Chinese chives, eggplants, assorted lettuce, green onions. They had turned down some live chickens and ducks.

"All the dead leaves and branches need to be cleaned so the vegetables can stay good longer," Aunt Daisy said.

"These vegetables last much longer than the store-bought kind," Uncle De-chen said, "without the fertilizers and pesticides and all the other chemicals."

I went to take a shower. Then I took out my phone. Perhaps I could call Auntie Wang. She should be up by now. But what do I say to her? Do I ask her to continue our conversation? But that conversation was in a dream. As my mind wandered, my hands followed their old habits: they clicked the email. Nothing important. Then I scanned the news. I immediately regretted that: it was hard to have any good news anywhere in the world lately. I didn't have the concentration needed for reading a book, so I joined the elderly at the table. I was not much of a help, but sitting there and watching them made me happy.

"Did you enjoy the trip to Cloud Gate, Rose?" Uncle De-chen asked, plucking at a bunch of water spinach.

"Yes, I loved it," I said.

"What's your favorite part? The fresh food? Even in Three Rivers, we did not have anything so fresh. Or was it the country scenery? Fresh air?"

"All of it. But most of all, I loved meeting Auntie Wang. She is like a living history book, one I wish I had more time to read." I wondered if I should tell them about the dream, but I wanted to talk to Hong-mei first.

"She is. She lived in the village her whole life and she is the last one in her generation. She knows more about the history of our two families than anyone else alive now," Aunt Daisy said. "Mom and Auntie Wang were best friends. We always visited each other for birthdays, weddings, funerals. At times of celebrations and times of sorrow."

"Yes," my mom said. "Every time I came back to Three Rivers, I would try my best to visit her."

"She's still sharp as a tack," Uncle De-chen said.

"I can tell," I said. "I wish there was more time to talk to her. I would like to visit her again when I'm here, to hear stories of the village and our families. She probably can tell us about Grandma Pearl's grandma."

"Yes, Auntie Wang will be the one," Aunt Daisy said. "None of us know anything. Mom didn't know. Grandma Iris might have tried to tell Lily and me, but we didn't listen."

"Do you think I can call Auntie Wang?" I asked. "Does she talk on the phone?"

As if by cue, the phone in the living room rang.

Uncle De-chen answered it. "What? How can it be? When? We will be back as soon as we can."

Aunt Daisy and Mom stopped what they were doing. My heart thrashed wildly in my chest. We all looked at Uncle De-chen, waiting for him to deliver the news.

"Auntie Wang passed away," Uncle De-chen said.

CHAPTER 18
THREE RIVERS, 1911

Lesser Heat: the thirteenth day of the sixth month and the thirteenth of the twenty-four solar terms. Torridity arrived.

How could I be so blind? Lady Han asked herself once again. She rose before anyone else in the household. She had trouble sleeping since she became aware of Jasmine and You-jun's intentions for each other. She had been combing through her memories for clues and signs. It had never occurred to her that this could happen. She held out hope that it was only a fleeting crush between two young people. But whenever she caught a glimpse of them, which she had been doing purposefully, she saw their gaze at each other, their longing stabbing her in the middle of her heart. Her agony kept her up until early morning, and when she finally dozed off, her sleep was cut short by nightmares. She doubled her prayers to Guanyin and stopped eating meat altogether, not just on the first and fifteenth days of the month, but every day.

She had to find a way to separate them. Even if it meant sending them away, at least until Jasmine was married off. Yes, that was precisely what she would do.

She stood on the covered front porch, mindlessly looking out to the sky above the walls that separated the house from the street. Then she heard a soft sound. Turning, she saw A-mei coming on the other side of the porch from the kitchen.

"You are up early, too," Lady Han whispered, smiling. The sight of her old friend was such a comfort. A-mei, and A-mei alone, knew and understood what she was going through. They made the plan together, and now they both understood that their plan might not work the way they imagined.

"The birds sing so loud, I can't sleep," A-mei whispered back, also smiling.

They stood on the porch, watching the sky and the early morning glow.

"Look at the red cloud. It'll rain today," A-mei said.

"That's the thing with Lesser Heat. Either rain and thunder and hot, or humid and hot. I guess today it's a hot day with rain and thunder," Lady Han said.

"It's going to be muggy." A-mei nodded.

"When is matchmaker Zhao coming today?"

"In the afternoon," Lady Han said. "Mrs. Fang and I agreed that the sooner Jasmine and Jian-da are engaged, the better. Mrs. Fang looks forward to having a daughter-in-law to take over the household so she can retire and enjoy herself. Madam Zhao is bringing betrothal gifts today. Master Han and I will accept the gifts and the two of them will be formally engaged."

Lady Han paused and took a deep breath, as if she were laboring by the mere act of speaking. She wanted Jasmine to be happy, but she must break the girl's heart in order to do that. She knew Jasmine would hurt deeply, not knowing why Lady Han would tear her apart from You-jun. *But I must not tell.*

"After that, you and I will help Jasmine get ready for her wedding. We will be busy, for there is a lot of embroidery and needlework to do."

A-mei opened her mouth to say something but swallowed her words. She wanted to ask if Jasmine knew, but she thought better of it. She knew the answer anyway. Although they were more like sisters and friends, A-mei never forgot that she was a maid to Lady Han, a fact she resented at times. Now was one of those times. Looking at her old Peony, who seemed to have withered in the past weeks, she had the urge to cheer her up and nurture her back to health. She, A-mei, was Jasmine's mother, too, and this was the best for her beloved daughter.

A-mei was part of the plan from the very beginning. They concocted the lie, set everything in motion. But they knew their hearts were pure and their deeds would have earned the approval of Guanyin. They did everything they could to make it a good plan, but that was only half of the possible success. The other half had to come from Heaven. Men strive, but God's rule. The other half had to come from the fate and destiny of each person involved. And they thought they had the blessings of Heaven. Until now.

The morning glow was disappearing. All kinds of sounds came through the wall and the gate: vendors peddling, neighbors saying good morning to each other, children crying. In the house, the cook had started the stove to make breakfast.

"We need to get ready for our visitor," Lady Han said.

A-mei nodded.

Together, they went to the kitchen.

In the room which Iris and Jasmine shared, the two girls were also awake, but they did not get up. Instead, they lay in their beds and whispered to each other, as they had always done.

"Madam Zhao is coming today, Iris," Jasmine said.

"How do you know?" Iris asked.

"Yesterday I heard Lady and Mother talking about it."

"They stopped when they saw me and sent me over to get Mother's embroidery tambour, but I heard Madam Zhao's name."

"She's been here so many times before. I'm sure Mother will turn her away, like all the other times," Iris said, stretching her arms overhead.

"But the way Lady and Mother were talking…it made me think somehow this time it is different. Sounds as though Lady had agreed to take Madam Zhao's offer," Jasmine said, also stretching.

Iris didn't say anything.

"Aren't you excited, Iris? Or are you worried?"

"I can't say. I knew this day would come. It's a dishonor to our parents and ourselves if we are not married by a certain age, so I know I should be happy if Madam Zhao brings proposals from good families. Mother will not marry us off to the families that are not good." Iris sat up on the bed, loosening her braids, ready to brush her hair.

"But still, I don't feel too happy. Once we are married, we are like water dumped out of our parents' home, gone. We are of no consequence to our parents anymore," Iris continued.

"I agree," Jasmine said. "I wish I were a son sometimes. Sons stay with their family and do not have to worry about moving to a stranger's home, living at the in-laws' every whim."

Both girls brushed their hair, then helped each other braid. Jasmine was about half a head taller than Iris. She talked more and faster, laughed more loudly, and forgot to cover her mouth when she did. She just seemed to be less lady-like. Iris was more poised and reserved.

To this difference, A-mei would say, apologetically, "That's my fault! Jasmine was raised a country bumpkin before Lady Han tried to straighten out the twisted branches."

"They are Yin and Yang," Lady Han would laugh.

The pair finally finished getting ready and headed to the kitchen.

There were only women in the house today. Lady Han had talked about having Master Han stay home for Madam Zhao's visit, but he would rather go to Chongqing with You-jun.

"Lady," he'd said to his wife the day before, "you are the head of the inner rim of the house. You can handle it. To be honest, I can't find anything to say to Madam Zhao. Just apologize to her and tell her I have a business trip that I cannot reschedule and you can decide for the family." And off he went, taking You-jun and Jian-da with him.

The women sat down and started eating their porridge, taking care not to make any slurping sounds. Jasmine had acquired proper table manners, but when there were only women and she was relaxed, she still ate too quickly. She ate two bowls and burped while the others were nursing their first bowl.

"Lady, Mother." Jasmine wiped her mouth and began, "I heard Madam Zhao is coming today?"

Lady Han and A-mei exchanged glances but pretended not to hear.

Jasmine continued. "I wonder whose family Madam Zhao will mention this time. I hope it's a nice family that deserves Jie Jie." She giggled.

Lady Han slapped down her bowl and her chopsticks. "You are old enough now, Jasmine. Don't behave like a little girl anymore. It's rude and embarrassing for a girl to ask questions about matchmakers."

The table fell silent. Jasmine turned bright red. Iris kept her head low, staring at her almost empty bowl. Her chopsticks wandered about in it, rearranging grains of rice.

Lady Han regretted her words and her harsh tone. She reached over to stroke Jasmine's hair. "Don't worry, everything will be fine."

"I didn't know Lady would get so upset. Jie Jie, I really do have a big mouth, don't I?" Jasmine was in tears when they got back to their room.

"Mother loves you. She never said a harsh word to you." Iris tried to comfort Jasmine. "She has something on her mind. Maybe she just doesn't want either one of us to leave the house. But she has to. We are not getting any younger." Iris sighed.

The girls stayed in their room that afternoon, except for going to the backyard garden for fresh air when Jasmine felt hot. But the air was not cool. It was, like A-mei said, muggy. Their excursion was cut short when the sky turned dark and the rain came.

When Madam Zhao arrived, both girls tried to steal a peek at the old woman. They had seen her before, during her other trips to the Han household, when she brought proposals to Iris. Madam Zhao was dressed loudly in a fuchsia jacket with golden trim and onion-green pants. Her rouge was two shades too red and shaped like two perfect circles on her broad cheeks. Even Lady Han, who never said a bad word about anyone, couldn't help commenting to A-mei once, after the matchmaker left, "The older she gets, the more brightly she dresses! Today was bright red and bright green, so ugly I almost cried over it!"

During those times Iris was usually called out, reluctantly, to bring tea to the matchmaker. The real reason was for the matchmaker to take a good look at Iris, to appreciate how beautiful, elegant, and mannered she was, so she might be able to paint a desirable picture of the girl to her potential mother-in-law. She stared at Iris, her small eyes measuring every move, and Iris felt like a soundless fly was following her.

Jasmine was usually not called but she was dying to see the old woman and to eavesdrop, so she would find some excuse to make an appearance: a tray of treats to carry, for example, with sunflower seeds or fruit, or teacups. She would follow Iris into the front hall where everyone was sitting so she too, could have a peek at the old lady. Afterwards, they would go back to their room and pretend to be Madam Zhao, walking unsteadily on her three-inch lotus feet, talking in a high-pitched voice, and dumping whatever treats she could carry into her pockets before she left. The girls would laugh so hard that Lady Han or A-mei would knock on the door and ask them to simmer down.

As soon as they heard A-mei go to the front door with an umbrella to help Madame Zhao in, and heard Lady Han thank the matchmaker profusely for coming out in such terrible weather, the girls put on their embroidered shoes and sat at the edges of their beds, ears perked, waiting to be called. But the call never came.

Lady Han, A-mei, and Madam Zhao sat in the front hall, whispering in hushed voices that the girls couldn't hear. Green Jade brought tea and treats for Madam Zhao, who did not forget to eat and drink. The intermittent thunder and the rain made eavesdropping impossible, though the girls tried.

The visit lasted only as long as it took to sip a cup of good tea. Madam Zhao got up and wobbled her way out the door, accompanied by Lady Han and A-mei. They whispered some more at the door. Then Madam Zhao climbed in the sedan chair Lady Han had called in and left.

Iris and Jasmine dared not come out, having been scolded by Lady Han earlier that day. They looked at each other, not knowing what to make of this visit.

"I don't know if this means something good or bad." Iris shook her head.

"Lady would not find you an unworthy family. Don't worry, Jie Jie," Jasmine said. But inside, she felt as unsure and uneasy as Iris.

CHAPTER 19
THREE RIVERS AND CLOUD GATE, 2017

Silence followed Uncle De-chen's news.

Aunt Daisy managed to say, "How can it be? Yesterday she was as alive as a tadpole in a pond at springtime. When did this happen?"

"They didn't know for sure. Remember this morning she was not up yet when we were leaving? They said she was usually up before dawn. When Wu Er went to knock on the door this morning, she said she was tired. When she still didn't get up for lunch, they went in to check on her. She was gone but still warm to the touch."

I couldn't believe my ears. Yet deep in my heart, I knew it was true.

I could see so clearly Auntie Wang's eyes, deep as two bottomless wells, despite the cloud of the cataracts. Lights flickered in them, drawing me in.

And then the lights went out.

I had just set my mind on looking for Grandma Pearl's grandmother. I just made discovering family history the new mission of this trip, not a mere distraction from my own heartbreaks. I would be in the dark again, not knowing where to begin.

#

The funeral for Auntie Wang was more like a wedding. People wore white from head to toe, including white head wraps and white shoes, and no one looked particularly sad. "The entire village came out for the celebration," Wu Er told me. Everyone tried to touch the coffin as Auntie Wang's sons and grandsons carried it through the village and out to the family plot. Several Buddhist nuns preceded the coffin, chanting sutras and beating the little wooden fish in their hands.

"Auntie Wang had such a long life, with so many sons and grandsons, and she died in her sleep. I heard that she even put on her longevity clothes herself before going to bed, you know, the shirt, pants, and shoes one wears to the afterworld, as if she knew that was the end of it. There is no better ending than hers, so everyone is trying to get some of that luck from touching her coffin," Hong-mei whispered to me as we followed the funeral procession.

"I thought they were supposed to cry. Don't some families hire people to cry at a funeral?" I whispered back.

"True, usually the more people cry at the funeral, the more face-saving for the family. It's an indication that the family has a flourishing number of descendants. The Wang family has enough people to cry if they want to, and the whole village probably will join in and the tears will be genuine. But Auntie Wang had specifically instructed people not to cry."

That was interesting news to me. "Why?"

"She was a devoted Buddhist her whole life. She fasted or ate vegan on the first and fifteenth of each month, gave almost all her money, the money her sons gave her, to the temple. All her devotion and virtues accumulated like a mount, and she will reach Nirvana through it. Tears at her funeral will only wash away that mount she had worked so hard to build. So no crying from anyone."

I said nothing. I was in awe of this tiny woman. I wished I had spent more time with her. On the other hand, it was like I knew her at a much higher level, far beyond the few hours we spent together. Some people you may not know, even if you spent a life together. Others, you might know to the core within just a few days, a few hours. Like Harriton. We spent a total three weeks together, when I counted the days, but it was long enough for him to be etched into my memory. Now add Auntie Wang to the list.

It was a beautiful June day. The air was warm but not humid. The breeze was strong enough to blow my hair but gentle enough for me to like how it touched my cheek.

The family plot was small. Plots like this were becoming rarer, since land was so limited and it was considered a waste to use it for burial. Even if the family did get to keep a plot, cremation had become much more common. It took less space to bury an urn of ashes than a body.

The coffin was lowered to the ground. We formed a queue to pay our final respects.

When it was my turn, I hesitated, but only a moment. My knees softened and I kneeled, my forehead touching the cold slab of the black tombstone.

"Goodbye, Auntie Wang," I said without uttering a word. "I'm so glad to have met you before you had to go."

We watched as the men in the village shoveled dirt to cover the coffin, and the women burnt paper money, a paper car, paper mahjong, and a paper cell phone.

My American self would have laughed at this—I did not see Auntie Wang having a cell phone when she was alive! But here, it did not seem odd to me at all. If Auntie Wang really were just heading somewhere for a long time, she would need a cell phone to keep in touch with the rest of us who were still here, and she would want to play mahjong along the way!

Back in the village, a banquet was laid out in the yard for everyone. It was like the birthday banquet we attended just two days before. Auntie Wang's sons took turns offering their toasts, praising their mother, and thanking the guests. Villagers shared jokes and stories of Auntie Wang. Drinking games followed, "Just as Mother would have liked," said one of the sons. "She loves it when people are having a good time."

Aunt Daisy, Uncle De-chen, Mom, Hong-mei, Shan, and I sat at the head table, with the Wang family, at their insistence.

"Did Auntie Wang really put on her longevity clothes herself?" Shan asked.

"She did. We prepared them a long time ago and stored them in the trunk in her room." Wu Er's mom Yan said.

I recalled the trunk in Auntie Wang's room. Was she already thinking about putting on the clothes when we talked?

"Wu Er said she looked as if she were in a deep, peaceful sleep. He said that he had never seen a dead person before but he was not scared at all. He knew right away that she had gone out of this world in her sleep," Yan continued.

The breeze seemed to have picked up and I shuddered.

Hong-mei, sitting next to me, sensed it.

"Are you okay?" She turned to face me. "Are you cold?"

"I'm fine, Hong-mei. Thanks," I said. "Not cold, just…maybe tired."

"Why don't you girls go to rest," Uncle De-chen said. "We'll stay up a bit and catch up with the relatives."

"Oh, I don't want to steal Hong-mei from Shan all the time…"

"What nonsense!" Shan stopped me. "Your cousin-sisters don't get that much chance to spend time with each other. Plus, I'd like to find out how the guys are going to divide their household, now that the matriarch of the family is no longer here. Go on!" He patted his wife's cheek affectionately. Good old Shan.

Hong-mei and I said goodnight to the family and excused ourselves to our room, the same one where we stayed just two days ago. The sheets were new and crisp. Yan had gotten everything ready for us.

Hong-mei and I sat down on our beds, facing each other. We could hear the talking and laughing drifting in from the courtyard, even though we couldn't make out the words. We didn't say anything for several minutes. Hong-mei looked at me in a way that made me think she was expecting me to say something. Finally, I began.

"This is going to sound strange," I said.

She didn't say anything. She kept looking at me, double-crossing her legs on her bed, sitting in a lotus pose.

"Auntie Wang visited me the night when we were here for her birthday. I mean, she visited me *in a dream*, but everything felt so real to me." I crossed my legs as well. We sat there, like two nuns sitting in their meditation poses. My voice sounded hollow and unreal.

I described the dream to Hong-mei, how I was soaked, and what Auntie Wang told me about Peony, A-mei, and the children they lost. How she said I resembled Iris in every way.

"Do you think my showing up in Cloud Gate killed Auntie Wang?" I asked the question that had weighed on me, however reluctantly.

Hong-mei uncrossed her legs and crossed them again, with the opposite leg on top this time. She must practice yoga regularly. I would ask her to take me to her practice.

Slowly she said, "No, you did not kill Auntie Wang. She knew her time was up, but she couldn't let go until you showed up. Somehow she thought her task was completed and she was ready to go. I still don't know what you should do, but she seemed to be sure that you would know what to do."

We both sat there, soaking up the thought. How would I know what to do? And why me? Because I looked like Iris?

"So Iris asked Grandma Pearl to look for Iris's mother," Hong-mei continued.

"Yes," I said. "Peony."

"But Grandma Pearl probably couldn't do that because of the Cultural Revolution," Hong-mei said.

"So she wanted us to do it by giving us dreams," I said.

"And we all thought those dreams were just coincidences. You know, we believe in things you can touch and feel and hold. We are materialists." Hong-mei smiled. "Now it's different."

"Then I showed up, not knowing much of anything about our family history, and wanting to know more," I said.

"A family's history is recorded in a genealogy book. I wish we still had ours. I had heard Mom had burnt it during the Cultural Revolution."

"But someone has to know something," I said.

"Do you think…" We spoke at the same time after a silence. And we both laughed at this coincidence. Hong-mei stopped, smiled, and let me finish.

"…That somebody in the Wang family might know something? That she might have mentioned something to them in the past? Why don't we go ask them right now?"

"We should do it tomorrow. It's been a long day for the family, and let's not add any more burden to them. The day after the funeral is the day to visit the temple. After the temple visit, all will be done, and that'll be a better time to ask," Hong-mei said.

Visiting the temple! Didn't Grandma Pearl mention the temple in our dreams? We might be able to find something there!

"Is it the same temple Aunt Daisy mentioned? The one she refused to visit when Iris died?" I asked.

"It is. There's only one Guanyin Temple in Cloud Gate, on the White Cloud Mountain."

The thought of the possibility to find something in the temple kept me up for a long time. When I finally fell asleep, I thought Auntie Wang would visit me again, but she did not. I had a short, dreamless sleep.

Everyone was up at dawn. I had become accustomed to the light Chinese breakfast: rice porridge, steamed bun, hardboiled egg, a small dish of pickled cabbage or daikon, or a small dish of fermented bean curd. It did more for my energy than my old staple—black coffee and whatever pastry I could grab on the way to work—had ever done.

This morning's fare was more elaborate than usual. There were also fried peanuts and cold cuts of stewed pork belly. The women in the Wang family must not have slept, going from a grand banquet to a splendid breakfast.

A drizzle started when we stepped outside. Soon, we were in a caravan of people walking to the temple. Some people had plastic ponchos on, some held umbrellas. Shan held a pink umbrella sprinkled with cherry blossoms, no doubt belonging to his wife. An American guy might have refused to hold a flowery or pink umbrella, but a Chinese guy was unfazed by either the pattern or the color. I thought about that time when Harriton and I were caught in a drizzle. We didn't have an umbrella, so he took off his windbreaker and we huddled underneath. The memory of the warmth of our bodies pushing against each other started to surface, but oh, what an ancient memory it was. Or had become.

I got under the umbrella with my mom. I took a deep breath and inhaled the scenery in front of me. Everything that morning, the green fields, the blue mountains far and emerald trees near, the gossamer drizzle and the misty haze, was like a Chinese painting in water and ink.

I held the umbrella, and my mom held me through the crook of my arm. We stabilized each other as we negotiated the narrow steps, climbing up to the temple. We walked in silence. I wondered if she was thinking about the times she came here as a little girl.

The temple was the only building perched on the top of White Cloud Mountain, and it took up the entire space. The main building was flanked by several rooms in each wing. There was a Guanyin statue in the main hall, behind a fence. An incense burner sat in front of the statue, outside of the fence, with burning incense sticks and candles in it. Next to the burner was a donation box. In front of the incense burner were three round red velvet cushions for people to kneel and kowtow. A bell sat under a small pavilion in the courtyard.

"Rose, come here!" Hong-mei called to me in a raised whisper. She was in the west wing of the temple.

"What is it?" I went over with my mom.

"Look at this portrait! It looks just like you!"

There was a row of portraits on the wall. They were framed as Chinese painting scrolls. The one Hong-mei thought looked like me was the third from the left. I looked at it carefully, and indeed it was like I stared back at me. I once had an art student paint a portrait of me in the Jin Li market in Chengdu, and it looked just like this one. Except in that portrait, I wore my American megawatt smile, showing my straight teeth that my parents had spent a fortune on. This lady, whoever she was, with her shaved head and nun kasaya, was not smiling. Or maybe she was, but so elusive I couldn't be sure.

"Who is this?" I asked the question we both had. My heart started to throb faster. The resemblance. Could this be…But she was a nun!

"Maybe we can find some record of these portraits and find out," Hong-mei said.

Just then the bell rang, calling us to the courtyard.

The family and the nuns had laid out soft cushions and chairs: cushions for younger people to kneel on, and chairs for older people to sit.

The nuns came out. The oldest one, Hui-Xin, Wise Heart, was in her 50s, I guessed. It was hard to tell because her face was smooth and unlined, but her body under her brown kasaya seemed old and frail. The others were much younger, and in fact, I was surprised how young they were. I wondered why they decided to become nuns. Did they decide on their own? Did their parents make the decision for them? Was the stay in the temple temporary or was it a lifetime commitment?

As I knelt on the cushion thinking, the nuns started the ceremony. Hui-Xin chanted while striking the wooden fish. The others struck the wooden fish without words. The rain had stopped. A gentle summer wind stirred waves in their kasaya and robes and carried their prayers away. The sounds of their prayers mixed with the rustling sound of the leaves soared high up in the sky and seeped deep down the cliff.

I believed at that moment that Auntie Wang was hearing and seeing all of this and she was happy.

We did not have time to linger after the ceremony. Auntie Wang's oldest son, Wei-guo, which meant "protecting the country," who came home from Guangzhou for his mother's birthday and stayed for the funeral would leave that night to go back, and he had an important message for us before he left.

Going down from the temple was harder because the steps were narrow and slippery from the rain. My mom and I supported each other until we slowly made it to the ground.

That afternoon, instead of in the courtyard, we had dinner in the dining room of Auntie Wang's house. It was just us from Three Rivers and the immediate family.

Wei-guo thanked us for coming all the way to the funeral.

"This means so much for the family," he began. "Father and Mother have always told us that the Han and the Wang were like one family. Now that the older generation is all but gone, I hope we can maintain our bond."

Aunt Daisy, being the oldest in our family, nodded solemnly and said, "Of course, Brother, we must do that. Our mom had always said that as well, and she visited Cloud Gate frequently. We will continue to do that. And we want all of you to visit us, any time!"

"And us, too," my mom said. "I know we are far, but a lot of people visit America now. We would love to have everyone visit us."

"Very good, very good!" Everyone promised.

Then Wei-guo said, "Cousin-sisters Daisy and Lily, it's now time for me to present you the treasure Mother kept for all these years. She got it from our father, who inherited it from his own father, our grandfather Tiger. She told me about it when Father died, for as the oldest son, I would take charge of it and give it to you after Mother passed.

"Mother told me that it belonged to the Han family. The year Aunt Iris died, she and our grandfather Tiger made the plan to save it."

He motioned Wu Er with his hand. Wu Er brought a small metal box. I couldn't tell what kind of metal it was, probably a tin box. I could see, from across the table, that the peeling paint looked like that of an old cookie box. Amazingly, this thing had a lock.

"Mother told me the box was buried under the locust tree in the yard. I had Wu Er dig it up this morning," Wei-guo said. "Regrettably, I didn't know this thing has a lock, and Mother never mentioned where the key was. But I don't think unlocking the box will be a problem. We just need…"

"The key is in my sewing basket."

My mouth was so dry that I couldn't speak. So I coughed and raised my hand like an elementary-school student. Everyone looked at me.

"The key is in Auntie's Wang's sewing basket," I managed, feeling foolish. It was a dream!

Wei-guo, Aunt Daisy, and my mom exchanged looks.

"How did you know, Rose?" my mom asked.

"Auntie Wang mentioned it to me. I didn't understand what she was talking about at the time." I didn't mention the dream.

Yan got up and left the room. She came back with a small key tied to a red string.

The room was so quiet, I could hear people's breath. Uncle De-chen coughed lightly.

Wei-guo put the key into the keyhole and turned. The lock clicked, obviously not rusted. Then he took a package out of the box.

Carefully he laid the package on the table. He unwrapped layers of varnished paper, then layers of cloth to reveal a notebook. From the inside cover of the notebook, he took out a small cloth sack and gently put it on the table.

Then he took the notebook in his hand, opened it, and read out loud:

"The Family Genealogy Book of Han, Number One Cypress Street, Three Rivers."

CHAPTER 20
THREE RIVERS, 1911

Greater Heat: the twenty-ninth day of the sixth month and the twelfth of the twenty-four solar terms. Hottest month of the year.

The heat hung in the air, from the moment the earliest bird went to look for the first worm of the day to the time when the last bird returned to its nest. Vendors of every kind stopped wandering on the streets. They parked their carts in the shade of trees and stretched their voices to call for customers. Soon, even the shouting all but stopped. "It is too hot!" they said, pouring water over their heads and down their throats. The only sound was that of the cicada, dragging the heatwave on and on.

If Chongqing was known as the Big Stove, then Three Rivers, true to its own nickname "Three Steamers," was the pot on it: everything was being boiled and roasted and steamed and simmered.

Everyone at Number One Cypress Street suffered the heat, too. The old magnolia trees provided the yard a good shield from the sun, making it the place to be, day or night. The covered porch offered another respite, but only early in the morning or evening when the sunlight did not hit it directly. In the night, bamboo futons were laid out in the courtyard for beds. This worked well because other than the old cook, there were no men in the house in the night. Master Han and You-jun were still in Chengdu, and the men who did manual labor in the house during the day went home after dinner. The only servants living in the house were the cook and Green Jade. The old school teacher had died the year before.

The women in the family, Lady Han, A-mei, Iris, and Jasmine, were not getting much work done. They took their embroidery to the porch after breakfast, which consisted only of cold porridge and pickles because anything else would add more heat to the body. But sitting on the porch last no longer than what it took to drink a cup of tea. It got hot and muggy quickly, and they moved under the tree. Soon they all needed to put down their embroidery tambour and needles and pick up their huge fans made of cattail. They wore the simplest white linen blouses with ample sleeves and plain white linen pants with wide legs that ended just below their knees. Any more adornment would make it hotter.

Since spring, Iris and Jasmine had been going to the rivers with Green Jade to wash the laundry in the morning, as Lady Han thought that the girls needed to be experts at all domestic chores. After using honey locust pods to wash the laundry on washboards, the girls pounded the laundry with wooden mallets, before rinsing everything in the running water. Their favorite thing to do was walking along the river after the work was done, chaperoned by Green Jade. Then Green Jade quit going for the walks because it was too hot. Iris didn't want to go either, but Jasmine gave no indication of stopping.

"It's the only time we can get out. It's too hot in the afternoon and not safe in the evenings," Jasmine said. "I like the fresh air, and I like to watch the barges and boats coming and going."

On one of the hot days, Jasmine was the only one who took a quick walk, while Iris and Green Jade waited for her under the willow tree on the river bank. Then the three of them hurried home.

At home, unable to do any work, the women sat under the magnolia tree, fanning themselves, when Jasmine said, "It's so hot, I wish we could go and take a dip in the river."

"I wish that, too," Iris said, "but of course we can't."

"When A-mei and I were little, younger than you girls are now, we used to go to the lotus pond in the village," Lady Han said.

"Really?" The girls were surprised. "Was that allowed?"

"Not really, but in the countryside, people did not pay as much attention to things like the proper behavior a girl should have." Lady Han said.

"We were able to go," A-mei said, "until your mother got engaged to the master. Then she needed to learn all of those proper lady's ways."

"In any regard, it was not nearly as hot in Cloud Gate as in Three Rivers, and we got too busy preparing embroidery. I was looking forward to being married into the Han household, so I was eager to do everything my future mother-in-law wanted me to do," Lady Han said.

A moment of silence followed. Lady Han and A-mei seemed to be lost in thoughts about the long-gone past. The girls seemed to be imagining what their mothers were like at that age.

Then Iris broke the silence. "So Cloud Gate is our ancestral hometown, and that's why we visit it often."

"Yes," Lady Han said, slowly swaying her fan. "Your grandfather was a legend in Cloud Gate. He was the only one from Cloud Gate who ever earned the highest rank in the imperial examination in the entire county. The emperor himself awarded him with silver, silk, and land. But he did not have the heart to be an imperial official. What he enjoyed most were the four treasurers of an accomplished scholar: chess, zither, calligraphy, and painting. And, of course, books. So he asked permission to be relieved from his official duty after only three years and the emperor granted it to him. He started the rice business, or rather, hired a trusted friend, a shrewd businessman to run the business.

"It was quite an honor when your grandfather and grandmother sent a matchmaker to our family. My parents, your other grandparents, were skeptical about marrying me off to a household that was much higher in status. If the door threshold was too high, my father said, it might not be a good idea to step over it. One could trip and fall."

"But your family was the best family in Cloud Gate," A-mei said. "Old master and old lady were determined to have a daughter-in-law from Cloud Gate, a place with good Feng Shui."

"I think they wanted a girl that was easier to deal with, far from her own parents, instead of having someone from Three Rivers," Lady Han said, "and it was also desirable to have a girl who was not a spoiled miss from a rich official family.

"No matter what it was, I was grateful for my good luck. Master Han was very kind to me, and I never received the ill-treatment a lot of young wives complained about. I wanted to be the best wife and daughter-in-law," Lady Han said.

"And you are," said A-mei.

They fell silent again. The only sound was that of the cicadas.

Jasmine broke the silence by saying, "I hope the family matchmaker Zhao selected for Iris is as good as the Hans. I'm sure it is, right Mama?" She looked at A-mei, then Lady Han. Iris blushed.

Lady Han stood up, as if remembering something important. "Aye, A-mei, let's go to the kitchen. Mrs. Fang is coming this afternoon for a visit. I want to make sure we have some nice cool plum tea ready."

The two of them got up and left.

Jasmine frowned. She turned to Iris and said, "Every time I try to get some information about your future in-laws, Mama and Lady Han go do something else. Why don't they want to talk about it? Ever since matchmaker Zhao was here, they are just hush-hush."

Iris sighed. "Maybe they didn't want us to ask? It's not good manners to ask about this sort of thing. Like you are eager to be married off to your husband's family. It's shameful. What else can we do but wait and hope for the best."

Jasmine said, "I'll find out one way or another."

Her opportunity came later that evening when Mrs. Fang came for a visit. The cook poured another round of well water in the courtyard to cool everything off, but it was still hot. People generally did not get out unless it was early in the morning or after sundown in the evening.

It had been a while since Mrs. Fang was in the Han house. She managed to look elegant, even though she had to constantly wipe her face with a silk handkerchief.

"Mrs. Fang, it's very nice for you to visit on a day like this, so hot! Could we offer you some supper?" Lady Han said.

"Thank you, but no, I have already eaten," Mrs. Fang said. She fanned herself like the rest of them.

"Then we'll enjoy some plum tea to cool off." Lady Han called Iris and Jasmine over to bow to Mrs. Fang, then told them to fetch the tea from the kitchen.

"I should have come sooner and more often, so forgive me, my lady," Mrs. Fang said. "I have a small household but still too many chores to take care of."

"That's very understandable," Lady Han said. "With Jian-da gone with Master and You-jun, if you need anything, just send Amah over and we'll see how we can help." Amah was an old servant in the Fang household, the only one in fact, and she was old and almost deaf.

"That is very kind of you," Mrs. Fang said.

"Of course!" Lady Han said. "Please don't be a stranger. We have always been like a family, and soon we'll become a real family through marriage, so you must not be overly formal and polite."

She said this in a soft voice, thinking the girls were out of earshot. But she had her back to the direction of the kitchen and did not notice that Jasmine had turned around after walking halfway to the kitchen.

Jasmine stopped, realizing she was eavesdropping. But Mrs. Fang saw her. She coughed and said, "Back so soon, Miss Jasmine?" and she was sweet as sugar in her voice and smile.

"Err…" Jasmine stammered. "Yes, Mrs. Fang, I just want to ask if you take sugar in your plum tea."

"What an observing and caring young lady!" Mrs. Fang nodded. "Just a tiny spoonful will be fine. Sweets make me sick, but plum tea is so tart without a little bit of sweetness."

"Yes, Mrs. Fang." Jasmine backed away, not looking at Lady Han.

Lady Han moved her willow chair, so she could see who was coming and going.

"My lady, have you still not told the girls about the engagement?" Mrs. Fang whispered.

"Well." Lady Han cleared her throat and whispered back, "I hope you don't mind, but I have my reasons. Jasmine is prone to be excited and I thought it would not be wise to get her excited. Have you heard the stories of young girls who stopped eating altogether once they got engaged, and wasted away? There have been several cases lately. I thought it was best to have a quick engagement, right before the wedding ceremony."

What she didn't say was: "The longer we wait for the actual wedding to happen after the engagement, the more likely something is to go wrong. When the night is long, dreams are many." She knew she had good reason to worry.

Before Mrs. Fang said anything, A-mei and the girls were back, carrying trays of plum teapot, cups, and bowls of watermelon slices and toasted watermelon seeds. They set the trays on the round stone table. A-mei poured tea for everyone and Iris and Jasmine carried the tea first to Mrs. Fang, then Lady Han. Then they sat down. Even though Mrs. Fang was a regular at their house, Iris and Jasmine were careful about how they sat: legs crossed, hands on the knees, heads bowed lightly.

Jasmine was dying to have some watermelon, but she waited until the bowls had been passed around before taking a piece after everyone else had done so. Then she took tiny bites. She sensed that Mrs. Fang was watching her intently. Although she found it annoying, she decided to forgo any watermelon seeds. There was no way she could remain dainty shelling the seeds with her teeth. She glanced at Iris, who was holding her teacup to her lips with her right thumb and index finger, her other three fingers free and softly curled—perfect orchid fingers—and the saucer with her left hand, looking so pretty. Jasmine sighed in her heart. Iris was graceful so naturally, but she had to remember and try hard to behave this way.

The rest of the evening, they talked about the weather, admired the embroidery work the girls did, and mentioned nothing else.

Once Mrs. Fang left, the girls took basins of water to their shared room to wash away the dust and sweat from the day before going back to the courtyard to sleep on the bamboo futons.

As soon as they were inside, no longer able to contain her excitement, Jasmine said to Iris, "Jie Jie, I know who you are betrothed to!"

"Really?" Iris continued what she was doing. She took off her shirt and pants. With only a brassiere and underwear on, she reached into the water basin for the washcloth. Jasmine grabbed her hands.

"Don't you want to know?" Jasmine asked.

"Of course I do. But I'm also afraid." Iris said. "What use is there to know? I still know nothing about what he is like. Is his face pleasant to look at or hideous? Is his manner mild or does he have a quick temper? I assume Father and Mother will not marry me to an illiterate, but will he be okay for me to read and write? When I think about all of these, I think it's better not to know."

"But you don't have to wonder about it anymore!" Jasmine said. "He's good-looking. He has great manners and a kind heart. And he loves to read and write with you!"

Iris opened her eyes wide. "Who is he?"

"Fang Jian-da! Master and Lady Han are marrying you to Jian-da!" Jasmine said, her grin wide as half of a watermelon.

"Don't open your mouth so big when you smile, Jasmine!" Iris pulled her hands back. "How do you know?"

"I heard Lady Han and Mrs. Fang talking about being a real family through marriage."

"Hmm." Iris frowned. "If it's Jian-da, why didn't Mama mention anything?"

"Maybe she's afraid that you would be too shy and not know how to act in front of the Fangs," Jasmine said.

"Well, there is just one problem," Iris said.

"What problem?" Jasmine stripped down to her underwear, too, and started to wipe her face and body with the washcloth.

"Jian-da has his heart set on you," Iris said, starting her own wash.

"Oh no no, Jian-da just likes to play with me because I'm more like a boy, another brother to him. He will love a girl like you. Besides, don't you know," Jasmine felt her face starting to burn, "I like You-jun. Jian-da knows that, too."

Jasmine continued, "Neither of us has to be married far off! We can all stay close. Don't you think that's so wonderful? I bet Lady Han planned his. She couldn't bear to have us married far away."

Iris didn't say anything for a while. She dipped her washcloth in the basin, took it out, squeezed out the water, and wiped herself carefully.

Finally she said, "I wonder how Father, You-jun, and Jian-da are doing in Chengdu and when they'll be back."

Jasmine dried her hands and went to the chest next to her bed. She came back with a piece of paper in her hand.

"Jie Jie, here, you can read this. You-jun sent this home to me."

"A letter? How did you get that?" Iris was surprised.

"Before You-jun left, he told me that he would write to me every week, and he'd send the letter to me by the barge that comes through town," Jasmine said, holding out the letter.

"That's why you go to the river every day," Iris said. "No matter how hot it is." She remembered that she was only wearing her brassiere and hurried to put on her sleeping clothes.

"Yes, Jie Jie. Don't be mad at me!" Jasmine said.

Iris sighed. "I'm not mad at you. But you know very well this is not proper, lady-like behavior. You'd be shamed to death if people found out. Our parents would be shamed. If you two fancy each other so much, he should ask Mother to send a matchmaker to your parents for a proposal and engagement."

"He said he had asked Master Han about it. But I don't know if Lady also knows."

"Well, I'll ask Mother tomorrow," Iris said. "Put on your clothes. Let's go to the yard now before Mother or A-mei come to check on us and ask why it takes us so long to get ready."

"You can read the letter if you want," Jasmine said.

"No, it's your letter. I am not nosy." Iris smiled and poked at Jasmine. "I don't want to be embarrassed by his sweet nothing words, ew!" She stuck out her tongue and left the room, laughing. Jasmine picked up the basin and went after her.

"What took you two so long? And what's so funny?" Lady Han asked.

"Nothing," the girls said together.

It was the most beautiful summer night. It was still hot, but because the hustle and bustle of the day had come to an end, minds had quieted, and with that coolness came.

Jasmine lay on the bamboo futon with only a shawl covering her navel, a place that should never catch cold. She couldn't sleep. She looked at the dark indigo sky, clear and crisp, with streaks of white clouds and millions of bright stars scattered around, as if a goddess had casually spilled her diamonds over velvet satin. Soon she heard the sounds of the sleeping people around her. Iris occasionally mumbled something in her dreams, Lady Han tossed and turned, and A-mei had soft, steady snores.

Jasmine wondered if You-jun was also up at that moment, looking at the same sky. She wondered if he lay awake thinking about her, just as she was thinking about him. In the quietness of the night, his written words became loud and clear, as if he were speaking to her. She had read his letter so many times that she remembered each and every word.

"Dear Jasmine, as promised, I start to write this letter to you as soon as I'm settled in with Father and Jian-da. We are staying at the Three Rivers Guild House in Chengdu, in the best rooms the house has to offer. Father's associates and Brother Liang Fei have been very considerate and generous with the arrangement they made for us. The kitchen in the house supplies us with excellent meals when we eat in, but more often than not we are invited out to dine with someone. An amah and her daughter, who reminds me of you, cleaned our rooms and laundered for us, making sure we are comfortable.

"Chengdu is not as hot and humid as Chongqing in the summer. In the morning, after a delicious breakfast, we all sauntered along the Jin River, taking in fresh morning air. It was quite a sight: people in Chengdu know how to enjoy a good life. There were people walking with their birdcages, people doing Tai Chi, and people playing Go. There are many tea houses and tea stands, all of which are full of people any hour of the day. I also saw foreigners. One is riding a...I will call it a machine on two wheels!

"After our walk, Father goes out to conduct his business, and Jian-da and I shadow Liang Fei as he goes to work at the Sichuan-Hankou Railway Company. This company is in charge of the funds for building a railway from Chengdu to Haikou, Hu Bei Province. Liang Fei said that the company has raised more than eleven million taels of silver! Think about that! What a huge number this is. It is apparently difficult to manage such big sum of money and make it work efficiently. I sense frustrations Liang Fei and his colleagues have, for the progress on the project has been extraordinarily slow, as 'the marching of a snail,' in Brother Liang's words. Too many people want to have a say in which route to plan and how the money should be allotted, etc. The situation got worse just recently, as the central government plans to seize control of all local railway projects so shares can be sold to foreign companies to raise money. Local shareholders from all walks of life consider this government plan a breach of contract. Rumors are flying about, and people are · confused and angry. Liang Fei and his friends have formed the Sichuan Railway Protection League, with the goal of resisting the nationalization, resisting borrowing money from foreign banks, and protecting the investment of common folk investors.

"Yesterday, we met Mr. Zhan Tianyou! He is the engineer who has been educated at Yale University in America, a mentor for Liang Fei. He is the first person to build a railway in China. I was awestruck meeting him. And I think that is what I will like to do: get a good education and build railways and factories in China. Only science and technology can make China strong like the West.

"Please forgive me for boring you with all the business talk. How are you doing at Three Rivers? Have you been going to the river every day? I'll write as much as I can, for how I would love to put a smile on your face—I imagine how your face lights up when this letter reaches you. I have no doubt you get along with Iris—my sister is the gentlest, kindest,

and most forgiving person I know! I hope Mother is not too hard on you, trying to make you another Iris! Can you hear that I'm laughing here? Father has written to Mother so she knows our whereabouts, and I hope she doesn't worry about us!

"*Before leaving Three Rivers, I spoke to Father about us. He seems to be happy about it, but you know how he doesn't bother himself with such 'domestic chores.' He said he would speak to Mother. I haven't got a chance to ask him if he has. I hope to have a proper engagement ceremony so I can call you and introduce you to other people as my fiancée. How I wish to travel the world with you! I know you are curious about the world just as I am. We'll climb mountains and walk on beaches. We will watch the sunrise and sunset. And we will enjoy the spring flower blossom, the summer breeze, the autumn leaves, and the winter snow.*

"*I should close now. Jian-da has just walked in and he asks me to send his regards to you and Iris. Poor fellow! He is pale and melancholy-looking. I think he's home-sick, and I know he worries about his mother. So do ask Mother to invite Mrs. Fang over often.*

"*I shall write soon again.*

"*Yours forever faithful, You-jun.*"

Jasmine smiled. "Yes," she said to You-jun without making a sound. "I would like that very much, traveling the world, holding your hand." She fell asleep.

#

The day broke early in the summer. People tried to get things done before the sun was too high and the heat set in. The chirping sounds of birds and the hustle of people woke Jasmine. She sat up, stretched her arms, and discovered that everyone else had already got up and stacked away their futons. She hurried inside and found them sitting in the kitchen.

"Jasmine, here you are!" A-mei came over when she saw her. "What a lazy girl you are sometimes! Come, I'll help you get washed up." She took Jasmine's hand and they went to the girls' room, where a basin of water was waiting.

A-mei wrung the washcloth, wet it again, and wrung it again. Then she put it in the basin, held out both her hands to take Jasmine's, and said, "Jasmine, my dear child, do you remember why we came to live here in Three Rivers, even though Baba and Tiger are still at Cloud Gate?"

"Yes, Mama," Jasmine said. "Master and Lady Han took me as their

156

gan nü'er. I will be married to a nice family as a lady, not a country girl."

"That's right. We all thought this is best for you, Master and Lady, Baba, and me. Now you are at the age of being betrothed, you must remember this and trust the adults for the choices we make for you, no matter what," A-mei said.

Jasmine tried to figure out what to think of this speech. Her heart almost jumped out of her chest. Did this mean...

"Mama," she managed to say, "I know."

When they came back to the kitchen, Lady Han and Iris were still sitting at the table. They avoided looking at her.

"Good morning, Lady, Jie Jie," Jasmine said, wondering what was going on.

They started eating. It was a quiet breakfast. The heat was rising by the time they were done.

After breakfast, Jasmine and Iris helped clean the table. Jasmine whispered to Iris, "Do you want to take a walk to the river with me?"

But Lady Han cleared her throat and called from behind them. "Girls, come and sit down under the magnolia tree. I have something to say."

Once they sat, Lady Han began. "It's been a while since we visited Cloud Gate. I thought it was too hot to travel. But it occurred to me that it's cooler in the countryside, with the mountains nearby. So we'll be traveling to Cloud Gate tomorrow. I have sent the cook to make the arrangements."

"Yay!" Jasmine clapped her hands. She loved to visit Cloud Gate. She felt freer there.

Iris didn't say anything.

"Iris and I will be back in several days, and Jasmine, you and A-mei will stay," Lady Han continued.

"Why?" This surprised Jasmine.

"Jasmine, my dear child," Lady Han said, "come sit by me."

Jasmine went and sat down.

Lady Han took Jasmine's hands in hers.

"You are betrothed now. I thought I would wait for a better time to tell you this but I don't know when a better time will be." She spoke softly. "You need to learn to behave like a soon-to-be bride, and staying in Cloud Gate will make it easier. None of this going to the river all the time business."

"Lady!" Jasmine's heart went to her throat. "You give You-jun and me your blessing?"

"No!" Lady Han dropped Jasmine's hands as if dropping hot charcoal.

"You are engaged to Jian-da," Lady Han said, looking away.

These words took the air out of Jasmine. Overcome by a wave of confusion and shock, she did not know what to say. Iris, who had learned this a few moments ago when Jasmine was getting ready, was on the verge of sobbing. Tears welled up in her big eyes. She lowered her head, her hands folded on her knees, and sat there as the saddest stone statue ever carved. A-mei, too, was almost in tears. She prayed that Jasmine remembered the talk she gave her, about how she must trust the adults for the choices they made for her.

Oh good heavens, what have we gotten ourselves into? A-mei thought. We wanted to save the kids, and who could save us?

Finally, Jasmine stammered, "But…but Lady! Isn't Jian-da engaged to Iris? We…"

Lady Han interrupted her. "When were you told that? Never. I have my plan for Iris, and she will be married to a prominent family in Chongqing."

"But why? Lady?" Jasmine was sobbing now. "Jian-da and Iris, You-jun and me, we will all stay close to home and be happy! Why do you have to set us up like this?"

"Enough!" Lady Han stood. "Listen to you! Shouldn't you be ashamed of yourself? Since the beginning of time, parents have made decisions for their children about important matters like marriage. You do not have filial piety when you think and behave this way. You will go to Cloud Gate and stay there until it's time for the marriage ceremony."

She left.

Jasmine and Iris embraced each other and cried into each other's shoulders.

"I'm sorry, Jie Jie!" Jasmine managed to say. "Jian-da, he…"

"Oh Jasmine, don't say that. I don't care for Jian-da or any men for that matter. I'm just sorry for you and You-jun…"

"Girls, girls!" A-mei held both girls in her arms. "Remember what I told you, Jasmine? Lady Han and I want the best for you and you must trust us. You like You-jun but he's not for you, and your feelings shall pass once you are married. You know Jian-da is a great young man and Mrs. Fang is very fond of you. Things will turn out all right."

Back in her room, Lady Han knelt in front of the small white porcelain Guanyin statue. She chanted her sutra silently and prayed to Guanyin. Save me, save us, You the Merciful One, the benevolent savior of the mass.

Then she went to her desk and replied to her husband's letter, adding a request in her reply.

CHAPTER 21
CLOUD GATE AND THREE RIVERS, 2017

A book of Han family genealogy?

My mom and aunt Daisy looked at each other.

"We thought..."Aunt Daisy began. "The record was lost. Destroyed."

Wei-guo smiled, as if anticipating this question.

"According to my mom," he said, "Aunt Iris was afraid that Cousin-sister Daisy and Cousin-sister Lily would get rid of it. It was the beginning of the Cultural Revolution; everybody was trying to get rid of everything carried over from the old-time, remnants of the Feudalism."

Aunt Daisy and my mom looked at each other again. My mom looked embarrassed, unnecessarily tucking and untucking her hair behind her ears.

"And we did," Mom said.

"I did," Aunt Daisy said. "It was my idea. You didn't know anything...or did you?"

"I knew. I was afraid, but I was also glad. I was afraid of being part of it because I knew Grandma and Mom would disapprove, but on the other hand like you, I thought family books were feudalistic remnants that needed to be destroyed. So I kept quiet, pretending to not know anything. You the strong-willed first child, and me the obedient follower!"

"Destroy the old to create new," Aunt Daisy said. "We were so naïve.

I have regretted this ever since. Number One Cypress Street did not have many old things left after the photo studio became a joint venture with the state in 1955. And I took the one thing we did have and tossed it in the woodstove."

"Not before Aunt Iris asked my grandfather to copy it," Wei-guo said. "They were taught by the same teacher when they were kids. My grandfather much preferred the simpler life of the countryside so he returned to Cloud Gate. For someone in the country, he was well educated. I have never seen it myself, but my mom said my grandpa's penmanship was extraordinary and it took him several weeks to complete the copying task. Then he buried it and only told my dad after the Cultural Revolution was over. Even then he said we needed to wait to hand it over."

We all leaned over to take a look at the book.

The book was definitely not from an ancient time. The paper was thin and yellowish, but not too fragile or antique-looking.

None of us reached over to pick up the book, despite the burning desire to know what was inside. I was afraid of touching it, and I also didn't think it was mine to touch.

"We need to preserve it," Shan said. "This book is precious. Nobody will burn it now, but we don't want to lose it to time."

"That's very true," said Wei-guo.

We discussed how to preserve the book. Somebody mentioned to laminate it, but that was vetoed by Hong-mei.

"I saw someone's picture got ruined by a mistake on the temperature setting. It came out dark as a piece of charcoal," she said.

Finally, Shan suggested that we scan and save the pages as digital files so that all of us, the next generation and beyond, would still have it. He'd do that as soon as he got back to his office, where he had access to a high-quality scanner. Everyone agreed that this was the best way to preserve it.

After that, we all said that Aunt Daisy should be the first to look at the genealogy book.

Aunt Daisy hesitated. Then she said, "Let me go wash my hands." She got up and went to the bathroom.

When she came back, we moved around the table to make room for her in front of the book.

She carefully picked up the book and read out loud, her voice and hands slightly shaking. "The Family History of Han, Three Rivers County.

Copied by Tiger Wang at the request of Iris Fang, November 1966."

Then she put down the book, gently turned a page, and said, "Tiger used regular printed script to copy the book. The writings were very small and neat, standard yingtou kaishu."

"Regular print script, not cursive script, tiny as the head of a fly," Hong-mei whispered in my ears. I was in awe. Tiger had to be in his 70s when he copied the words, and I imagined how he hunched over the book Iris brought, under the 60-watt bare light bulb, reading glasses perched on the tip of his nose, a writing brush in his hand, and ink nearby. How he diligently labored over it for weeks.

Aunt Daisy looked at the book for a few minutes. Then she said, "This page is the Forward. It looks like there are several of them, written at different times. I think we'll need to take our time with the book."

I was reluctant, but Wei-guo had to catch his train, and Shan and Hong-mei had to work the next day. I suspected that Aunt Daisy also needed time to process the shock: the return of the lost family book she thought she was responsible for destroying.

Auntie Wang had given me the key. I must take great care to see what doors the key would open. I must know why she chose me. When we started reading the book again, I'd better be prepared with a pen, a notebook and my laptop, *and* a calm, absorbing mind. Waiting a little would be better.

Wei-guo carefully put the book back on the varnished paper, re-wrapped it, placed it in the metal box, and put the lock back on. Then he said, "Look, we almost forgot. There's something else."

We had all forgotten about the small cloth sack. "I believe this belonged to Aunt Iris," he said and handed it to Aunt Daisy.

Aunt Daisy handed it to my mom. "Lily, your turn. I looked at the book first."

My mom opened the sack and took out a square of silk. She carefully unfolded it. In front of us was a beautiful silk handkerchief. The silk was ivory white and embroidered with two flowers, one light yellow and the other light mauve, perching next to each other on the same stem, accompanied by lush green leaves. The colors were still vivid and the stitches neat and tight.

"Bingti Lian, Sister Flowers," Hong-mei said. "It's beautiful."

Wei-guo put everything in the box, picked it up with both hands, and handed it to Aunt Daisy, who received it with both of her own. Could the answers to our dreams about Grandma Pearl's Grandmother Peony lie in that small metal box?

I couldn't sleep that night. I stared into the darkness, and a small clock on the wall filled the room with faint but clear sounds, clicking away the minutes and hours.

When I finally drifted into sleep, I saw many girls and women going in and out of the room. They talked and giggled and cried, but I couldn't make out exactly what their words were. I could tell that Daisy, Mom, and Hong-mei were among them. I saw myself, but I was in a long dress, a style from the last century. I was holding hands with a girl that I couldn't place in my head. Then I saw the lady from the portrait in the temple. She had come to life and she was floating to me on a cloud, smiling. I ran towards her, dragging my friend with me, but my feet were heavy as lead. I opened my mouth, but no sound came out.

"Rose, Rose!" It was Hong-mei, gently shaking me. "Wake up! It's time to go! Are you having dreams again?"

I sat up and rubbed my eyes. "Hong-mei, everyone was in there," I said.

"Where?" She was packing up her toothbrush.

"In my dream," I mumbled.

"Did Auntie Wang tell you about the key in that dream you had on the day she died?" Hong-mei knew.

"Do you think that's unbelievable?"

She paused. "I don't know. But I start to think we should find out."

We smiled at each other. So we would.

On the way back, Uncle De-chen gave us, the younger generation, a good lesson about Chinese genealogy. It turned out that he was a history buff, and he had enjoyed reading and studying the genealogy, or Jia Pu, of famous families in history.

"Jia Pu," he began, "is the recording of the family history, of course, but far more than that. It is also like a small encyclopedia of the time and place that the family has gone through. One will learn the birth and death of family members, marriages, the successful and important members of the family, the family traditions of weddings and funerals, and so on, but all of these will also show us what the society was at the time, the customs, people's preferences and beliefs."

According to Uncle De-chen, most of the Jia Pu that survived today were from the late Qing Dynasty and the Republic days. The number was small because most people burnt theirs like Aunt Daisy did during the Cultural Revolution. A family genealogy book could have as many as twenty chapters, starting with the name of the book, followed by a forward, the format used in the book such as who were recorded and how many volumes had been recorded, samples of writings from ancestors, achievements and awards of prominent family members, family relations, family rules and traditions, properties owned, inheritances, who had all pitched in to make the book, etc.

Uncle De-chen said, "A Jia Pu is not just a family tree with boxes connecting to boxes. It's a storybook of the family."

"It's like a scrapbook with words." I made an analogy.

I couldn't wait to read the Han family genealogy book, my Jia Pu. Would it tell me the stories of Grandma Pearl, Great-grandma Iris, and Great-great-grandma Peony? Would it tell me about myself? If my story would be added to this book, how might it be written? Losing my job and Harriton uprooted me, and I'd been adrift like the puffball of a dandelion flower swept by a gusty spring wind. Could this be my chance to find out where I belong and how to set down my root again?

CHAPTER 22
THREE RIVERS, 2017

When we got back to Three Rivers, Shan and Hong-mei went to work. Mom, Aunt Daisy, and Uncle De-chen sat down at the kitchen table and started to clean the vegetables they brought back from Cloud Gate, a routine they had every time after they visited Cloud Gate, I realized.

I wanted to start the genealogy book right away, but I also understood that we should wait for Hong-mei to be home when we did that. It was the book for the whole family.

So I lay on the couch and connected to my phone. I wanted to look at job ads on the Chronicle of Higher Education. I'd been thinking about finding a new job closer to LA, closer to my mom. But an e-mail from a listserv caught my eye, from one of the professional organizations I belonged to. Hoping to find job postings, I clicked it.

There was an embedded video, and it was Harriton, giving an interview about a new blog he had launched at the professional conference, our conference that he alone attended this year. Dressed in a dark plum-colored shirt and a light beige jacket, he was devastatingly handsome. He talked with his hands, as always, his long, lean fingers gesturing elegantly to aid his points, which he articulated in his usual gentle and deep voice. He smiled and nodded. He made self-deprecating jokes. He delivered one clever pun after another, making the interviewer, a young woman who was probably not far out of college, giggle non-stop. He was doing so well in a world without me.

I closed my e-mails and put my phone aside. I joined in the vegetable cleaning and storing chores.

Shan not only scanned the book and saved it on two flash drives, but he also brought a copy he printed. The original copy was carefully wrapped and put back in the metal box.

"My boss wasn't around today. I figured it was okay to make good use of company resources," he said. "I work very hard all the time!"

After dinner, Shan went downstairs to watch a soccer game on TV with neighbors. Mom, Aunt Daisy, and Uncle De-chen went for their usual evening walk. I asked my mom and aunt if it was okay for Hong-mei and me to start the genealogy book while they were gone—I couldn't wait anymore. I was very glad they said yes.

Hong-mei and I did the dishes quickly and cleaned the dining table. Then we sat down next to each other with the book, a note pad, and pens in front of us.

"Shall we?" Hong-mei asked.

I nodded.

"The Family History of Han, Three Rivers County. Copied by Tiger Wang at the request of Iris Fang, November 1966," Hong-mei read the cover.

Then she turned the page. "Forward, by Han Zhuo, also known as Jin-Shu, in the fifth month of the twenty-fourth year ruled by Daoguang Emperor.

"So his family name was Han, his given name was Zhuo, and he styled himself Jin-shu," Hong-mei explained.

"Ok, which year was that?" I fired up my phone and looked it up. Emperor Daoguan ruled between 1821 and 1851, so the year was 1845.

"So," Hong-mei counted with her fingers, "Zhou would be our great-great-great-grandfather?"

"The one who ranked first in the imperial examination in the whole Sichuan province?"

"Yeah, I think so," Hong-mei said, "the Jieyuan, top examinee in the triennial provincial exam."

Then she read: "It is with gratitude to the Heaven, the Earth, the Emperor, my father, my mother, and my ancestors, that I take the privilege to write and compile this family history book of Han in Three Rivers County. Our previous family book was unaccounted for because our family had moved to Sichuan Province from Ma Chen, Hubei province in the mass migration during Emperor Qianlong's reign, as told to me by my Father the Excellence. Now I have grown up and have fortunately passed the imperial exams at the county level, college level, and most recently the provincial level, in which I was able to honor my ancestors by placing first. On the verge of being appointed an official position in Three Rivers and being married to the virtuous daughter of the Chang family, I took my duty as the only son of the Han family to start this new family history book.

"Every member of the family will thus be recorded truthfully and accurately, including daughters and daughters-in-law. Once I am blessed to have sons and grandsons, I shall commend them to continue the recording so generations later our descendants will continue to know our ancestors and our family principles and traditions."

My mom, Aunt Daisy, and Uncle De-chen came back.

"What have you girls discovered so far?" my mom asked. "We cut our walk short so we won't miss much of the Jia Pu reading."

Hong-mei read the passages again.

"I remember Mom told us about the family's moving from Hu Bei province," my aunt said. "We were part of the migration wave. More than a million people had migrated to Sichuan during that time, and half of them were from Hu Bei. The emperor had encouraged the migration because there was a population shortage in Sichuan due to peasant uprising and natural disasters."

"I remember Mom telling us about the migration, too, but this is the first time it was actually confirmed by the writing of our great-great-grandfather," my mom said.

Shan came back. "We lost, again." He grumbled. "Sometimes I thought I played better with my company league than the professional team!" Then he asked Hong-mei, "Ready? We both have early meetings tomorrow."

"Okay," Hong-mei said. Then she turned to me and said in an apologetic tone, "I know you want to read the book, Rose. So do I. But Zhuo wrote the book in the old-style words and prose and it's not as quick and easy as I thought it would be. Tomorrow it's a workday, but this weekend, we can pore over the book. How about that, Rose?"

"Sounds good!" I did feel tired, thinking about the book, Auntie Wang, and Harriton. "I'll look at my notes and fill in everything before I start to forget."

We hugged each other, and then Hong-mei left.

I took the copy of the book and notes with me to my room, which was Elise's room before she went to college. Her high school was closer to her grandparents so she had stayed with them during the week. The room had a nice student's desk and shelves of books. Aunt Daisy put the metal box in the safe in their bedroom.

I sat down at the desk, turned on the desk lamp, and went over my notes. Drawing a map of the family, I realized that Zhuo was Peony's father-in-law. Peony, the ancestor we were supposed to be looking for! Zhuo specifically mentioned that "daughters and daughters-in-law" would be recorded, which probably was a big deal back then, because when daughters got married they were no longer considered part of the family, and a daughter-in-law almost always had the lowest status in a family. I would be able to read what happened to Peony and Iris! This thought filled me with anticipation and excitement. Auntie Wang's key would soon open a new, no, an old world for me, a world where the essence of me had come from.

#

Saturday morning, I woke up to an empty apartment. Mom, Aunt Daisy, and Uncle De-chen had gone somewhere, probably the park to exercise, since it was too early to go to the market. They had pork buns in the steamer for me. I took my breakfast to the balcony, sat down, and watched people on the street below.

When I worked, I tried my best to make time for exercise, but seldom did I have the time and opportunity to just sit and be quiet and watch life go by. Now watching the narrow street crowded with cars, bikes, mopeds, and pedestrians, I saw a beautiful picture of down-to-earth living. I wondered what stories these people had, whom they loved and lost, and what hopes and dreams they had. I wondered how things had changed or remained since the time Zhuo and Peony and their children walked those streets. It was night in the States, and I wondered what Harriton was doing at this moment. For a while, I would read our old e-mail communications when I couldn't get him out of my mind. I reached for my phone.

Hong-mei found me on the balcony. She was dressed in a tank top and tights, wore no make-up, and her short hair was secured by a wide hairband. The sight of her lifted my spirits.

"Ready?" she asked.

"For what?" I put away my phone.

"The Diaoyu Mountain and visit to the fortress? You forgot?"

"Oh yes!" We had made plans when I first arrived in Three Rivers for Hong-mei to take me there this weekend. I had forgotten about it.

"If we still have steam left after that, would you also go to my yoga class with me? I never asked, but somehow I just know that you practice yoga, too," she said.

"You are a true detective, Hong-mei!" I joked. "Yes!"

"Of course," she said. "Don't you think it's weird? We see each other every couple of years, but I don't feel estranged from you. Like I actually know what you are like. As if we were meeting each other for tea each week or something."

"It's the blood, Hong-mei," I said.

"It must be!" She laughed. "And we'll be back in time for lunch, and be energized for reading Jia Pu!" She read my mind.

"Sounds like a lovely plan you've got for us," I said, "but what about Shan? You are ditching your husband?"

"He's got back-to-back soccer games to play. Then he goes out with his buddies for beer. It's watching soccer and playing soccer for him," Hong-mei said. "He may join us for dinner. He said that you don't come here often so I should hang out with you as much as I can."

"What a nice guy!" I said. I considered the possibility of Harriton and I being a married couple like Shan and Hong-mei, but I couldn't picture it. Not that Harriton wasn't nice, but he possessed a different kind of niceness. I wondered if I had been looking for the wrong thing in a guy all along, if I would like to be married like Hong-mei. Perhaps he knew it, too, when he chose his wife.

"He is! I'm lucky. Do you have workout clothes to change into? If not, I brought you a set."

"Oh, I have, but I'd love to take yours! My friends with sisters always talked about how they share their clothes and now we can, too!" I said.

I quickly changed. Hong-mei's clothes fit me perfectly.

On the drive east to Diaoyu Mountain, I said, "Tell me the history of Diaoyu Fortress again, Hong-mei." I had been there once before a long time ago, but I didn't remember much.

"Oh, yes," she said. "It's the site of an ancient battlefield between the Mongols and the Song army in the thirteenth century. The legend says that the fortress was under siege for more than five months, but the Mongols could not capture it. After that, the battles between the Song Army and the Mongols lasted for thirty-six years. It was the only place a Mongol Khan had been killed during their ambitious campaign to conquer Asia. According to some historians, had the Mongols succeeded in Diaoyu Mountain, the world map might have been drawn differently."

"Amazing." I felt a sense of pride being connected to this place.

We started to climb towards the main gate, Huguo Gate. There was a light drizzle that did not require an umbrella, and there were not many tourists. I was mesmerized by what I saw. A fine mist had enveloped the mountain and the rivers, and everything in that mist seemed to be floating and drifting—the trees, the ships, and boats, the white pagoda tower on the shore.

"You are lucky to witness one of the Eight Sceneries of Three Rivers, the most elusive one: Mist over Diaoyu," Hong-mei said.

"It's so tranquil," I said. "Who would think this was a battlefield some seven hundred years ago?"

"The fortress had been damaged and restored, but look," Hong-mei pointed, "you can still see the traces of the old stone walls under the new ones."

We were greeted by two young men dressed in Song period army outfits who gladly posed with us for a selfie. We passed the Huguo Temple, freshly restored, and judging by the numbers of incense sticks and candles in the incense burner, amply worshipped. We stopped at the arsenal, the magnificent, wide-open training campground, and the numerous stone carvings and sculptures of Buddha and his disciples.

I was especially interested in the reconstructed Song Jie, or Street of the Song Dynasty. My dissertation was about the art of architecture of the Song Dynasty, and this street was a miniature replica of the theme. I walked the street and imagined how people lived there, carrying about their business, under siege by the Mongol army. I took pictures of old artifacts and texts etched on various stelae, an old habit of mine—I always collected information that could potentially inspire a research project. My mom had commented once that photos of my trips were boring, nothing that could be put in a Christmas letter.

I was a little disappointed to see that tourist businesses—a tea house, a fast food joint, and a souvenir shop—had occupied several houses. An older gentleman sold hard malt candy under three Huangjue, white fig trees that had grown right out of a large boulder. He beat a small gong to get the attention of potential customers, and he used a hammer and a chisel to carve out a portion for them, always a bit more than they had wanted. The modern commercial activities brought me back, abruptly, from the thirteenth to the twenty-first century.

"Do you have any steam left, Rose?" Hong-mei asked.

"Yes, I'm good," I said, wondering about her question. It couldn't be...but it was!

Through the curved door, we entered a courtyard, and through the black-stone paved courtyard, we entered a yoga studio. The yoga class was intense. Hong-mei obviously was a regular here, and she introduced me to the teacher, a lady in her 60s, I guessed, and other students. We didn't talk very much and the class began. Towards the end of the class, when I had worked enough to be pliable in a pigeon pose, I had tears in my eyes. I laid my head on the mat.

When we got back in the car, Hong-mei sent our selfie to Shan.

"Hong-mei, when you met Shan, how did you know he was the one?" I asked her.

"Well, I didn't. When I met him, I was still stuck in my own trap. I was still thinking about the guy who broke my heart."

I nodded. I remembered the story she told me about the student leader she fell for.

"I didn't think I could love anyone else the same way, and I didn't. The kind of love that you want to live one minute and die another minute—I did not have that. So I did not think I was in love with Shan. He was just always there. When I got sick, he brought me soup. If I mentioned a movie I wanted to see, he bought tickets before I asked. When I went shopping, he sat outside the dressing room and waited. Just things like that. One winter, he went away for work quite often, and I realized I missed him dearly. The following spring we got married. I didn't even think we had ever said 'I love you' before that." She smiled at me. "We are very boring, Rose. But we are good with each other, and we can be completely relaxed and be ourselves."

"This is probably the best kind of love. A love that doesn't roll through like a storm, but rains like a spring shower. Storms damage. Showers let the water soak through and moisten the soil and make things grow," I said.

"Mei Mei, you sound like a poet." Hong-mei glanced at me with a smile and turned to focus on the road, her hands on the steering wheel. "What about you? Is there anyone special?"

I had not told anyone about Harriton. What could I say? "I'm having a long-distance affair with a married man who dumped me?" I didn't think so.

But sitting in the car with my cousin-sister, I said, "There was this person…"

When we came to the apartment building, Hong-mei turned to face me and said, "I know this has been said many times before, but Rose, trust that he showed up in your life's journey for a reason. He was true when he said he loved you. And when he could no longer be there with you, there must have been a reason. Knowing this does not reduce your pain, but it may help you heal." She paused, then continued, "Thank you for sharing this with me, Mei Mei. But let him go. It's time."

"Yes, Hong-mei," I said through my moist eyes. "I know, and I will." I just need some more time.

#

Uncle De-chen had already made Dandan noodles for lunch when we got back to the apartment. We sat down to eat. My mom asked, "Hong-mei, where did you girls go?"

"We went to Diaoyu Fortress, Aunt Lily," Hong-mei said. "Rose's favorite is the Song Street."

"Of course," my mom said. "Her doctoral dissertation was about the art of architecture of the Song Dynasty. It won an award!"

I was shocked. I thought my mom didn't pay any attention to whatever I was doing in graduate school because I did not become a doctor. But I did not show my surprise. I smiled at her, and she smiled back.

After we finished eating and cleaned the table, Hong-mei and I washed the dishes. Then I went to my room and brought out the family record copy.

I laid it out on the dining table, and Hong-mei and I sat down. My mom, aunt, and uncle sat down with us.

"No mahjong?" Hong-mei asked.

"Not today," Aunt Daisy said. "We are here to read the family book with you girls."

We perused the pages and learned our past. A past we thought long been flushed away by the river of time.

The Han family, like many others at the time, was given land and reduced taxation by the government as incentive to migrate to Sichuan. The journey from Macheng to Chongqing was relatively short and the family settled in what was to become Cloud Gate. They were able to make a good living.

Zhou Han, my great-great-great-grandfather, had exhibited talents in reading and writing at a young age. He was able to recite Sanzi Jing, the Three Character Classic, when he was five. His father decided that he was material for passing the Imperial Examinations someday and spared him from farm work and manual labor. Instead, Zhou's father hired the best person he could find around Cloud Gate to teach the young boy how to read and write. Soon, Zhou was outdoing his teacher, and the family hired a master from Three Rivers to continue his education. The master came once a month and was paid in cash as well as in rice, vegetables, and home-made goods.

The efforts paid off. Zhou went on to pass the imperial exams at the county level at age 18, continued forward to pass two more levels of exams, and earned first place in the provincial exam. The emperor awarded him land and silver and an official position in Three Rivers, an equivalent position to a mayor. He married the daughter of another prominent family from the nearby Copper Ridge City and had one son. That seemed to be the one regret he had, that he did not have many sons.

Zhou grew disenchanted with official life. He preferred reading, writing, and composing poems to dealing with official duties and socializing with other officials, many of whom he found dull and lacking in scholarly knowledge. He wrote to the emperor and asked to be relieved of his official duties so that he could "return his hometown to spend his retired years in the idyllic countryside." His wish was granted, but instead of returning to Cloud Gate, he started a rice business in Three Rivers. He built the first house on Cypress Street, by the hundred-year-old cypress tree. When his son, my great-great-grandfather Yu-wen married, new rooms were added to the house to make space for the newlyweds.

Yu-wen was born in the Third Year of Daoguang Emperor (1848). Although well-educated, he did not focus on scholarly pursuits. Instead, he expanded the family rice business. Number One Cypress Street became one of the most important addresses in Three Rivers.

Yu-wen married Peony from Cloud Gate, a beauty "who not only knows her way around needles and threads and all the womanly arts, but who can read and write as well as a man, yet who retains her modesty and remains demure as if she was capable of neither," the book said.

The job of writing the family book was handed over from father to son when Yu-wen married.

"That was pretty easy to tell," Hong-mei said.

"How so?" I asked.

"Well, Zhou did not mention much about his wife, other than where she was from. Yu-wen, on the other hand, clearly loved his wife and held her in high regard. Look at all the praise he lavished on her."

"And she is the one we are supposed to look for," I said.

"Look, here's something about Grandma Iris!" Aunt Daisy pointed at the book.

She read, "Iris, the first child born to Master and Lady Han (Yu-wen and Peony) is a shiny pearl in her parents' palms. She was born in the fourteenth year of Guangxu Emperor's reign. She is educated by the family tutor as if she were a son and she could read and write as well as one. She was taught by her mother and her embroidery skills were well known in Three Rivers and the surrounding area."

"And here are the records of the other two Han children," Aunt Daisy said, sounding surprised.

"Two other children?" My mom frowned. "We thought Grandma Iris was an only child."

Hong-mei and I looked at each other. When Auntie Wang visited me in the dream, she mentioned that Peony and her maid A-Mei each lost a child. So Hong-mei and I knew there were two Han children. But a third child?

Aunt Daisy continued to read, "A second daughter was born two years later, in the sixteenth year of Guangxu Reign, but unfortunately died at birth. This child was not named because of her short time with the family.

"A son, You-jun was born in the eighteenth year of Guangxu Reign. He was the pride and joy of his parents. His grandparents doted on him to exhaustion from the time he was born until the time they passed.

"In the summer of the thirtieth year of Guangxu, we took in Jasmine (born in the sixteenth year of Guangxu), the lovely child of Tiger and A-mei Wang of Cloud Gate, as a gan nü'er. This was a happy occasion for all, but in particular, it was a joyous time for my wife Lady Han and Mrs. Wang as the two had been like sisters their whole life.

"The three children have brought so much noise and laughter to Number One Cypress Street."

"A son in the family! Grandma Iris had a brother, and a gan mei mei!" Aunt Daisy put down the book, frowning. "Why didn't she say anything? Or did we just not listen and hear her?"

I looked up the years mentioned: Iris was born in 1889, You-jun in 1893, and the baby who died at birth and Jasmine were born in 1891. Jasmine was taken in by the Hans as a gan daughter in 1905.

The writing ended here. A blank page followed, but it was not the last page of the book.

"That's strange. I did not hear anything about Yu-wen passing away at a young age—why did he stop writing?" Aunt Daisy said.

She turned the page, then said, "Ahh, here, we have writings again." She read out loud:

"I, Iris, as the only offspring remaining in the Han Family, take the duty to continue the writing of our family book. Although my surname has been altered due to my marriage, I believe my father and mother would not mind me undertaking the task. I shall write truthfully and to my best ability about the events that have transformed my beloved home and family, so that our sons and daughters in the coming generations are not ignorant of the Han Family history. I am not a son but I shall keep glorifying the family name.

"The family events I am about to write affected me deeply. It is my hope that my writing will not only continue our family book but also make me discard the anger and bitterness that has torn me apart so I could be whole again."

The date was 1931.

So this is it, I said to myself. Something happened to the family. Something that made all of us have that dream. And Iris is telling us what happened, in her own writing, from so long ago.

CHAPTER 23
IRIS, THREE RIVERS, 1931, SPRING

On a stroll along the riverbank the other day, I noticed the appearance of some tiny, most tender buds on the willow tree, in a shade of pale baby-duck-yellow. So a new spring is here. Oh, how I always welcome the new spring.

A spring day like this reminds me of days past and memories lost. The scenery is the same today as then, but the people, alive or dead, are no longer the same. I think about my family. The events that unfolded twenty years ago altered our family and the destiny of each one of us so profoundly that I feared there would be no more springs in Three Rivers and at Number One Cypress Street. But of course, another spring does come. And just the same, one comes each year after that. It comes anyway, no matter who is still here, and who has gone forever.

The world has changed. No longer do we have an emperor. We have generals and warlords instead. First, it was Yuan Shikai, who wanted to be an emperor. Now General Liu Xiang rules our province. The railway between Chengdu and Chongqing is still not built, but I have heard about a flying machine the General has purchased.

Twenty years ago, I never would have dreamed of being the one writing the family book. I can read and write, as Father often said, as well as any men, even better than most, but the task to write the family book always belongs to the first son of the family, the one who bears the family name, as soon as he is married. But what happened that year extinguished Father's spirit, and You-jun never married.

It took me twenty years to pick up a brush. Putting words on paper became easier after time has put distance between me and the past. Last winter, Mother gained her entrance to the West Pure Land. When the news came, I wept. I had the urge to pour everything out on paper. But still, I needed the sprouting life of a new spring to give me the final motivation. Spring, summer, autumn, and winter, the four seasons will always come and go, even when people are gone forever. What we can hold on are memories and stories. I need to tell the stories and keep the memories alive.

Perhaps Father and Mother would have wished for all who lived to remain silent, to never mention what happened, and to forget everything. We must not tarnish our reputation as the best and perfect family in Three Rivers. But how could one forget? It is the true ending of our family if we forget; after all, don't all families wish for at least one son so their names and legacies can be carried on? I don't bear the family name anymore, but I will do as a son to carry my family's story.

As Father wrote, I was fortunate to be born into a family in which there was no shortage of food on the table or clothes on my back. Father never treated me as a deplorable daughter, for he had an enlightened mind. He hired the best tutor in Three Rivers to teach me how to read and write. He poured affection on me, always bringing me novel trinkets from his many business trips.

Mother taught me everything about domestic responsibilities a woman must take, as much as what the tutor had taught me about books. Mother herself could read and write, which was something I had not observed in other women in her generation. Her reputation for both her domestic and scholarly skills, and her filial piety to her mother-in-law accompanied her from Cloud Gate to Three Rivers.

My grandfather, the old Master Han, doted on me as well. He often asked me to recite poems and verses from the Tang and Song Dynasties and praised my excellent memory and diligent work. My grandmother, the old Lady Han, whom we called Old Ancestor, almost never spoke to me, as if I were invisible. I thought this the proper way a grandmother treated her grandchild, until I saw how she loved You-jun. Then I understood. I was not a boy. My grandmother had wished me, the firstborn, to be a son.

I was told that Mother lost a child when I was very young. I remember nothing more than the frenzy in the house waking up that day. But I learned bits and pieces growing up, from conversations by grownups, and I pictured what happened from that. Father was not back yet from his business trip when the baby died. Mother remained in her room and did not wish to be bothered by anyone, other than her old friend and maid, A-mei. But A-mei was sent to take the dead baby out of the house, as it was customary for the burial of a child to be done without parents. If children die before their parents, they have committed the act of lacking filial piety. Parents should not mourn them in formal funerals for this hinders the chance for the dead children to be reborn into decent families, as human beings. A-mei would not return for a few years. I was left with Grandfather and Grandmother and the new maid, Green Jade.

Grandfather read and played with me. Grandmother had a frown that made me quiet. She gave orders to Green Jade and other servants and complained about having to take charge of the household work, because my mother was supposed to be doing that.

My father came back on the third day after the baby died. Grandmother stopped him at the threshold and told him not to visit my mother right away.

"She needs rest," Grandmother said. "She needed not cry so much over the baby—it was only a daughter. I hope rest will make her recomposed and recover quickly enough to take up her proper duties as the lady of the house."

So Father came to me instead. He played with me and helped Green Jade put me to bed. He told me stories at bedtime. I remembered one particular story, called "Three Huangjue Trees on the Rock."

The rock stood on the main street of Diaoyu Fortress, before the place was under siege from the Mongols. The three Huangjue trees grew straight out of the rock, forming a canopy of leaves and branches that provided cool shade for the people. Many years later I heard the story again, when the men in the house and a guest visited the Diaoyu Fortress. Jasmine, my gan mei mei, and I could not go because we had bound feet and could not climb the mountain.

The trees could grow out of a rock because they came from the seeds that were given by Guanyin, the Merciful Goddess. Guanyin had inhabited the body of an old beggar woman, who was shunned by most people. But a mother and daughter, who were poor and barely supported themselves by selling homemade rice cakes at the foot of the rock, took pity on this old beggar woman. They gave her food and let her sleep under their shabby umbrella while they stayed under the blazing sun. The beggar woman revealed herself as the Most Merciful of all the Bodhisattvas and gave the mother and daughter three seeds to be planted on the rock, before she departed in a rainbow-colored cloud. The seeds grew overnight, and the mother and daughter were shielded from rain and sun ever since. And the trees provided a good resting place for Song soldiers when they fought the Mongols.

The moral of the story, my father said, was to always be kind and take pity on those who were poor and unfortunate, as all good deeds would be rewarded in the end.

My mother finally came out of her room. It must have been very difficult for her without her closest friend and maid, but my father stayed home for a while, having delegated all his business travels to his associates. I, for a very short time in my life, had both mother and father with me, at home, and I was too young to understand the pain they must have been going through, so I had a very happy time. Perhaps the happiest time of my life. Or one of the happiest. I was very happy, too, when Jasmine came to live with us and became my sister.

I must mention two families that are of great importance to us. They are not part of the Han family by blood, but they are part of us by bonding.

The first is the Wang family in Cloud Gate, A-mei's family. A-mei was my mother's maid and confidante since they were girls. When Mother married Father, A-mei came with her. The older I became, the more I thought that they were like sisters, especially after I acquired my own sister. By the time I was old enough to observe people and things around me, I saw that Mother and A-mei kept their distance when other people were around, especially when grandmother was near, as one was the lady in the house and the other was the maid. But if it was just them and me in mother's room doing embroidery, they laughed and talked nonstop, like sisters.

A-mei stayed in Three Rivers most of the time even after she married into the Wang family, only going back to Cloud Gate during busy farming times such as planting and harvesting seasons, or important holidays. The longest time she was absent from our house was when she went home with the dead baby.

Mother told me that A-mei's husband Old Wang was also a childhood friend of theirs. "The Wang family is like our own family," my mother said, over and over again, as if she were afraid we would forget.

The Wang family and the Han family became more connected when A-mei came back from Cloud Gate after that long absence. I would have forgotten her if not for the fact that mother and Green Jade mentioned her all the time. From mother, I learned that A-mei did not return right away because she had two babies during the time she was away: a daughter, Jasmine, and a son, Tiger. It so happened that my grandmother was living mostly in the Huguo Temple by then. The older she got, the more diligently she worshiped to prepare herself for her journey to the West Pure Land. My mother needed help with the household, and who would be a better choice than her old friend A-mei? Jasmine and Tiger were old enough to come to our home. Tiger was not used to life in Three Rivers and he later returned to Cloud Gate. I did not know back then that one day we, Tiger and me, would be the only two left, and how we would need to help and hang on to each other as sister and brother.

Jasmine became my friend the instant she walked into Number One Cypress Street. I was overjoyed when Father and Mother took her in as their gan nü'er. We became sisters. My brother You-jun loved Jasmine, too, but it was a different kind of love. A love that did not bring happiness to them or the family. But we did not know that when Jasmine walked into our house on that fateful day, a girl so beautiful as if she had descended from Heaven.

The second family important to us is the Fang family in Three Rivers. Mr. Fang was an old friend of father's, but he, unfortunately, caught a very bad flu and passed away when his son was only a toddler. The widow and the child managed with the rent of their land from the countryside but could not afford much more. My father took pity on the little child and included him in our private school. Jian-da grew up with us and we all loved him—his melancholy disposition, his gentleness, and his observant and caring manner. He was the opposite of my brother in nature: one was soft and one was hard. One waited and calculated, and one rushed and acted.

Mrs. Fang was a regular visitor to my mother. I was a little afraid of her when I was a child and tried to avoid her when I was older. I felt that her eyes followed me around and I was afraid of making a mistake or doing something embarrassing, as I understood that she was observing me as a future daughter-in-law. From the moment I understood that girls were to be married out of their parents' house, I understood my destination might be to end up at the Fangs. I could not say that I was unhappy about the arrangement. Jian-da was kind and handsome, and he was the only boy, or later man, that I had ever met, other than my father, brother, old Uncle Wang, Tiger, a handful of my father's friends, and our household helpers. I understood that the worst thing that could happen to a girl was to be married to the wrong family, with a husband who could beat her as he wished or marry as many concubines as he wanted, or smoked opium. I knew I would not end up like those girls if I was married to Jian-da. I guessed that Mother would choose Jian-da for me. She had mentioned many times that our family did not need to marry me out for money, because we had enough. She wanted me to be with someone who would be kind to me, and this someone was not just the husband. This someone was also the mother-in-law.

It is difficult for me to remember when the trajectory of our lives shifted. Was it when Jasmine walked into our house in her simple, cream-colored cotton jacket, red pants, her long braid reaching to her slender lower back? Was it when You-jun jumped into the lotus pond and Jasmine said she would jump in with him if he didn't come back? Or was it when Jasmine was sent back to Cloud Gate when You-jun was away in Chengdu? When I close my eyes, all the people and events float in front of me as if I were watching a puppet show, but I cannot remember what the main act was.

If I had written it down back then, I might have remembered more clearly. But words only come to me now, after twenty years. After Mother was gone forever. After I myself have a grown daughter.

Both Jian-da and You-jun fell in love with Jasmine, or at least what I understood as love. But Jasmine loved You-jun. I couldn't say that I was jealous. I loved Jasmine, too. But if loving someone meant that a person would disobey her parents and jump in the river for him, I admit that I did love anyone like that, not even Jian-da. All I wanted was a quiet life, with food on the table and clothes on my back, a husband to take care of and, if I was blessed enough, sons and daughters to carry on my husband's name.

I trusted that my parents would find me a suitable husband if Jian-da was not in my destiny. But Jasmine was different. She wanted to decide for herself whom she should be married to, and she would disobey parents, the worst kind of unfilial crime. And even die for what she desired.

Everyone except Mother and A-mei thought we would have two perfect couples among the three families. My mother was against marrying You-jun and Jasmine. She had a good reason, which nobody except for A-mei knew at the time. She even went against Father's wishes. My father had suggested that Jasmine be returned to the Wang family so a betrothal gift could be sent to them. But Mother would not hear that. The mother I knew until that point was very gentle, a pious lay Buddhist who made a habit of visiting the Guanyin Temple in Cloud Gate, despite the distance, eating vegetarian dishes on the first and fifteenth day of every month, and offering daily incense to the small white porcelain Guanyin statue in her room. I did not know my mother could be so headstrong and immune to the pleading of You-jun and Jasmine. And Jasmine was the same way, being headstrong, just like Mother. People always said I resembled my mother, but that was only in appearance. Jasmine was the one who'd gotten her heart, as we would learn soon.

Mother decided to marry Jasmine to Jian-da and send You-jun to America. She found me a rich family in Chongqing. What if her plan had worked? What would the families be now? I do not know. One can never know what did not happen.

I only stumbled upon the reason behind my mother's decision by accident. Here, I'm trying to write it down, but I don't know if I can. I don't know what words to choose and how to form sentences.

CHAPTER 24
THREE RIVERS, 2017

We sat at the table in stunned silence. It had taken us the whole afternoon to finish reading Iris's writing. Hong-mei and my mom helped me with translation, and I recorded it all on my laptop.

"I remember seeing a grave with the name Jasmine at the family plot in Cloud Gate," my mom said, "but I don't remember Mom or Grandma mentioning the name at all. Yet here is Iris's writing about Jasmine. And it looks like Jasmine died. Do you remember anything, Daisy?"

"I don't," said Aunt Daisy.

Hong-mei carefully flipped the pages. "Yes, there are more."

Just then, Shan came in to take us out for a feast on roasted whole goat. Once I heard a joke that an American came to Chengdu and swore to eat all the delicious food throughout China in a year. Five years later, he still had not finished all the yummy things in Chengdu! I was sure the same joke would be true about Three Rivers; I had not been treated to the same meal twice since I arrived. For breakfast, one day it was rice vermicelli in chicken broth, another day it was steamed rice flour cake. Lunch could be beef noodle soup or Dandan noodles. Dinner was the most important meal, and so far, I had had Three Rivers wild fish banquet, hot pot of various varieties, and all kinds of dishes of meats, organs, and plants. It was surprising to me that a small city like Three Rivers would have so many different gourmet foods, until I discovered that until the end of Ming and beginning of Qing Dynasties, Three Rivers had the second largest population in Sichuan province, second only to Chengdu.

With so many delicious foods, perhaps it was not surprising that Sichuanese love to eat. I joked with Hong-mei that if I could not find another art history teaching job, I might write a book called "Sichuanese Women Don't Get Fat," like the same title about French women. There were equal numbers of restaurants and dress shops all over Three Rivers as well as in other Sichuan cities where I had been. The restaurants were always full; it did not matter if it was a luxurious eatery where waitresses dressed in finely tailored qipao uniforms catered to guests' every whim and wish, or a simple hole in the wall on every street corner. Sichuan girls ate all things at all times, and they wore their clothes the same way as they ate, be it Christian Dior or something someone made in a home dress shop that was smaller than most American living rooms, they were beautiful and elegant.

On this day I would not have liked to be interrupted in the reading of the family book. But one main goal my uncle and aunt had for us was to eat all the good food in Three Rivers. Roasted White Goat was a famous dish that had been popular for hundreds of years. and the reservation had been made before the turn of events. Nobody had dreamed that we would stumble upon our genealogy book!

Shan drove me, my mom, and Aunt Daisy along a winding country road. Hong-mei drove the other car with her dad. After about forty-five minutes, we ended up in a farmhouse. The place was called River Fish, but no mistake, there was a whole roasted young goat in front of us. The goat had been roasting the whole day. Shan specifically told the cook to be light on spices so I could eat it. As soon as I held the piece of leg meat he put on my plate with my gloved hands and bite into it, I understood what he meant. A lot of Americans eat spicy stuff, like Mexican food. But Sichuan pepper was something else. It numbed my tongue quickly. Even with the "light spiciness," I had to gobble down sliced watermelon to blunt the burn in my mouth.

"Here." Hong-mei pulled a piece of Dove chocolate from her purse. "This works great!"

There were several people I didn't know at the dinner table, which was not a surprise. For a family that had lived here for generations, there were so many relatives, old friends, and new acquaintances. Someone besides family was almost always present at an outing like this. Mom was usually busy talking to people she hadn't seen for a while, and I just ate. My Mandarin was not sufficient to carry a good conversation with people, and the fact that their native tongue was Chongqing dialect—so they and I both had an accent speaking Mandarin—did not make it easier. But on this trip, discovering the family record book, I truly wished that I were fluent in my ancestors' language.

Hong-mei brought someone to introduce to me. He was perhaps in his late fifties, very thin, deeply tanned, with wrinkles carved in his forehead. I had seen him somewhere before.

"This is the owner of this restaurant, Old Brother Zhou," Hong-mei said. "Auntie Wang's nephew."

That was it; I must have seen him at Auntie Wang's birthday party and funeral. He had her eyes.

"Ni hao!" Old Brother Zhou shook my hand. "Auntie Wang and my mother were sisters."

"Very nice to meet you," I said. "I'm very glad to have met Auntie Wang."

"Pretty amazing lady, wasn't she?" Old Brother Zhou said.

I agreed.

"I heard you and Hong-mei are perusing your family book?" he said.

"Yes. It's so interesting. There is so much family history that we don't know," I said.

"I heard Auntie Wang talking to my mom about the Han family once," he said.

"Oh! What about?" Hong-mei asked.

"It was the day of Pure and Brightness one year. After sweeping the tombs of my grandparents and the tombs of Wangs and Hans, Auntie Wang went to the Guanyin Temple. She went on this trip every year. I was too young until that year to pay attention to what my mom and my aunt were talking about. It turned out that not all the ancestors of the Han family were buried in their family plot. One of them actually cut her hair and became a nun, and her ashes were kept in the temple with those of the other nuns. So on the tomb-sweeping day, the Han family would take an additional trip to the temple, not just to pray and burn incense but to remember an ancestor. And you know the Wangs and Hans were like one big family, so Auntie Wang always went as well," Old brother Zhou said.

"Which ancestor was this?" Hong-mei and I said together, hopefully. "Did Auntie Wang ever say?"

"This I'm not sure of," Old Brother Zhou said.

This was not part of the family record we'd gone through so far. Would Iris write about it? Could this be Grandma Pearl's grandma, Peony, the person she wanted me to look for? My heart skipped a beat at this thought. Yes, in the dreams, didn't Grandma Pearl mention the temple? So did Auntie Wang. And the portrait in the temple Hong-mei and I saw.

Old Brother Zhou, Hong-mei, and I continued our conversation. We talked about my impression of Three Rivers and Cloud Gate and whether I could get used to living here for long periods of time. He asked about the political systems in the U.S., the presidential elections, the NBA, and soccer in the U.S.

This was a typical situation I had run into traveling around China: people, no matter their educational levels or where they lived, were interested in what was going on outside China. They were very curious. I wished I could say the same about my countrymen. Maybe I could stay here longer. I could teach English and learn Mandarin at the same time, and produce scholarly work. Mom had hinted she might move back to China and stay with Aunt Daisy when the day came and she could no longer move about easily.

I pushed the thoughts about family history to the back of my head so I could concentrate on my conversations with people around me and enjoy the food. And I knew I would pay a visit to the temple in Cloud Gate, soon.

#

Sunday morning came. Uncle De-chen made tangyuan, sweet sticky rice ball for breakfast. "I made the fillings myself, much better than what you can buy," he said proudly.

"What's in it?" I love tangyuan, even though it is so sweet and rich I could only take three or four at a time. My mom said that my dad could eat twenty at one meal when he was a young man.

"This one is made of white cane sugar infused with roses from our own garden, black and white sesame paste and seeds, chopped walnuts, lard, and peanut butter. The key is to have the right proportion of everything so it will be sweet but not too much, rich but not greasy," Uncle De-chen said.

"I think yours is perfect, Uncle De-chen," I said.

"Your uncle used to grind the sticky rice flour by himself, too. We had a millstone for that," Aunt Daisy said.

A millstone was made of two stone discs with grooves on them. The top disc had a hole through which to feed grains of sticky rice that had been soaked in water. The miller would turn a handle attached to the top disc to grind the grains. The ground flour and water would then flow through an opening at the bottom groove into a bucket.

"I saw a millstone in Chengdu once," I said. "It was at a restaurant, and guests could experience how to grind rice and other grains. It was fun to try it for a few minutes, but it must be hard work to actually grind flour by oneself."

"It was hard work," Aunt Daisy said. "Today even most Chinese kids have never seen a millstone. Everything you can buy. Things have changed so fast, especially in the last twenty years."

"Not as good as home-made. I try to make stuff by myself as much as possible. Otherwise, what is one to do, after retiring?" Uncle De-chen laughed.

A thought crossed my mind. Peony, Iris, Jasmine, and all the other people in the family book, they must have made all these traditional foods at some point and enjoyed them with family and friends just like we did. How things changed, but yet remained the same.

As soon as Hong-mei and Shan came, we started reading the family book. Shan stayed. "I heard the story was getting interesting," he said.

"Yes, we are reading what Iris wrote," his wife said.

I had my laptop in front of me. Hong-mei, my mom, and Aunt Daisy crowded at the other long side of the dining table, across from me, and Uncle De-chen and Shan each sat at the short end of the table.

Hong-mei started to read Iris's writing, and she stopped and translated for me when I needed her to.

In the next couple of hours, Iris's words transported us back in time, through the joys and sorrows of our ancestors. We came face to face with the family secret, so unexpected, so heartbreaking.

CHAPTER 25
CLOUD GATE AND THREE RIVERS, 1911, PART 1

The Beginning of Autumn: the fifteenth day of the second sixth month (the leap month) and the thirteenth solar terms of the twenty-four seasons. Autumn begins.

Jasmine sat in front of the window, an embroidery tambour in her quiet hands. She was not working on her embroidery, a pillowcase with butterflies, and spring flowers. She stared out the window, looking at nothing in particular.

She had been back at Cloud Gate for two weeks. Lady Han decided to send Jasmine to Cloud Gate the day after she told the girl that Jasmine was betrothed to Jian-da. They all went to Cloud Gate for a few days, but Lady Han went back to Three Rivers with Iris, and A-mei and Jasmine stayed.

"I'll tell Mrs. Fang that you are under the weather and need good rest," Lady Han said. "Breathing fresh country air is good for you. You can work on your wedding dress and your trousseau, and visit the Guanyin Temple and pray. You will find peace and accept your fate, what's best for you. You will forget about your fit of passion and be calm."

The night before Iris went back to Three Rivers, Jasmine wrote a short note to You-jun and asked Iris to post it for her. In the note, she let You-jun know that she was staying in Cloud Gate.

"Come get me and take me with you. Anywhere you go, I will go with you."

Jasmine muttered these words again. Every day, she sat here, waiting for You-jun, or at least some word from him. But there was nothing.

"Jasmine." A-mei came in, holding a bowl. "You haven't been eating well for some time. Come, take this chicken soup. Your father slaughtered a fat hen this morning. Tiger helped him clean it, and it took me a whole morning to simmer it. Come on, take some."

Jasmine turned her head, forced back her tears, and said, "Mama, what date is it today?"

"It's the fifteenth day of the leap month, the Beginning of Autumn, daughter," said A-mei.

The wedding was set for the auspicious day of the twentieth day of the seventh month, a little over one month away.

Jasmine lowered her head, and the tears she tried to hold back poured out like raindrops through a leaking roof.

"I wish I was not taken in as a gan nü'er," she said bitterly.

"Jasmine." A-mei wiped her daughter's tears with a handkerchief. "You should be grateful for your good luck. Master and Lady love you as their own child. A person must always be grateful for even the smallest kindness from others and return the favor many times more. As they say, a drop of water should be reciprocated by a gushing spring. And you should be happy that you are getting married to such a nice family as the Fangs. Jian-da is intelligent and kind, and everyone can see that he likes you. Mrs. Fang will retire, and you will be the lady of the household. A girl cannot dream of anything better than this."

Jasmine sobbed softly, not saying anything.

"I know what you are thinking," A-mei continued, "but one day you will understand. One day when you have children and settle into the roles of wife and mother, you will understand why your parents have made this choice for you. You will enjoy your life and you will forget about the past."

"What if I can't?" Jasmine said.

"I promise, you will. Everyone does," her mother said. "Everyone forgets. Time puts everyone and everything in the right place, eventually and always. Time does the trick for all of us. Now take the soup and change your clothes. We'll go to visit the Guanyin Temple today. Baba and I want you to get out and get some fresh air."

Jasmine took a few sips of the soup and changed into her outing clothes, an indigo cotton tunic, and bloomers. She followed A-mei out of the house, through the narrow front yard, where a rooster and a couple of hens wandered under a wooden table, looking for worms. They went on the narrow path weaving through small patches of farm plots.

When A-mei was in Cloud Gate, she tended the vegetable plots with other women. Old Wang and Tiger, who was a grown-up young man of eighteen, took charge of the rice fields. It was a busy time for the men; they needed to harvest the spring rice and plant fall crops within a short time span. Jasmine saw her father and brother from a distance and waved at them. They waved back. After a while, she turned and saw that they were still standing, watching her.

Soon they came to the lotus pond. Jasmine said to A-mei, "Mama, I want to sit down and rest for a little bit." A-mei agreed that it was a good idea. Autumn had just begun but it was still hot in the late morning under the sun. They sat down under the willow tree, dabbed the sweat from their foreheads. A-mei rubbed Jasmine's feet.

The lotus flowers had long withered. Ducks played in and out of the pond.

Several children ran out from behind the willow tree and started skipping pebbles over the water. Two boys challenged each other to jump into the water, and they soon took off their shirts and did just that. The girls screamed at the adventure, and they clapped and cheered when the boys re-emerged.

Jasmine watched them, misty-eyed. She saw herself, Iris, You-jun, and Tiger in these children, and she remembered the moment when she ran to You-jun after he came out of the water. She remembered how she had wanted to jump in the water with You-jun, and what You-jun had said to her.

"I will always come back to you."

But would he?

It was the fifteenth of the leap month. The sky was cloudless. There would be a full moon tonight, the same full moon.

That day when the four of them came to the lotus pond, the last night when she and You-jun sat under the full moon—it all seemed to have happened in another lifetime.

They began walking again and slowly came to the foot of the steep steps leading to the Guanyin Temple.

"Jasmine, we'll hire a huagan to take you up today," A-mei said.

"But Mama!" Jasmine was surprised. "Lady Han never took a huagan! She said we must show our sincerity and eagerness to worship Guanyin and taking the steep steps with our three-inch lily feet was exactly the way to show it!"

"I know, I know. But Lady Han had specifically told me that it is okay for you to be carried up by a huagan, because she wants you to be in good spirits and health when you get married. She gave me extra money to buy extra incense and donate to the benefaction box. The dowry for you had provisions for traveling and payment for hiring a huagan is included."

Two men and a huagan stood waiting, as if they had been summoned.

When they got to the top, A-mei thanked the men, paid them, and asked them to wait in the shade of the trees.

There were no other visitors that day; it was a busy farm day and not a holiday. The master nun Hui-Ming and a young nun, a girl who had just taken the oath to be a nun but had not had her hair shaved, were sweeping the courtyard. A-mei asked the young nun to bring some tea to the huagan carriers. Incense burned in the old bronze burner in front of the main temple, and plumes of smoke were gently scattered by a breeze. The large, ancient trees provided shade for the rooms and the courtyard, and Jasmine sensed the instant coolness.

Hands folded together in prayer, A-mei went up to the master and bowed to her.

"Master," she said, "my lady, lay Buddhist Peony, sends her best regards."

"Thank you." The master bowed back.

"Master," A-mei continued, "my lady requested that you counsel her gan nü'er, my daughter Jasmine, before her wedding."

Jasmine came forward and bowed to the Master, her hands in prayer in front of her chest.

The master nodded, walked to the side chamber, and sat on a mat, cross-legged, her hands counting her prayer beads. Jasmine followed and knelt on a mat facing her.

"Young benefactress," the master began. "Congratulations on your upcoming wedding."

Jasmine stared at the ground in front of her, saying nothing. Tears welled in her eyes.

"What's the matter, child?" the master said.

"I..." Jasmine started to sob silently. Finally, she said, "Master, isn't it destiny that brings husband and wife together? If so, how does one know one's destiny?"

The master didn't say anything. She stood up and said, "Come with me, child."

Jasmine followed her into the temple. In front of Gaunyin, on the altar, hundreds of candles were lit, their flames flickering gently.

"Can you tell me which one of these candles shines the brightest?" the master said.

Jasmine opened her eyes wide and shook her head. "No. They all look the same."

The master smiled gently and nodded.

"If one is not able to tell which one is the brightest of these candles, how could one then tell which person is her destiny? Whatever we accept is our destiny."

#

Back in Three Rivers, the Han household was getting ready for the wedding. More precisely, they were helping the Fang family to get ready since the Fang household had only Mrs. Fang and an old amah. Lady Han made daily trips to the Fangs to help with all the details: guest list, menu items, decoration of the newlyweds' bedroom, and so on.

This day, however, Lady Han stayed at home, anxiously waiting. Master Han was expected to arrive home.

Lady Han had written him, urging her husband to return by himself. "Leave You-jun and Jian-da in Chengdu and entrust them to Mr. Liang Fei. Come home as soon as possible. I must speak to you." She had never asked her husband to hurry home in all these years. Master Han would have thought this urgent message meant that his parents were gravely ill, had the old Master and Lady still been around. He told the worried boys to continue working and studying with their mentor Liang Fei while he went home for some business. He promised them that he would return in a few days.

Lady Han waited by the front gate. She had lived in a lie, and she had to tell her husband the truth before he found out a different way. Paper could not wrap a fire. Sooner or later he would know, when he questioned why she chose Jian-da, not You-jun, as Jasmine's husband. It was one thing never to mention it, but a whole other thing to lie if he asked.

As soon as Master Han came through the gate, she took her husband's hand and led him into their bedroom. She had already prepared a basin of fresh water for him to wash his face and wipe away the dust from three days of traveling. She helped him change into comfortable house clothes and called Green Jade to bring a pot of freshly brewed tea and two teacups. Then she closed the door.

"Wife, what's the matter?" Master Han asked.

"Jasmine and Jian-da's wedding is set on the twentieth day of the seventh month. It happened fast and I want to have a word with you about it."

"So fast?" he said. "You know Jasmine and You-jun like each other, and to be honest I don't know why you must separate them and marry Jasmine to Jian-da, and do it so quickly."

Lady Han did not answer. Then she got up from her chair, knelt in front of her husband, put her head in her hands, and started sobbing uncontrollably. She tried her best to keep the sound muffled.

Master Han was shocked. He tried to help his wife to her feet but she stayed down.

"Husband." Lady Han looked up at her husband, her tear-streaked face pale as a ghost. She muttered through her sobbing, "It has been twenty years, and in all that time I did not know what and when to tell you. I thought I'd saved our child. I did not expect this today…"

"What are you talking about?" her husband asked.

"Jasmine and You-jun can never be husband and wife. They are sister and brother. Jasmine is our daughter, not a gan daughter, but a blood and flesh daughter of ours," she said, and she put herself on the floor.

Master Han fell back into his chair, staring at his wife, his eyes wide and his face red.

Iris had heard that her father was home. She had just gotten to the door of her parents' bedroom and was about to knock and call out, "Father, are you home?" when she heard her mother's words.

Their voices were low and muffled. Iris thought that she should turn around and leave, but an invisible force fixed her. She dropped her hand that was reaching the door, but her feet, heavy as lead, did not belong to her. She heard every word, and every word struck her as if thunder exploded directly above her head, piercing through her eardrums on a cloudless day.

"Flawless," Master Han muttered at the end of his wife's story, "like a dress made by fairies. Or almost. What if You-jun was also a daughter? Would you have done it again? "

Lady Han didn't answer. She turned her head to look at the Guanyin Statue.

He looked at her and gasped. "Of course, you planned again. You know it doesn't matter, right? You know I didn't care if it's a boy or girl. I love all my children!"

"But it does matter! It matters to me and to Old Ancestor. It matters we have a son to bear our family name. It matters that my daughters won't be drowned or despised!

"And Guanyin had mercy on me, and I had You-jun, a boy! Please, Husband!" Lady Han inched forward towards her husband on her knees. "Punish me if you will! I lied to our parents and to you, an unforgivable and unfilial act. But please! Look at the faces of our children, forgive me, and help me right the wrongs! Help me save the children again this time from their blind passion."

Master Han held his head in his hands for a long time. Finally, he rose from his chair, and using both his hands, he gently pulled his wife up.

"You did lie. But how can I blame you? I know you are a lay Buddhist and you have the heart to love all living beings. You saved Jasmine. But why marry her to Jian-da? Why not somebody far away? Wouldn't that make it easier for everyone? Chop down the tree, and no more crows will caw."

"I…I can't bear to send her to a faraway place again. And this time, it'll not be old Wang and A-mei. It'll be with strangers I know nothing about, and she'll have a husband and a mother-in-law above her! I can't bear the thought." She sobbed.

Her husband sighed again. "Then, why tell her this early? Why not let her get married, let her think it's You-jun all the way up to the last minute when the groom lifts the bridal veil? Make it cooked rice, and there's nothing anybody can do anymore."

"Oh husband! I can't do that to my daughter! I don't want her to find out on her wedding night that her husband is Jian-da. I know a lot of brides do, but not our daughter! A moment of weakness in my heart made me tell her. As they say, as a woman I have long hair but short wits! I just pray that nothing happens before the wedding."

Master Han exhaled deeply again. "There's no turning back now," he said. "I may not blame you, but society's judgment can destroy our family reputation. As the saying goes, splashing saliva can drown a person. Let's keep this among us who already know it. We may have to tell the children, but only if it's absolutely necessary. The more people who know, the easier the word will get out."

#

Iris dragged herself back to her room. She sat on her bed, trying to make sense of what she heard. She had always noticed a strong bond with Jasmine, and she was not surprised that they were sisters. Real sisters, with the same blood running in their veins. She wished more than any other time that she had been a son. *Only if I'd been a son, mother would not have to scheme with A-mei and send Jasmine away and pretend she died,* she thought, *and Jasmine and You-jun would not have to be like this today*...The more she thought, the more she felt hopeless. She had been missing Jasmine terribly since Jasmine was sent away, but now she was glad Jasmine was not here. She did not know how to face her.

At the dinner table that night, Master and Lady Han noticed that Iris seemed troubled. Her eyes were puffy and red. They didn't know that Iris kept thinking that all this would not have happened had she been a boy. *It was her fault.* Master Han was sad to see his daughter this way. His wife avoided his gaze, picking up a piece of chicken with her chopsticks and putting it in Iris'srice bowl. Master Han had never been interested in domestic things such as finding spouses for his children. But now, looking at Iris, he thought that she was sad because she liked Jian-da, and Jian-da was getting married to Jasmine. He promised himself to look into his business relations and find Iris a good family to marry. He would take this one into his own hands.

After dinner, the three of them sat in the courtyard, sipping tea and enjoying a beautiful full moon, perfectly round, like the full happiness of a family with everyone together. Like that night of the Mid-Autumn Festival, a long time ago, on the river.

That night when the three of them dined together was the last time they sat with each other. Many years later, Iris still dreamed about that night. And in her dream, she was a child again, and she was with her whole family: father, mother, sister, and brother. But in every dream, no matter how hard she tried to keep them, they all left her. One last glance, one last nod, one last smile, and one last sigh. One by one, they dissipated like the morning mist over the rivers. She cried, she screamed, and she chased. But there was no one left to be with her.

Iris had always taken Jasmine as her sister, but everything changed the instant Jasmine *was* her sister.

Iris became the unknown and unwilling bearer of the family secret.

CHAPTER 26
THREE RIVERS, 1890 AND 1891

Lady Han knelt in front of the white porcelain Guanyin statue in her room. She couldn't do this for long, however. Her belly was getting big. She asked Guanyin for the most important blessings of her life, a son. She couldn't make the long pilgrim trip to the Guanyin Temple in Cloud Gate anymore, so she prayed in her room several times a day.

She held on to the side of the bed and pulled herself up. The baby kicked. It was a strong kick, the kind of kick a boy made, she thought. Hoped. She walked to the porch, where A-mei was playing with Iris, who was about one and a half. The girl wobbled to her mother and wanted to be picked up. Lady Han did, and Iris showed her a red string knot she was making with A-mei.

"That's very pretty, Bao Bao," Lady Han said. Then she saw her mother-in-law, the Old Ancestor, appearing at the end of the porch. She put down Iris, held her tiny hand, and walked over. "Bow and say good morning to your grandmother, Iris."

"G'morning!" Iris said in her baby voice. Her grandmother nodded, but didn't say good morning or pick her up. A-mei came over and took Iris. "Good morning, Old Ancestor." She bent her knees. "I'll have Green Jade take Miss for a walk."

"How are you today?" the old woman said to her daughter-in-law after

A-mei and Iris left.

"Doing well, thank you, Mother," Lady Han said. "Just prayed and burned incense."

The old woman nodded again. She had been disappointed that her first-born grandchild was a daughter. The Han family was blessed in many things except for a large family. For several generations, the family had one son in each generation. Some had daughters, but one son was all the Old Ancestor had. She made sure that her son married a girl from Cloud Gate, which had the best Feng Shui, hoping that would bring her several grandsons. Since the first was a girl, for the second, "let it be a boy," she said.

"Let me feel the baby," the old woman said, putting her hand on Lady Han's belly and running the hand around. Lady Han tried not to shudder.

"Good kicking," her mother-in-law said. "Strong. Must be a boy."

"Also," the old woman continued, "We both prayed so much. At least I'm very pious in my praying. I could not imagine why Guanyin would not bless us with a boy."

"That's true," Lady Han said. She didn't utter her real thought. As a body of flesh and blood, a lowly woman, how could she even know if she did something wrong in her prayers, or offended the Goddess, or if she had committed a sin so grave in her last life that she was punished with only girls in this life? Or maybe whatever she had done was just simply not enough. There was just simply not enough time in a mortal person's short life on this earth to do all the right things to please those who controlled her fate.

The old woman went on. "The way you carry—big protruding belly but barely changed behind—that's a sure sign of a boy as well. Everyone says that."

"Oh, I'm so glad to hear this!" Lady Han said. But she felt exactly the same as with her last pregnancy, when she had a girl.

"We'll have a boy. I won't need to deal with the kind of headache some families have."

The old woman was referring to the many stories of newborn girls, especially the second or the third-born of the family, dying suddenly. But she knew as well as anyone else that the baby girls did not just die themselves. The families killed these girls. The easiest method was to drown them. Just grab their ankles and dunk them in washbasins. It was not uncommon to have a ten-year gap between the first-born girl and the son that came next. All the girls in between had perished.

Lady Han hesitated but spoke. "If those rumors are true... I don't understand how anyone could do that to a person, even if the person was a useless girl. A Buddhist would not even want to step on any ants when walking!"

Her mother-in-law shot her a dark look. "They may not have a choice. How many families are fortunate enough to feed all those additional mouths? Even us. The Han family is blessed enough to have plenty, but not enough to waste on someone who will not bear the family name at the end. Not only that, we would have to pay for another dowry."

The old woman left for the Huguo Temple in the Diaoyu Fortress. Lady Han sat alone like a stone for a long time.

#

One unusually hot afternoon in late autumn, Iris was fussy and could not be comforted and she kept crying. Old Ancestor showed her face at her daughter-in-law's room and said, "What's wrong with this girl? Her screaming is disturbing my peace and my prayer. Might as well give her away if she cannot be quiet! Or should have drowned her as soon as she was out of your womb!"

This was the last straw. Lady Han decided to act. She asked the cook to brew some zisu tea. She fed the drink to Iris to cool her heat and aid her digestion, and called A-mei over and told her to take Iris for a walk. The rocking motion of walking and sounds of the rivers always made Iris calm, and the herb drink worked wonders when the baby was fussy due to tummy ache or other small ailments. A-mei went out with Iris, and by the time they came back, Iris was asleep, and Lady Han had come up with a plan.

Lady Han put Iris in her crib and told A-mei to sit down. She took a quick look around, making sure no one was nearby. Her in-laws were still taking their afternoon nap, and the cook and other servants were taking the chance to rest themselves. Master Han as usual was out of town on a business trip.

Closing the door behind her, Lady Han sat next to A-mei. "A-mei," she began, "You know that I never think or treat you as a maid, right? You have always been a sister to me."

"Of course, I know that, Peony. Why do you mention it now?" A-mei said.

205

Lady Han put a hand on her belly. The baby kicked. It liked to kick whenever the belly was touched.

"Because of this child. I don't know what will happen to it if it is a girl," Lady Han said.

"Peony! You will be blessed with a son. Guanyin will bless you!" A-mei said.

"I hope so. But what if I'm not blessed? What if I don't deserve a son?" Lady Han's voice shook.

"Oh, Peony! You will! You will be blessed!" A-mei took Peony's hands and squeezed them hard.

"I have to think about something, just in case. I don't want the Old Ancestor to drown it if it's a girl." Lady Han whispered.

A-mei didn't know what to say.

"I have a plan, A-mei, but I need you to help me." Lady Han said. And she told A-mei the plan.

"I have some savings no one knows about, not even Master. This plus the jewelry my mother gave me as my dowry should be enough," Lady Han concluded.

"And, Old Wang, what do you think, A-mei?" Lady Han asked. "Will he be on board?"

"He will, you know that, Peony," A-mei said. "We grew up together, and ever since we were kids, he would always do things for you and for me. He would climb a ladder and pick the stars if I told him to!"

Lady Han nodded.

"I'm only worried…if we are discovered…" A-mei said.

"I know this is very risky. I know if we are discovered my reputation of the perfect, obedient daughter-in-law and wife will be gone forever. The reputation of the Han will be gone forever. Master is not the mayor of Three Rivers, but even the mayor consults with him for official business. He is everyone's number one guest for both weddings and funerals. So I know I must do everything I can to keep that reputation. But if Guanyin does not bless me with a son, she may have mercy on this daughter. If it is in the girl's destiny, we will succeed. If it's not, I know at least I tried. Men strive, Gods rule," Lady Han said.

And Guanyin did give her blessing. On the day of the Pure and Bright when the girl was born, the stars aligned and everything fell into the right place.

Master Han was on his way home for the birth of his second child, but there was an unusual torrential rain which did not normally happen that time of the year—April, the day of Pure Brightness—and his trip was delayed three days because floods washed away the road he was taking.

Old Ancestor was away in the Diaoyu Temple. She had been going there regularly to burn incense and to pray. She also stayed there periodically, as short as a day or two, or as long as a week. It was the time for her to immerse herself in sutras and be away from the world. And this time, she had one particular wish in her heart, which was to pray and to ask to be blessed with a grandson.

Old Master Han was never a worry; his only interest was his old books.

Old Wang and a nephew of his, who was mute from a childhood illness, secretly arrived in Three Rivers and stayed nearby.

And the girl herself came into the world under the cover of the darkness of the night. The night watchmen's clapper and gong and the tow men's singing obscured her crying. The men came, took her, and boarded a small riverboat and left before dawn. All was done in less time than it would take to sip a cup of good tea.

In the morning, A-mei went to the Old Ancestor in the temple. She told the old woman that her daughter-in-law had delivered a baby in the night, and it was sudden and there was no time to call for the midwife. The baby did not survive. Yes, it was a girl. And she, A-mei, would take the dead baby away as soon as possible so no bad luck would be brought to the family. After that, A-mei would help her husband Old Wang with the busy farm work in Cloud Gate. And yes, she would make sure to burn enough money for the girl to use in the other world so she wouldn't need to come back and haunt her family or be born back into this family. The old woman wept, not for the loss of a granddaughter, but for not having her wish fulfilled. She told A-mei to take care of all those things before she would be back in her home.

A-mei hired a new maid, Green Jade, to help with household work in anticipation of a new baby. She told Green Jade to take over and left for Cloud Gate. The hiring of Green Jade turned out to be the best thing for the family in the coming years.

#

In the years that followed, Lady Han was able to see Jasmine regularly on her monthly trips to the Guanyin Temple in Cloud Gate.

"I need to do better with my praying," she said to her husband and mother-in-law. "Show Guanyin how pious I am, how much I'm willing to travel to pray to Her."

In the village, she played with Jasmine, whom the Wangs did their best to raise as a young lady, and not a rough farm girl. She daydreamed about having Iris and Jasmine together and raising Jasmine as a proper city girl from a prominent family. *I would be the luckiest mother the Heaven allows, with all my children by my side*, she thought.

As soon as Jasmine turned seven, she, A-mei, and Tiger came to Three Rivers to stay with the Han family. The Old Ancestor spent most of her time in the temple by then, and after she passed away, Lady Han suggested and Master Han agreed, and thus the Han formally took Jasmine in as their gan nü'er. Now Lady Han could provide and compensate for her as much as she did with Iris. No one needed ever know what she had done. The prosperity and reputation of the Hans were assured. And she had all her children by her side.

CHAPTER 27
THREE RIVERS, 1911

Ghost Festival: the fifteenth of the seventh month. The gate of the Heaven opens.

White Dew: the seventeenth of the seventh month and the fifteenth of the twenty-four solar terms. Dew curdles due to the coolness of night.

The fifteenth of the seventh month, the Hungry Ghost Festival, had always been a busy time for the Han Family.

This was the one day in the year when the gate of heaven opened and all those who died that year descended upon the living world, enjoyed another meal, and once again tasted the deliciousness of earthly food before they departed forever. No dead person should be denied this opportunity; otherwise, it would become a ghost, stuck between heaven and earth, roaming around and causing terrible ills: crops would not bear seeds and no harvest would be made; women would not conceive and babies might die in their infancy. The Hans had always prepared a feast for the Hungry Ghost Festival.

This year, the date fell five days before the wedding between Jasmine and Jian-da. The wedding preparations were almost complete. It was easier to hold the ceremony in the Hans' house since it was bigger and had more servants than the Fangs' house. The newlyweds would be transported to the Fang household after the ceremony to start their new life together.

Despite the extra task of preparing for the wedding, Lady Han told the rest of the household that nothing should be skipped or simplified. Even though no one died during the year, it was extra important to remember filial piety and pay tribute to the dead Han ancestors. It was equally important to satisfy the hunger pangs of the other ghosts, however unrelated, who happened to be wandering in the neighborhood, seeking food. The last thing the Han family needed was some mistreated ghosts who could come back later and seek revenge.

Jasmine had returned from Cloud Gate a week ago. When Lady Han saw Jasmine, she twinged as if someone had stabbed her in the heart. Jasmine was pale and thin, like a branch of a willow tree that could break any time from the blow of a strong gust of wind. Lady Han went over and took Jasmine's hands. "Daughter, you are home! Come and have some rest and let me take a good look at you."

To her comfort, her daughter smiled and seemed happy to see her. "Mother," she said, instead of "Lady" as she usually called Lady Han. "I missed you and Jie Jie. It is good to be back."

Iris rushed over to help her sister sit down on a bench in the courtyard, fanning her with a silk fan. Nights were cooler but a cloudless sunny afternoon was still hot.

Both Lady Han and Iris remembered A-mei and hurried to help her bring in sacks and baskets. The sacks contained the embroidery Jasmine had done while away at Cloud Gate: handkerchiefs, table settings, shoes, shoe insoles, curtains, and several sets of new dresses, shirts, and pants. The baskets held fresh farm produces.

They sat down in the courtyard and sipped tea. For a moment it was just like old times, as they sat, talking and laughing. Only each knew that it was not the same anymore. And it would never be the same. The last time they sat like this was less than a year ago, but it seemed like another lifetime.

In the days that followed, Iris kept Jasmine close company. Lady Han sometimes asked Iris when Jasmine was out of earshot how her sister was doing. Iris said that Jasmine was doing well. She was calm, though she did not mention anything about her wedding, as if this homecoming was just to come home and stay, not to become a bride in a few days.

Iris did not tell Lady Han that the day when Jasmine came back, as soon as they were alone in their shared room, Jasmine asked if Iris had mailed the letter she wrote to You-jun and if You-jun had written back.

"I sent it," Iris said.

"Did…did he write back?" Jasmine asked, her eyes seeking answers in those of her sister's. She lowered her head from the look on her sister's face.

"Maybe he's too busy," Iris said, "or maybe the letters were lost. Things like that happen all the time."

"Do you think Lady has them?" Jasmine thought about a possibility.

"No. I went to the river myself every day. Plus, Mother never mentioned getting anything," Iris said. "I think she would be upset if You-jun wrote to you, and I would know about it."

Jasmine remained silent. She did not seem to be overtly sad. She kept busy with her embroidery, ate her meals without much fuss, even smiled once in a while. And she was like that for the remainder of her days.

Lady Han and A-mei noticed the change. "Jasmine is more like Iris now," A-mei said one day.

"Probably for the better," Lady Han said.

They both hoped that Jasmine's resigned nature meant she had finally grown into a proper lady as she was about to become a wife. They convinced themselves that Jasmine's silence was an indication that she had accepted her fate. Had Jasmine stayed sad, they might have had no choice but to tell her the truth, why she could not marry You-jun. But some things were best left buried. Something so big, a plot that was unfilially hatched to deceive one's mother-in-law and husband, should never come to light. The more people who knew, the more likely the truth would spread as a wildfire. Lady Han's reputation would be gone forever, and she would have no face left in front of her children. So they were relieved that they did not have to say anything to anyone. For the moment, at least.

Master Han came home the day before the Hungry Ghost Festival. Jian-da came with him but went from the boat straight home to be with his mother. He sent his best regards to Lady Han through Master Han. You-jun stayed in Chengdu, preparing to sail to America to study civil engineering in a few weeks. Working for the Railway Protection League with Liang Fei sparked his interest in the subject. He wanted to come home, but Master Han was stern in rejecting his plea. You-jun only knew that his father was going home for the Hungry Ghost Festival, and Jian-da was to attend his sick mother. Master Han promised his son that he would arrange for You-jun to come back to Three Rivers for the Mid-Autumn Festival, which was only a month away, before You-jun left for abroad.

On the day of the Hungry Ghost Festival, a large banquet table was laid in the courtyard. Lady Han, A-mei, the cook, and other servants rose before dawn to slaughter a rooster, a fat hen, and clean several fish. Butchers delivered fresh pork and a whole young goat, the famous Three Rivers white goat. Farmers delivered fresh vegetables. After a whole day's work, they made bowl after bowl of food.

The process was not without incident. Normally, Lady Han issued commands and did not get her hands dirty. On such an important occasion, she decided that she would do some of the work. But she was having difficulty concentrating on the task at hand. Her heart beat like a water bucket being pulled up and down in a well. When she was helping the cook clean fish, her hands slipped. The sharp fish scale went the wrong way and scratched a deep, bloody groove on her hand. She had to quit the kitchen work after that.

As the lady of the house, Lady Han's other job was to set the table. Her hands trembled as she carefully put out the best china from Jin De Zheng. There were more bowls and plates for the dead than for the living. The seats of the dead were marked by their name plaques, which were moved over, or "invited over," from the altar in the front hall of the house.

After everything was ready, Master Han called their ancestors to the feast. He called the names of his grandparents, parents, and dead uncles and aunts, one by one. He asked them to enjoy the humble feast the family had made and forgive the family if any mistakes were made or anything was not to their liking. Next, he called all the other ancestors, the ones who died before he was even born and whose names were unknown to him, to come and enjoy the feast. Finally, he called to the North, the South, the West, and the East, to all who needed to taste the earthly fare one more time, to come and be their guests. He poured good rice liquor into a small glass and shed the liquor on the ground, one drop after another, to toast all who came and enjoyed the meal.

By the time the living could eat, which was after all the dead had been fed and satisfied, it was almost dusk. No one dared to eat very much, for fear of being the one who took portions from the dead. They took a couple of bites in their mouths and were ready to release lights on the river, one more act to comfort the wandering ghosts and to point the direction home for those who were homeless.

The whole family went down to the riverbank. They picked the location where all three rivers merged to one, right across from their house. It was a popular location and a large crowd had already gathered there. The water, lit with hundreds of candles carried by paper boats and lanterns, twinkled as if the Milky Way had tumbled to the Earth. There were small roadside fires as well where paper money and other offerings burned. Releasing river lights had always been the Han children's favorite activity. This year, with just Iris and Jasmine, no boys around, the whole ceremony was more subdued.

As they stood, watching the lights they released drifting away, Master Han overheard a conversation that caught his attention.

One man said to another: "Brother Zhang, did you hear about the strange drifting wood chips people caught today? They were brought by the river current and carried messages from Chengdu."

The other man said, "Indeed, I heard about that. The wood chips were wrapped in varnished paper, and they carried messages for people who are part of the Railway Protection League."

Master Han turned and saw that he knew the two men. They recognized him and exchanged some pleasantries.

Master Han said, "I overheard your conversation about some messages from Chengdu?"

Zhang said, "Brother Han, indeed. It was a peculiar way to get messages to spread, but something major happened in Chengdu today. General Zhao Erfeng set a trap to arrest the core members of the Sichuan Railway Protection League. When people found out about this they organized a protest outside his office, and he ordered firing into the crowds. Lots of people died, even more, wounded. The remaining members wrote the messages on woodchips and threw them in the river to let the messages be carried away by the water."

The other man said, "Brother Han, you go to Chengdu all the time. Have you seen anything like this coming?"

Master could not feel his tongue. He muttered, "Not really." Then he excused himself, found his wife and daughters.

"Come with me," he whispered, but before they responded, he turned and walked fast towards home. Women with bound feet could not catch him, but they did their best to hurry along.

Once they all sat down, Master Han told them what he had heard. Iris and Jasmine did not comprehend what this message could mean, but they did remember that You-jun worked for the Railway Protection League. Lady Han lost strength in all her limbs. She said quietly to herself, *That's why my heart jumped up and down so much today.*

Master Han said, "We need to find out more information. Don't worry, I'm sure You-jun and Liang Fei will be safe. I'm going to the mayor's house right now to see if he has any official word. Official posts travel much faster than private posts. If he hears nothing tonight, I will request he send a telegram tomorrow to Chengdu to find out more."

He left. Nobody else moved.

He returned quickly. The mayor did not have any more information than the rumors they already heard. But he promised to send a telegram to Chengdu first thing next morning as official business and see if he could find out any information. The most important was to see if You-jun was safe. The major also sent one of his most trusted men on a fast horse to Chengdu overnight. If the man found You-jun, he was to make sure You-jun came back to Three Rivers safely, by whatever means. Master Han thanked the mayor and left a sack of silver dollars on the mayor's desk.

There was nothing they could do but wait. Master Han did his best to stay composed and calm. He ordered everyone to bed, even though no one could sleep. Everyone had the same thought: they wanted You-jun home. They wanted him home now.

Lady Han kept incense in front of her small Guanyin statue burning all night. She knelt, holding her prayer beads, and said the sutra with utmost piety. *I do not care anymore if he comes home before the wedding. I will tell him the truth. I will tell Jasmine the truth. Punish me however I deserve, but please send my son home!* A-mei stayed kneeling with her. They did not go to bed.

Iris and Jasmine stayed in their room and lay on their beds in the dark. Iris heard sobbing and asked, "Jasmine, do you want to come to my bed and let me hold you?" Jasmine came to Iris's bed without saying a word. Iris held Jasmine and felt her sister shaking like a leaf in a hurricane. "Don't worry, don't worry," she comforted Jasmine, even though in her own heart, she saw the light of her brother's life going dim.

"Jie Jie, I have been feeling terrible since this morning. I knew something bad was going to happen," Jasmine said.

"Don't say that," Iris interrupted her. "We don't know yet. You-jun always has the best luck. Remember that time when he was jumping over a flash flood creek with some other naughty boys? The boy before him was bigger but he fell in and never came back. But You-jun did. He always turns bad luck to good. Watch, he'll come in through that door in a day or two."

Morning came and went with no news. A whole day came and went, still no news.

Around noon on the day of White Dew, the man named Zhang came to pay a visit. The ladies stayed at the back of the house, but they all tried to listen to what he had to say.

"My wife's nephew just came back from Chengdu. He was near the massacre site and took off as soon as he could. I came as soon as I heard the news he brought. I'm so sorry to be the bearer of bad news and I still hope that I'm mistaken, but it seems that Young Master Han was indeed in the wrong place at the wrong time."

Master Han's face went white. "Thank you for coming," he said to the man. Zhang bowed several times and offered his help. Master Han thanked him and told him that he would send someone to fetch him if needed.

Lady Han passed out upon hearing the news. Several servants moved her to her room to lie down. Iris and Jasmine were in shock, but they had no tears and did not know what to do.

"What do we do now, Master?" A-mei asked.

"Nothing. Not yet. We still don't have the official word. This nephew did not know You-jun, even though he was also from Three Rivers. It might very well be a mistake," Master Han said, his voice shaking.

But the official word came soon enough. Before dinner, the mayor himself came. As soon as Master Han saw him, he knew. He sat down on his chair, and the strength that had held him up in the past several days drained all at once.

CHAPTER 28
IRIS, THREE RIVERS, 1931

The reason that You-jun and Jasmine could never be husband and wife was because they were brother and sister. Blood brother and sister. Mother and A-mei made a plan to take Jasmine away when she was born because they were afraid that Grandmother would drown Jasmine. I wish I could say that my mother and A-mei had been paranoid. Nothing like that was ever recorded, but rumors always circulated about what people had done to newborn baby girls. I shudder to think what if Jasmine had been the firstborn daughter and I had been the second.

It was in Jasmine's destiny so she was saved. She came to the right place at the right time, as they say. Mother and A-mei's plan worked. Nobody other than the two of them and A-mei's husband Old Wang knew who Jasmine really was. Mother longed to bring Jasmine back, to give her everything a family like ours can provide for their daughters. The Wangs had a good living by managing the farmland for the Hans, but Cloud Gate was a small village compared to Three Rivers, and as the daughter of a tenant, Jasmine's marriage prospects were not great. Besides, Mother longed to have the daughter she was forced to give up be near her again. But she couldn't just bring Jasmine home. How would she explain this to people? How could she let people know that she lied to her mother-in-law and her husband about this daughter? She had to find a way. And she did.

She and A-mei did. As soon as Grandmother passed away, she held a ceremony to take Jasmine in as a gan nü'er. All would have worked perfectly, except that You-jun and Jasmine fell head over heels for each other. Nobody had thought about this possibility.

I remember the instant connection with Jasmine the moment I saw her. I liked how carefree she was, always laughing and curious about things. And she told me that I made her calm because I was much slower in action when she was rushing. Mother said we were like Yin and Yang, complimenting each other. We always had so much to say to each other. I grew up with You-jun and Jian-da, and for the first time, I had a sister to share and to keep secrets, and to laugh and to cry together. Now I knew it was because we had the same blood running through our veins.

Was it the same blood that connected You-jun and Jasmine? The same blood that made them recognize each other in a way no strangers could even imagine? The kindred spirit. I never told anyone the incident by the lotus pond in Cloud Gate, when Jasmine was ready to jump in the water for You-jun, and when You-jun told her that he would never leave her. What I saw in their eyes shook me and scared me. Would it have made it better if I had told Mother back then what I saw? Would Mother have been able to steer the future in a different direction?

Mother finally told Father the truth about Jasmine, and Father helped to continue her plan. Mother's reputation, the family reputation, must be maintained. He went back to Chengdu and arranged for Jian-da to come back to Three Rivers for the wedding. You-jun stayed in Chengdu and prepared to go to America to study.

My parents' plan was to marry Jasmine and Jian-da before You-jun came home for a visit. Once the rice was cooked there was nothing else anyone could do. The wedding was set for the twentieth day of the seventh month. Mother sent someone to bring Jasmine and A-mei back from Cloud Gate to Three Rivers a few days before White Dew. Old Uncle Wang and Tiger still had work to do after harvest and were to arrive a day or two before the wedding.

Father came back and brought back Jian-da with him. But none of us saw him. He went straight home to avoid seeing his future wife. Admittedly, unlike most marriages, they already knew each other, but it was still better they didn't see each other.

Father said that You-jun would be home in a month for the Mid-

Autumn Festival before he set out to America.

Jasmine asked me about You-jun. She was quiet after she heard that You-jun had not written to her. She did not mention him anymore, and I thought she had accepted her fate.

But on the day of the Hungry Ghost Festival, the fifteenth of the seventh month, five days before the wedding, everything changed.

Jasmine told me as soon we got up that day that her right eye was twitching, that something bad was going to happen. As they say, twitching of the left eye, money went; twitching of the right eye, misfortune came. I told her that it was probably because she was one day closer to being a married woman; she was just nervous, and rightfully so. But inside, I was uneasy myself. Then Mother cut her hand scaling fish and everything in the house seemed to be off and ready for some disaster to happen. Perhaps it was just the ghosts. It was the day for them to roam the earth. Perhaps they had turned everything, the air, the people, the hearts, ghastly.

Then Father hurried us home from releasing the river lights and told us that something bad had happened in Chengdu. General Zhao Erfeng ordered soldiers to open fire on protesters from the Railway Protection League, and people were killed. You-jun was working with Mr. Liang Fei at the League. We were very worried. Father went to the mayor to see if he could find out more information. We hoped and prayed that You-jun would be okay.

I do not remember what I did in the time we waited for the news. I think Mother was in her room the whole time, kneeling in front of Guanyin. We waited for two days before the news came, confirming our worst fear, but it felt like a lifetime. Nothing seemed real and everything seemed like a dream. Mother's hair went almost white and Father aged ten years. Jasmine was quiet. She had been quiet for some time and to be honest, I don't think Mother and Father had enough energy to pay attention to her. Because she was so quiet, she was like a shadow only. She had become one of the ghosts, I thought. I was horrified by this thought and I tried my best to kick it out of my head. I kept an eye on her, but I did not know what to say to her.

Yes, You-jun perished in the railroad massacre. My heart bleeds even now as I write these words. The only son of the Han family, the one to bear the family name, was gone at the age of eighteen.

Just as I cannot remember what happened during waiting days, I cannot remember what I did after we confirmed the news. All I remember is that it started to rain that night and the rain lasted for five days. The non-stop water pouring down from the Heaven washed away roads and drowned our hearts. I remember the chaos in the house. Mother fainted at the news. Father left for Chengdu immediately to bring You-jun's body back to Cloud Gate for burial. We prayed that his body had been recovered and kept for his family to retrieve. Thank Heavens it had been. Mr. Liang Fei was the one who made sure we had You-jun back. He was as heart-broken as us, and he told Father that he would feel guilty towards the Hans for the rest of his life.

Because You-jun was only a boy and the youngest in the family when he died, my parents were not supposed to mourn him or hold a formal funeral for him. They could not even bring him home. Because he was not married, he was not supposed to be buried in the family plot with all the ancestors. He just needed to be put in the ground as soon as possible so he could be on his way to finding another family to reincarnate in.

Uncle Wang and Tiger walked into the chaos. Father arranged for You-jun to be buried in the Wang family lot, so Uncle Wang turned around and went straight back to Cloud Gate to prepare everything before he could rest his tiring feet. Tiger stayed to help and was sent to the Fang's house to inform them of the news. He came home and said that Jian-da broke down at the news and was inconsolable.

"I have never seen a grown man cry like that. He kept saying that You-jun should have come home. He kept saying it was all his fault that You-jun died. He said he had betrayed his best friend," Tiger told me, misty-eyed.

I knew what Jian-da meant. Nobody told You-jun that Jasmine and Jian-da were to be married. You-jun thought Jian-da went home to Three Rivers because Jian-da's mother was sick. Jian-da did not tell You-jun because he was in love with Jasmine. He probably had hesitated, had pondered, but he went along with the plans made by my parents.

I wanted to tell Jian-da that he should not blame himself. Heaven and Earth have a plan and a destiny for all who live in between. We are the chess pieces, and the players are never ourselves. I did tell Jian-da this many years later, and we both accepted the plan Heaven and Earth made for us. But at that time, I asked Tiger to go back to the Fang house and ask Jian-da to come help with all that needed to be done. But when Tiger went to the door, Jian-da was already there.

Only when I saw Jian-da's pale, unshaven face did I think about Jasmine. Should I keep her away from her future husband? Would the wedding still take place? I yelled. In my whole life, this was the first, and the last time, that I ever raised my voice. "Where is Jasmine?"

Nobody knew. We had forgotten about the silent, transparent, ghostly shadow. A-mei was by my mother's side. Old Wang and Tiger did not even see their daughter and sister before they were swept up by all the things needing to be done in the household. Why did I not pay attention to Jasmine? When did I take my eyes off her? And for how long?

I still ask myself these questions. In my dreams Jasmine comes to ask me, with her eyes but not words, "Jie Jie, why did you not keep me?"

I screamed Jasmine's name and ran from room to room looking for her. I tripped and got up and ran again. I had no tears, and my voice went hoarse.

But she was not in the house.

I ran out of the house to the street. The relentless rain came down so quick and so dense that it slapped me like thousands of tiny whips. I could not see but I could hear. I heard the rain and the wind and my own voice calling my sister.

Lightning flashed right above my head, as if to tell me where my sister went. I knew then where Jasmine had gone. I ran as fast as my bound feet and my aching legs could carry me, and I fell. I struggled up and kept running. I was soaked. If a child had seen me then, he would have thought me a river ghost.

In front of me was the point where the three rivers came together. In this downpour, I saw a different kind of beauty than I had ever seen before. The rain had connected the sky and the water. It was hard to tell where one began and where one ended. The river took all the water that came from the Heavens above and carried everything away. I collapsed on the riverbank, which was in danger of flooding soon.

Eight years before, when we visited Cloud Gate to sweep our ancestors' tombs, Jasmine had said to You-jun by the lotus pond, when she thought he was drowning, "If you did not come back, I would have jumped in to find you."

He did not come back.

And she jumped in to find him.

Jian-da came running after me. He pulled me up to higher ground, holding over my head an umbrella, which was soon torn by the wind. He did not call Jasmine aloud, but I knew he must have been calling her in his heart.

The rain and the rivers drenched us, head to toe. Our hearts and our souls had forever gone damp.

Jasmine's body was recovered about ten li downstream after the rain stopped. I did not see it, but our maid Green Jade said that fishermen saw a double rainbow as soon as the rain ceased, and Jasmine's body was under it.

None of us could bear to see her. I went through her things and discovered a set of white summer clothes was missing, a light linen tunic, and wide-legged pants. She must have worn those when she ran out of the house. It was an odd set of clothes to wear at that time of the year. Over the years I have thought about why she would do that, and I concluded that the clothes must have special meaning for her. Or perhaps she was dressed in all white, mourning for You-jun. Under my pillow, she tucked the sister flowers handkerchief I gave her when my parents took her in as their gan nü'er. The small square of silk was neatly folded. I understood that was her good-bye. I unfolded it with my trembling hands and held it to my heart.

What I could not forgive myself for was that not only did I not keep an eye on Jasmine, but also that because of me, she died thinking You-jun had forgotten his promise. When she asked me if You-jun had written to her, I told her no, he had not. The truth was, after I discovered who she really was—my blood sister—I thought the best thing to do was for her to forget You-jun. I held on to the letters, letters he had sent to Jasmine, just as he had promised. There were four of them. There was also one later, arriving after his death.

Jasmine was considered a Wang, and she was buried in the Han family plot without a funeral, for the same reason You-jun was buried in the Wang family plot. She and You-jun were not even in the same burial place after they died. They had been separated eternally. Their stars crossed each other's path, shining so brightly for just a moment, and then they went in the opposite directions and went dim.

I held my own ceremony for Jasmine on the day of Autumn Equinox, a few days after she was buried. Autumn Equinox used to be a holiday for us, when we would gather with relatives and friends to celebrate the end of another harvest season. It was one of the last nights of the year when one could still be outside without catching a cold. But that year, there was a Han family only in name. Number One Cypress Street was an empty place. Mother went to the temple in Cloud Gate with the intention of staying, despite my pleading for her not to. Later, I visited her once, hoping for her to change her mind, but she did not even acknowledge me as her daughter. She lost Jasmine, and as a result, she didn't want me anymore. All she wanted was to be parted from this earthly world. I never visited her again. A-mei went with Mother and stayed in Cloud Gate. She continued to visit Mother, and so did Tiger. Father disappeared into the tea house frequently, as he did after the funerals.

I decided that the night of Autumn Equinox was the right time to say my own farewell to my sister. I don't know why I did not do the same thing for You-jun. Maybe because he was a man, even though he was my brother? Maybe I didn't want to hold the ceremony for Jasmine and You-jun together? Later, I found out that Jian-da had done the same for You-jun. He said his goodbye to his best friend and asked for forgiveness.

Have our actions helped Jasmine and You-jun rest in peace?

I washed myself with rose-scented water and wore my best silk dress. I went to the garden in the back of the house, where as children, You-jun, Jian-da and I, and later Jasmine, and for a while, Tiger used to play. The trees, the swing hanging between the branches of a fir tree in the middle of the garden, the pavilion, the pond—everything was the same. Jasmine and I had loved to swing; sometimes we pushed each other. Sometimes the boys pushed us. But that day, it was only me. The crescent new moon had risen, floating behind the bamboo. The air was crisp and cool. Tired birds had returned to their nests and autumn insects were singing their swan songs. I thought that if Jasmine were there, she would be happy with the night, and she would approve my choice.

I lit three sticks of sandalwood incense, Jasmine's favorite. I held them in both hands and bowed to the East, the South, the West, and the North, and then deeply, I bowed to Jasmine. I put the sticks in the incense burner I took from Mother's room. I also lit a long white candle. Then I laid out several dishes of delicate snacks: sliced rice cake with walnut pieces, a Three River specialty, sunflower seeds that I shelled earlier, roasted peanuts, and oranges. All of these had been Jasmine's favorites. For drink,

I brought freshly squeezed sugar cane juice and a bottle of my father's best rice liquor. I brought two small glasses.

I poured the liquor into one glass and juice into another and offered a toast to spirits of all directions by decanting the fluids on the ground. I thought it was okay not to call my ancestors, for sure they would not have liked to be disturbed for Jasmine's sake. Then I poured the liquor again. This time I held it up to the moon that was slowly rising, and I offered it to my sister.

"Mei Mei," I whispered, "please accept this offering. Even though I'm older and I should not mourn you, I, your Jie Jie, am here to say goodbye. May the liquor and juice I poured quench your thirst and these snacks I prepared ease your hunger. I was heartbroken to let you go, but I pray for you to be released from your suffering and to reincarnate into a good family and have a good life. And in another life," I hesitated for a moment, and then continued, "I pray for you to be with the one you love."

Then I poured everything under the fir tree, next to the swing. I took foods from each of the snack plates and sprinkled them over the liquid as it disappeared into the earth.

After standing silently for a moment, I opened the cloth sack, which Jasmine made for me, and took out the four letters from You-jun. They were still sealed.

"Jasmine," I said, "You-jun kept his promises. He should not have, but he loved you. I loved you, too, but I deceived you. Please forgive me."

Tears poured out of my eyes. Suddenly I had not only sadness but also anger. An anger that surprised and overwhelmed me.

"Mei Mei," I said, "you foolish girl. Why did you leave me, Mother, A-mei, and everyone else? Do you love You-jun only, but not any of us? I'm so mad at you." I covered my face and sobbed uncontrollably. I felt so alone. I would have many happy moments later in life after that night, but that loneliness never left me. Through my tears I whispered to Jasmine again, "But I lied to you and made you suffer, too. We are even. Now please accept this and forgive me."

I lit the letters with the candle, one by one, and let them burn to ashes. My intention was to gather the ashes and bury them under the fir tree, but when all four letters were burned, a gust of wind came suddenly from the west and scattered the ashes.

"Was that you, Mei Mei? Was that you who came to collect what belonged to you?"

I did not hear any answers. But I believed it was her.

I sat down on the swing and moved myself, forward and backward, pretending that Jasmine was pushing me.

And I knew nothing would ever be the same.

CHAPTER 29
THREE RIVERS, 1911, FALL AND WINTER, AND YEARS BEYOND

After You-jun and Jasmine were buried, Lady Han knelt in front of her husband. She told him that she was responsible for all the misery and misfortune that had descended on the Han family. She was punished for her unfilial act, her lies. She was determined to devote the rest of her earthly life to Guanyin the Most Merciful. She was sorry but she had to give up all her earthly desires and possessions and responsibilities in order to do so.

Master Han didn't say anything. He slumped in his chair, staring at Lady Han. After a long while, he got up and walked out of the door without a word. This time he didn't pull his wife up.

So Lady Han went to Cloud Gate, climbed the steep steps of White Cloud Mountain, and entered the temple, never looking back once.

Master Hui-Ming, Wise and Bright, received her.

"Master, please allow me to stay." Lady Han bowed deeply.

"Certainly, benefactress Han. We're happy to share our homely vegan meals and chant sutras."

"Not for a month or half, but…for the remainder of my days in this shell of flesh." Lady Han kept her head down and her hands in prayer.

Master Hui-Ming paused and nodded but didn't ask questions. "Namo

Amitabha," she said, bowing back.

A-mei went with Lady Han and begged her friend to reconsider. The one child who was still alive was in need of her mother. But Lady Han said to A-mei, "My dear friend, my sister, I'm so sorry. Please take care of Iris for me. I loved all my children. I did everything I could do for them as a mortal person. This is the last time I'll speak to you as the old Peony. May Guanyin bless you. Namo Amitabha." She held her hands in prayer in front of her chest and bowed her head to her dear friend.

True to her words, the Lady Han known to everybody was gone. Not in body but in spirit.

The first and only time Iris went with A-mei to visit her mother in the temple, she was very emotional. She asked her mother in a manner she had never had before.

"Why? You prayed and prayed. But it did not work, did it?"

A-mei was shocked. "Shush!" she said. "Don't blaspheme against Bodhisattva!" She thought that the poor girl had gone mad after all she had been through.

But Iris was not done.

"And now you are leaving me behind. Do you love only You-jun and Jasmine, but not me? Please! Mother! Go home with me!" Iris clung to her mother's robe.

But her mother only chanted her sutra and counted her beads. Tears rained down her cheeks like a river and wet her robe, but she carried on.

A-mei pulled the girl by her hand and nudged her to kneel in front of the Guanyin Statue.

After this incident, A-mei continued her trips to the temple, but Iris never went back.

Iris got very sick. Perhaps it was from the night when she held her own ceremony to say goodbye to Jasmine. The cold air had found a way of seeping into her body, weakened by her grief, its pores pried open for the invasion of all things evil and unhealthy.

In her illness, she spent hours sleeping, but her sleep was interrupted repeatedly by dreams of Jasmine and You-jun. In the dreams, all three of them were playing together, but a sudden storm would separate them as she watched Jasmine and You-jun swept away by waves insurmountable as mountains. She struggled but could not grab their hands that reached out for her to rescue. She woke up crying and sweating.

She also had dreams of Jasmine looking at her with her eyes deep as old wells, full of questions yet no words.

Green Jade took care of the household. She had come from a good family, but her parents died. Her father's debtor was selling her to repay the debts when A-mei saw her at the roadside, a straw stuck in her hair, a marker that the girl was for sale. A-mei liked that the girl was clean, her clothes old but in good repair, her eyes bright and her manners calm, even under that circumstance. A-mei was right. Green Jade was kind, clever, and hard-working. She learned quickly, and she was a great amah for Iris. Both Lady Han and A-mei liked her and treated her well. As she grew, Green Jade felt lucky that she ended up in the Han household. She could have been sold as a child bride or worse, into a brothel. This was her home now. She swore that she would pay back the kindness of the Hans when she could and now she had the chance. She practically raised Iris with Lady Han and A-mei, and it pained her greatly to see Iris so lonely and so sad. Grief had driven Iris's parents away, him to a teahouse, and her to the Guanyin Temple. Iris had no one but Green Jade.

Green Jade asked a doctor to visit Iris regularly, brewed the herb medicine diligently, and did her best to feed Iris the herb drinks. But Iris needed help. She needed someone to talk to. Maybe then she would be able to see the world as a whole again, and maybe then she would start to eat and get better. Green Jade wished that grief and sorrow had not captured Master Han and Lady Han this way. They lost a son, the most important heir, but still, they should remember they had a daughter, the always good, obedient Iris. The Wang family was far away. So Green Jade thought about Mrs. Fang.

Mrs. Fang had always wanted Iris to be her daughter-in-law, not Jasmine. She thought Iris had a better personality and nicer demeanor. Iris was calm and grounded, more obedient, and more down to earth: all the qualities Mrs. Fang wished for in a daughter-in-law. Jasmine, she thought, was too energetic, having too many ideas, and not as poised as an upper-class lady. And she thought that was because Jasmine was not a real Han daughter, even though the Han family held an elaborate ceremony to take her in as a gan daughter, and even though Jasmine was taught how to read and write, and grew up not in Cloud Gate but in Three Rivers.

When Lady Han told Mrs. Fang that she intended to marry Jasmine, not Iris, to Jian-da, she said it in a way that Mrs. Fang could not refuse.

She said that she had a fortune teller look at the birthdays of the children, and the fortune teller suggested that Jasmine and Jian-da would be a much better match. She told Mrs. Fang that she was planning to give Jasmine a bigger dowry than she would give Iris, because she didn't want people to gossip that she was stingy with her gan daughter after taking her in with such a high-profile and elaborate ceremony.

Mrs. Fang knew that the Han Family had been generous with her and Jian-da since her husband passed away. Jian-da received the same education through the private tutor for the Han family. Mrs. Fang might have been able to provide a living for her son, but not the same education. She decided that if Jian-da was okay with the arrangement, she would accept it and be grateful to the Han family. If Jian-da did not want to marry Jasmine, then she would have a good excuse to ask for Iris.

To her surprise, Jian-da looked overjoyed when his mother mentioned Lady Han's proposal. He only said, "Mother, for marriage one must obey the wish of his parents and words of the matchmakers, so please decide it for me." But Mrs. Fang saw that he was obviously relieved. She saw the twinkle in his eyes and the smile that took over his usually melancholy, handsome face. Everyone, including Jian-da himself, had thought that Iris would be the one marrying him.

After You-jun and Jasmine died, even though no one said anything to her, Mrs. Fang realized that Jasmine must have loved You-jun. She was angry at both Lady Han and Jasmine. Lady Han had to know about this, she thought, and Lady Han deceived me. For Jasmine, she thought that her impression of her was right: the girl was not composed and rational. She was too emotional, and she lacked finial piety—killing herself was one of the most unforgivable, unfilial acts.

Mrs. Fang went to see Iris at Green Jade's request. As soon as she saw the poor girl, the one she had always loved and wanted to have as her daughter-in-law, she could not help but became a mother to the girl. How could Lady Han abandon Iris and the entire household to become a nun after what happened? Her resentment of her old friend grew. *What a terrible, calculating mother,* she thought. Indeed, they never spoke to or saw each other again for the rest of their lives.

Mrs. Fang spoke to the doctor and gave advice to Green Jade about what to do. She and Green Jade helped Iris get outside on the days when the sun was warm and the wind was calm, so Iris could get some fresh air, as the days were getting shorter and colder.

Mrs. Fang told Jian-da what happened during the day and how Iris was doing when she came home, usually at dinner time, but she did not ask Jian-da to visit Iris. Jian-da shut himself in his room most of the time. To be polite, he sat at the table and ate with his mother, but he could not tell what he had eaten or how it tasted. In his mind, he kept repeating the night before he came back to Three Rivers from Chengdu, the last time he had seen his best friend alive.

Jian-da tried to tell himself that what he did was not a selfish act. He was just following the orders of his mother. But deep down, he knew that he should have told You-jun. He knew that he was jealous of Jasmine's love for You-jun, and he wanted Jasmine to be *his* wife.

But he did not want You-jun to die! And he understood why Jasmine died. He hated himself for betraying his best friend, and he was saddened that Jasmine did not love him. Instead, she loved You-jun, with her life.

#

One day, as Mrs. Fang was going to Number One Cypress Street for her routine visit to Iris, rain started to come down heavily. Mrs. Fang slipped and fell on the moss-covered stone walkway in front of her house. So she stayed home to recover and sent Jian-da over to check on Iris.

Jian-da had not seen Iris since the day when he ran after her down to the river bank, looking for Jasmine. She had been so far from his mind that he had almost forgotten her. He took the basket that held a clay pot of stewed chicken soup with him and went to the Han house.

How the house had changed! The heavy black door with a red door ring was the same. The old cypress tree was the same. The stone-paved courtyard was the same. The large magnolia trees in the yard were the same. Yet the house was so different: the air was stagnant, and there were no sounds of living.

Jian-da knocked with the door ring, but no one answered. When he pushed the door, he discovered it unlocked. He invited himself in.

"Hello?" he called out. Still, no one answered.

He hesitated. It was inappropriate for him to go to Iris's room, even though he knew where it was.

He decided to sit down under the covered porch and wait. As soon as he sat down, Green Jade came from the direction of Iris's room.

"Miss just went down for a nap," Green Jade said.

Jian-da asked Green Jade to feed Iris the soup he brought and was going back when Iris called from her room, "Who is it, Green Jade? Is it Mrs. Fang?"

"It Mr. Fang," Green Jade answered. "Can he come in for a visit?"

She motioned for Jian-da to go in.

"I should just take off and let her rest," Jian-da said.

But then they heard Iris saying, "If it's not too much trouble."

Jian-da followed Green Jade to Iris's room.

Green Jade said, "I'll be right back with some tea, Mr. Fang." She went to the kitchen.

Jian-da sat down on the chair next to a small nightstand and looked at Iris. His heart jerked at what he saw. Iris sat on her bed, propped up by a large pillow, with a blanket drawn all the way under her chin. She had lost a lot of weight in the past weeks, and her pale face seemed to have shrunk an entire circumference, from round to angular. The blanket was burying her.

Iris looked like Jasmine.

Jian-da had known Iris much longer than he had known Jasmine, and he didn't think they looked alike. To him, Iris's features were always softer, and Jasmine was sharper. Perhaps their personality differences had made their faces distinguishable. Even identical twins could look different to people who knew them, if they had different personalities.

But now, Iris looked like Jasmine.

And this room was also Jasmine's room, and he could feel the essence of her, still lingering.

"How have you been, Iris?" Jian-da asked, his mouth dry.

"Doing better each day," Iris said, "thanks to your mother and Green Jade. I plan to visit your family to offer my gratitude as soon as I'm strong enough to walk a few blocks."

Jian-da told Iris that his mother had slipped and fallen.

"Oh!" Iris sounded worried. She struggled to get up and said, "I should go see her."

"No, no." Jian-da stood and tried to stop Iris from getting up. "She's doing okay. She asked me to tell you not to worry."

Green Jade came back with the tea. Jian-da and Iris were embarrassed. They sat down as earlier and didn't have much to say.

Finally, Jian-da said, "You should get up and walk around to breathe some fresh air and gain strength. If you'd like, I'll come each day and accompany you on your walks."

"That would be so appreciated," Green Jade said before Iris said anything.

So Jian-da went over every day and took Iris for a walk. Green Jade followed a few steps behind as a chaperone. Initially, it was only during nice weather. Then they went out under an umbrella in the rain. At the beginning, they walked around the courtyard, since Iris had to sit down every few steps to catch her breath. Slowly the walks grew longer. They went outside the house and walked along the river. The river walks started in the morning, when the trees still had their leaves of colors, and then shifted to afternoons when those leaves dropped. But they avoided the back garden where they used to play as children.

By the next spring, Iris had recovered enough to run the household. One spring day, all the flowers were blooming, the magnolias were almost past their prime, but the cherry, peach, and apple flowers were magnificent. Iris and Jian-da were on their way out when an invisible hand drew them to the back garden. Many years later, when she recalled that day, Iris believed that Jasmine had led them there.

In the garden where all of them, Iris, Jasmine, You-jun, Jian-da, and Tiger used to play, they broke into tears. Iris had not cried like that since the day when they went down to the river in the rain to look for Jasmine. They embraced each other and cried in each other's arms. Jian-da recounted the night before he came back to Three Rivers and how he had betrayed his best friend.

Jian-da had received a letter from his mother, in which she wrote about the wedding, and asked him to come back with Master Han. Master Han, then a conspirator of Lady Han's plan, told Jian-da that he should not mention this to You-jun.

"Their birthdays and Eight Characters were not good matches," Master Han said, "but they were blinded by their passion. You are helping them and our family if you don't mention a word to You-jun. Once you and Jasmine are married, everything will fall into the right place and You-jun will soon forget her. He will have so many new things to learn and new people to meet once he goes to America."

Jian-da was bothered by his conscience. *This was deceit*, he thought to himself, *but what was the alternative? Since Master and Lady Han had made up their minds, he would only make things difficult by telling You-jun.*

The night before he came back to Three Rivers, he and You-jun stayed up late, talking about the Railway Protection movement and You-jun's plan to go to America. At that time, the movement had a lot of energy and momentum, and they were both excited to be part of the effort trying to build the railroad financed with only domestic money. Master Han was patriotic and supported this effort. None of them knew that the government led by General Zhao Erfeng planned to strike down the movement and danger lurked ahead.

Before they called it a night, You-jun asked Jian-da to send his best wishes to Jian-da's sick mother and he asked Jian-da to take a letter to Jasmine.

Jian-da felt the tiny droplets of water on his forehead. He was glad that in the dim light it was hard for You-jun to see his red face. "Maybe it's not as convenient," he said. "I probably won't see her." This was true. He would not be allowed to see Jasmine before the wedding.

"Jasmine is probably still in Cloud Gate," You-jun said. "Just give it to Iris."

"You-jun died, and it was my fault." Jia-da finished telling his story.

"No, Jian-da, it was not your fault," Iris said. "And you were not wrong for loving Jasmine."

Jian-da cried again. He took a folded envelope from inside of his shirt pocket and handed it to Iris. Iris knew right away what it was. The fifth and last letter from You-jun to Jasmine. They burned it to offer it to Jasmine, just as Iris did with the other four letters. And again, a wind scattered the ash of the words.

Jian-da pulled Iris into his arms for another embrace.

"Let me take care of you, Iris. I'm still here. I'll make up for everything." he whispered in her ear.

Iris nodded. This was her fate, after all.

Jian-da went home and asked his mother to send a matchmaker to the Han house and propose to Iris. Master Han was in the tea house and the matchmaker had to track him down there. He agreed on the spot.

Jian-da and Iris were married in a simple ceremony. They insisted on having both Jasmine and You-jun's names on placards at the wedding, on the banquet table. Master Han cried. The day after the wedding he wandered out like a Taoist monk, only to return home many years later when he knew his time in the world was ending. He died peacefully surrounded by his daughter, son-in-law, and little granddaughter, who was born in 1913. Iris named her Pearl, so the girl would be pure yet strong. She did not want to name her daughter after a flower. Iris also told Jian-da, "Let's raise her not like a deplorable daughter, but like a child, like how we were taught how to read and write."

Mrs. Fang moved into the Han house with Jian-da. The Fang house was rented out. Mrs. Fang was an easy mother-in-law and did not interfere with the household management.

Iris kept close ties with the Wang family in Cloud Gate and visited often, at least once a month. She went to see the Wangs, but not her mother. A-mei would tell her how Peony got along in the temple and she would listen. As the years went by, Iris found herself resenting Peony less, as she mothered Pearl and watched the girl grew, sometimes with great agony, worrying about the choices she made for her as a mother. She thought how hard her own mother must have tried, and how helpless and hopeless she must have felt. She couldn't muster enough courage to visit the temple until it was too late. The year Pearl turned seventeen, Peony passed away, and Iris forgave her.

CHAPTER 30
THREE RIVERS AND CLOUD GATE, 2017

Hong-mei finished reading Iris's story.

We sat there. Nobody said a word for a few minutes.

I tried to picture what Iris had described. I tried to imagine what she was going through. But how could I? She had lost two siblings at once. And then her mother. I considered losing my dad a few years ago and later losing Harriton as my greatest losses. But Harriton shouldn't count. He never belonged to me, and how could I say it was a true loss?

My mom and Aunt Daisy dabbed their eyes with tissues. Uncle De-chen coughed.

"I had no idea what Grandma went through," my mom said.

"And we almost destroyed her story," Aunt Daisy said.

"Incredible," Shan said.

"I have a hard time believing this happened in our family," Hong-mei said.

"It explains a lot about why the Han and Wang family are so close," Shan said. "You-jun was buried in the Wang's plot, and Jasmine was buried in the Han's plot. Yet there was also a small unmarked grave in the Wangs' plot."

"For the baby who supposedly died," Aunt Daisy said. "That's why we heard Iris and Tiger were the only ones left, and why Grandma kept telling us that Uncle Tiger was like a brother to her, and we should always treat the Wangs as our own family."

"I did not know the family had such a close tie to the 1911 Railway Massacre in Chengdu," Uncle De-chen said. "This event was considered a trigger to the Xin Hai Revolution, the revolution that ended the Qing Dynasty and started the Republic."

He went to his bedroom and came back with a book.

"Here," he said, "this is a history book on the Sichuan Railway Protection movement."

We passed it around.

"Yes," Shan said, "I remember learning about this in school. There is a Railway Protection Monument in Chengdu."

"In People's Park," Hong-mei said. "The monument is a landmark you'll see whenever you visit the park. I've seen it several times but never made an effort to visit it."

When the book came to my hands, I took my time flipping through the pages. I looked at the pictures carefully. Could You-jun's face be in one of them? If so, how could any one of us even recognize him?

My own family, a tiny drop of the long flowing river of the Chinese history.

I pained for my ancestors. Peony made the choices because she loved her children. Her choices caused enduring sorrow for Great-grandma Iris and cost her Jasmine and You-jun. But shouldn't the society and its time bear the brunt of the blame? What would the family story be if Peony, Iris, Jasmine, You-jun, and everyone else lived in a different era? In an era when girls were treated equally as boys? Peony would not have to worry about hiding Jasmine. Jasmine and You-jun would live until they had their own families. Peony and Master Han would enjoy the togetherness of children and grandchildren at an old age.

I wished that You-jun's letters to Jasmine had survived. We would be able to see through his eyes what had happened. Still, the letters were for Jasmine only, and I was glad that Iris in her own way delivered the letters to Jasmine. I thought about the letters, no, emails, between me and Harriton. They were memories of a past that did not exist or matter anymore. Maybe they should be gone with that past.

I asked Mom and Aunt Daisy what they remembered about Iris and Jian-da, their grandmother, and grandfather.

They remembered Grandma Iris well. In their memory, she was a small, thin woman with bound feet, quiet but funny. She loved her granddaughters and always told them so. In summer Grandma Iris sliced watermelons and put them in a bowl, then placed the bowl in a bucket of cold well water so they always had chilled juicy fresh watermelons to eat after school. In winter, she put two big sweet potatoes in the ashes of a stove when they left for school, and by the time they came back home, they had hot, steaming roasted sweet potatoes waiting. She made them each a new pair of winter shoes every year.

"The shoes were so beautiful. They had embroidered tops stuffed with soft cotton and layered cloth bottom, thick and soft," Aunt Daisy said. "They were fit to be placed in a glass case in a museum."

Iris also made shoe insoles for almost everyone she knew. "They were beautiful as well," my mom said. "Each pair had different cross-stitched patterns and thick white trim. You can't find them anywhere nowadays."

"I wish we had saved a pair or two," Aunt Daisy said.

The only time Iris had been tough on them and scolded them sternly was to warn them not to burn the family genealogy book when she heard that the Red Guards were doing just that. Had she not taken an extra measure to have Uncle Tiger copy the book, we would not be sitting here with new revelation and understanding of our family history. I would not be learning how despite sorrows and anger, one must continue to love and forgive.

My mom and Aunt Daisy did not remember Grandpa Jian-da well. He died in 1950 when Daisy was seven and my mom was five. All they remembered was that he was even more silent than grandma, but he loved them and showed his affection with toys occasionally, such as seashells and wooden yo-yos.

In her writing, Iris told the story of how she and Jian-da did the best they could to maintain the Han and Fang households, but could not keep their family fortune. Years of war and looting by bandits had caused huge inflation. To make matters worse, Mother Nature had taken her toll on people, too: there had been alternate years of drought and flooding, and their farmland in Three Rivers had not been able to bring any income. The 1936-1937 Sichuan Famine due to drought was particularly devastating: not only was there no harvest, but hungry people rushed the rice shops everywhere, including those belonging to the family.

So after Mrs. Fang died, Iris and Jian-da sold the Fang house and much of the rice business. Green Jade married a former servant and they were the only two helpers still with the family. Iris, and Pearl as she got older, did most of the cooking and washing. Iris cared for her father Master Han, who came home after wandering about and died when Pearl was three or four. Green Jade's husband went back to his hometown in the North sometime after, and reluctantly she went with him. At first, she had asked people to write letters to Iris—she never learned how to read and write—and Iris heard that she had a son and a daughter and lived a happy life. But in time they lost touch.

In 1933, Pearl married Ching-Yu, a school teacher who grew up an orphan. They lost two infant children to dysentery, and Pearl also suffered a miscarriage before they finally had my aunt Daisy in 1943, and my mom Lily in 1945.

Grandpa Ching-Yu learned to take pictures with a camera that was given to him as a wedding gift by a friend of his father-in-law Jian-da, Mr. Liang Fei, who survived the railway massacre, emigrated to the U.S., and came back for a visit. The Liang family later sponsored my mom's moving to the U.S. in 1972. Mom said that they told her that they were fulfilling a promise made long ago.

In addition to taking pictures, Ching-Yu became interested in the chemistry of developing negatives and photos. He turned Iris and Jasmine's old room into a dark room for that purpose. Jian-da and Iris had the old master bedroom and Pearl and Ching-Yu moved into Yu-jun's old room.

As more friends and neighbors asked to have their pictures taken, Pearl and Ching-Yu decided to turn Number One Cypress Street into a combination of business and residence. The business was called Three Rivers Photo Studio and it did well. A favorite place for people to take pictures was the back garden, with its many flowers and trees, a beautiful rockery, a pond, a pavilion, and lots of bamboo. I have seen some of the old pictures of my mom and Daisy when they were little girls. The most interesting thing for me was how colors were painted on these black and white pictures: pink cheeks and red lips, and green leaves and flowers of various colors. Grandpa Ching-Yu did the work himself first, and slowly the business grew and he hired helpers and trained them. Even Grandma Pearl learned how to develop pictures.

Grandpa Ching-Yu never quit teaching, despite the success of his photo business. He considered himself a scholar first and businessman second. According to my mom, Grandma Pearl had mentioned many times that this had been one of grandpa's best qualities. "Our family has always had businesses, but in our hearts, we are scholars who always appreciate an elegant poem praising the short life of falling spring flowers, an exquisite landscape painting depicting the beauty of nature, and calligraphy that was like flowing clouds and running water."

All the talk about how the family had always valued scholars made me realize something in myself: this must be why I fell in love with Harriton. He was the kind of scholar my ancestors would have approved!

Hong-mei and I had never met Grandpa Ching-yu; he died in 1960 during the Three Years of Great Famine. "He was starved to death," my grandma said.

The city government purchased more than fifty percent of the family business in 1956, under the policy of controlling the national economy by state-owned companies. Businesses, both big and small, became state-private joint businesses, big ones such as the then-largest department store in China, Shanghai Yong An Department Store, and small ones such as the Three Rivers Photo Studio. Grandma Pearl and Grandpa Ching-Yu worked for the new joint business, receiving a monthly salary and retirement benefits, which were not very much. Iris, considered too old to be a part of the regular workforce, helped with the household work. Later, Daisy went to the countryside to be re-educated, as millions of young students did, and Grandma Pearl used all her connections and even bribery to bring her back. The job waiting for Daisy: working at the Three Rivers Photo Studio.

I thought about Number One Cypress Street now. The old cypress tree was still standing, but no residents in that tall apartment building knew anything about what the place used to be. I was glad that Grandma Pearl did not know any of this: she died in 1993, before the construction of all the high rises.

"I have a hard time believing this happened in our family," Hong-mei repeated. "And Lady Han became a nun."

"She renounced all the earthly relations and concerns," Aunt Daisy said.

"Why did she become a Buddhist nun? I had a sense that she was a pious lay Buddhist, but leaving her only surviving child and her husband and her best friend to become a nun seems extreme to me, even cruel," I said.

"Plus, all the offerings and prayers did not protect her children as she so desperately wanted to," Hong-mei echoed me.

"Rose and Hong-mei," my mom said, "we may never know why. Maybe she thought she was not pious enough. Or maybe she was tired of all the sufferings and she wanted some peace, and that's the kind of peace she could see."

"That is what faithful people do," Uncle De-chen said. "No bitterness. Disappointment in life only makes them more devoted. Buddhism believes that our sufferings come from our desires. Being alive is to suffer, because nothing in this world is permanent, no matter how much we try to hold on to it. And one way to avoid suffering is to give up all the desires, desire for love, family, materials, and become a Buddhist monk or nun. Even a number of Chinese celebrities have done that in recent years."

Hong-mei looked at the book again.

"Here are recordings of the date of Iris and Jian-da's wedding; Pearl's birth; Master Han's passing. Look, here's a sentence, dated 1966, at the bottom of the page."

She read it out loud:

"I have held bitterness against my mother for many years. I thought she did not love me. But after I became a mother and raised my own daughter, I understood more about a mother's love. She did not love Jasmine more than she loved me. But she lost Jasmine from the time Jasmine was born, and that tore a hole in her heart. Losing You-jun ripped that hole wide open and shattered her. Nothing could ever repair that. The only thing she could do was to renounce all the earthly relations and concerns that had brought her suffering and pain. As my own ending is drawing closer to me, I forgive her. To honor her wishes, I will not write anything more about her, but I command that all the descendants of this family that will come into existence in this world shall never forget her."

"So Grandma Iris visited Lily and me in our dreams to let us know," Aunt Daisy said.

"And Grandma Pearl visited Rose and me in ours," Hong-mei said.

"Grandmothers to granddaughters," my mom said. "Special bonds."

"And I am the chosen one to complete the task," I said, my eyes moist.

"The one who has drifted the furthest from the family root, the one who knew and understood the least of our history, and the meaning of love, forgiveness, healing, and letting go."

"But also the one who has it all," Hong-mei said, wrapping her arms around my shoulder. "Peony's clever mind, Iris's good looks, and Jasmine's pure heart."

"You know me," I smiled through my tears. "Let's visit the temple tomorrow."

#

That night, I had a hard time falling asleep. The lives of Master Han, Lady Han, Iris, Jasmine, You-jun, and Jian-da went through my mind, as vivid as if I were watching a movie. I saw how they lived at Number One Cypress Street here at Three Rivers and in Cloud Gate. I saw how they visited the Diaoyu Fortress and the White Cloud Mountain. I saw how they laughed and cried and loved. Their blood ran in my veins, and their DNA was in my cells.

I saw a middle-aged woman gliding to me. I could see myself in her, especially when she smiled. She had a gray unadorned cotton tunic, black pants, and small lily feet. Her hair was combed and twisted into a tight chignon. She said to me, "Rose, you are here."

"Peony? Lady Han?" I asked. "Great-great-grandma?"

She smiled and did not answer, but turned around.

I followed her. We crossed a busy street and went into a magnificent house that had a stone-paved courtyard, lots of rooms, and a beautiful back garden. Then, we came out through the thick black door and were now in a boat on the river. The water was smooth as glass, and a gentle breeze caressed my face. I saw a white pagoda tower on the shore; then it disappeared and was replaced by blue mountains covered by fine, white mist. In the blink of an eye, we were off the boat and walking on narrow country roads winding through small plots of land. I saw the gate, the lotus pond, and finally the steep path leading to the Guanyin Temple perched on top of the cliff of White Cloud Mountain.

"Great-great-grandma!" I called out. I understood she was taking me through the places of her life. Tears ran down my cheeks. All the places, except Number One Cypress Street, were still there, beautiful and silent. How long would they remain? Would they ever let their silence be broken and let all the love and loss they had witnessed spill out?

243

She turned around. She had donned a nun's kasaya, her dark hair gone. She sat down, her legs folded in a double lotus, her hands counting her wooden prayer beads. She motioned me to sit down. I did and waited for her to speak.

"Don't cry," she said softly. "You wanted to know why I came here and stayed."

I nodded.

"It was a natural path for me. Just as when we were on the way here: we took the path in front of us, and it brought us here.

"I had thought I could change the path. I thought that if I made good plans and worked hard on them, I could carve out a new way. I thought I did, but then that new path was washed away from under my feet."

"You did what all mothers would have done, for the love of their children," I said.

"What is love?" she asked me, her voice hollow, like the sound of a bell drifting in from far away.

"Is love a desire to keep a thing or a person? If it is, by default it will cause suffering: the deeper the love, the worse the pain. Because not being able to have the thing or the person is suffering, but having them means one will inevitably lose them—more suffering.

"It was too late for me to understand this, even though I had been trying to learn the truth. I had been praying to Guanyin, but my heart was not open, my eyes didn't see, and my ears didn't hear."

"But because of your love, Jasmine lived, and she came to know your love," I argued.

She trembled at the name but regained her composure quickly.

"Only to endure more desire and more suffering. And cause the suffering of others, just like this earthly world, one generation after another, always and forever."

We sat there in silence for a while. I heard the drumming of the wooden fish and a ringing bell in the distance.

"Do you still? Believe in love?" she whispered.

I thought about Jasmine and You-jun, Iris and Jian-da, my parents, Uncle De-chen and Aunt Daisy, Hong-mei, and Shan. And I also thought about Harriton, his wife, and me. And I thought about different kinds of love: Peony and her children, Peony and A-mei, Iris and Tiger, Iris and Jasmine, and Hong-mei and me.

"Yes, Great-great-grandmother," I whispered back, tears streaming down. "I think I do. But…"

There was a sigh, barely audible.

I looked up and saw that Lady Han was gone. I looked everywhere, behind the large pillars in the front of the temple, behind the altar, in the side rooms, and she was nowhere to be found. The closer I looked, the less I could see.

"Great-great grandma!" I called out. "Peony! Lady Han!"

I sat up, but there was no one in my room, only the undulating drapes caressed by the breeze coming through an open window.

I whispered and finished my sentence."…but I also learned love means letting go." To let go when a path came to an end. To go on and continue to live the best one could, like Lady Han, like Iris and Jian-da, but never to forget.

I went to the desk by the window, opened the drapes, and let the moonshine in. My laptop was on the desk, its power flickering an eerie green light. Without turning on the lights, I turned on the laptop. I opened the folder H. Then I highlighted all the files, right-clicked them, and hit "delete." I opened the e-mail folder with the same name and did the same thing.

Iris burnt the memories. And I did the same with the stroke of a key.

Bye, Harry.

#

In the morning, the four of us piled into Hong-mei's car. She drove us out of the city into the country. I told them that Lady Han had visited me.

"She asked me if I still believe in love," I said.

"What did you tell her?" Daisy said.

"That I do, still," I said. And I added, "Just like she did still believe in Guanyin."

"Oh, and Mom," I said, "I saw a job ad for a community college near LA. I want you to take a look at it with me when we get back."

My mom, sitting behind me, reached her hands, and cupped my cheeks from behind. "Haode, Mei Mei," she said.

We went on the bridges over the three rivers and onto the wide, smooth, four-lane highway. In the next hour, I saw everything I had seen in my dream, and I climbed the same steep steps to the Guanyin Temple.

The abbot Hui-Xin, Wise Heart, was sweeping the courtyard. Seeing us approaching, she stopped her broom and smiled at us. Then she held her hands in prayer, lightly bowed to us, and said, "Mrs. Wang had said that you four ladies would be back in about a month after her funeral."

She looked at me and said, "You must be the one she was talking about, a girl who looked like Iris. Come this way."

"Wait," I said, holding my hands in prayer in front me. "Excuse me, but can we light some incense first?"

She nodded.

We each took three sticks and lit them on the burning red candles. I held mine up to the sky, lowered my head for a moment, before putting them in the incense burner. These are for you, my ancestors: Peony, Master Han, Iris, Jian-da, Jasmine, You-jun, A-mei, Tiger, and Old Uncle Wang.

Then we followed her to the west wing of the temple, to the wall with the portraits. We saw this wall on the day of Auntie Wang's funeral.

"This one." She pointed to the third portrait.

Unlike my memory from last time, the lady in the portrait seemed to have a smile on her soft, kind face, after all. My great-great-grandma, Lady Peony Han, the tenth abbot of the temple, Master Hui-Jue, Awaking Wisdom, looked at us as we looked at her.

AUTHOR'S NOTE

About Three Rivers and Cloud Gate

Three Rivers is based on Hechuan (合川), my mom's hometown, and my birthplace. I never lived there, and I only visited it a handful of times, most recently in the summer of 2018, shortly before I finished the first draft of this book. All the descriptions of physical features of Three Rivers in this book are true, at least to the best of my knowledge. I heard many stories about Hechuan growing up, and these stories got into my head and inspired my imagination.

Cloud Gate (云门) is a small town near Hechuan, where an uncle is from. I only visited the place when I was very young, but I loved the name. I imagined it as an ancestral home for my characters, drawing pictures stored in my head from my visits to other countryside places in Sichuan.

The Early Railways in China

I found the history of early railways in China fascinating. I hope you, dear reader, indulge me by allowing me to share my fascination.

The first railway, a mini-track of five hundred meters or one-third of a mile, was built in Beijing by a British businessman in 1865. It did not go well with the locals who thought the steam engine running on the track was an iron dragon of some sort, a wicked magic creature made by the foreign devils. Dowager Cixi Empress ordered the tracks to be dismantled. But the British were not deterred. They built another railway in the commercially developed Southeast ten years later, put it in operation, and sold it to the Qing government, which promptly dismantled it, again. But people who had ridden on the train were hooked. Reformers in the government presented the idea of building "China's own railways" as a key step to allow the country to become modern and prosperous. In 1881, the first such railway, "China's own," was built, except that the Empress Cixi ordered the trains be pulled by horses and mules because the loud rambling engine noses "were bothering the sleep of royal ancestors in the underworld." But the Empress did taste the sweetness of speedy travel in luxurious cars when a railway was built between her Palaces in Beijing in 1888, and, soon after, the reformers had the green light to build whatever railways they wished had they gotten the money.

Constructing railways in Sichuan was proposed in 1881 as well when China lost in the Sino-French war and the gate to southwest China was forced open. All the Western superpowers at the time, France, England, and the U.S, requested to have the rights to build railways in Sichuan.

Having enough funds to do so was a big problem. A government-owned company was established in 1904 to raise and manage money for the railway project, and one of the main principles adopted by the company was that money would come from the following sources: the government, both federal and local, private businesses, and even ordinary people. It was decided that no money should be borrowed from any foreign countries. According to the Boxer Protocol signed between the Chinese government and the Eight-nation Alliance in 1901, China was to pay 450 million taels of fine silver (approximately $333 million or £67 million at the exchange rates of the time) as indemnity over the course of 39 years to the eight nations involved during the Boxer Rebellion, of which 2.2 million taels came out of Sichuan each year from various forms of taxation, including taxation on outhouses (called the shit tax by the locals). Borrowing money from these foreign countries was like adding insult to injury.

By 1911, more than 76% of the money, over eleven million teals of silver had been raised from taxation of ordinary people in the form of "shares" of the railway. It was not exaggerating to say that all the common folks in Sichuan had always held a stake in the railway project.

But things did not work out as planned. Some in the central government who had firmly believed that no funds should come from any foreign banks changed their minds, as they saw that the current railway company was fraught with corruption, misuse of funds on business unrelated to railways, and inefficiency. The progress of actual construction was extraordinarily slow—the groundbreaking happened five years after the inception of the company! This idea of change caught on and became the doctrine of the central government, which sent out orders to the provinces to proclaim that the railway project would be nationalized and it was necessary to borrow money from foreign banks in order to complete the construction at a reasonable speed. Stocks would be issued to those who had paid their shares, without cash back or compensation for funds lost or misused.

This move created a huge outcry. By then the Constitutionalists, most of whom had recently returned from overseas and who brought new ideas to make China prosper, who wanted reform of the Qing Dynasty but not revolution, had taken hold of the board of the railway company and decided to resist the take-over from the central government and borrowing money from foreign banks. They formed the Sichuan Railway Protection League on June 17, 1911, at a rally attended by four thousand people in Chengdu. Soon the movement spread throughout the entire province, men, women, old, young, children, social dignitaries and even prostitutes participated. Strikes were everywhere: shops and schools closed. The sewer waste from Chengdu, which had been carried out of the city each day to the countryside to be used as fertilizers, piled up inside of the city. Things had gone from bad to worse, leading to bloodshed on September 7th (Gregorian calendar; or fifteenth of the seventh month) in Chengdu. Surviving members of the Railway League wrote messages on wood chips and threw them in the water to spread the news, as described in the book.

Historians have different views about the Sichuan Railway Protection movement. The official view, sanctioned by the government was that the people who were part of the movement were national heroes, whereas those who wanted to borrow foreign money were traitors who wanted to sell the sovereignty of China to foreign powers. But in recent years, more historians have questioned this simplistic view and suggested that part of the fuel for the movement was a narrow nationalistic view of the world, fear of change, and a focus only on local vested interests.

Regardless, no one disputes the importance of the movement. Mr. Sun Yat-sen, the Father of modern China, was quoted saying that "...without the rebellion of the Sichuan Railway Protection League, the Wuchang Uprising (the first successful uprising after a series of failures in the Revolution of 1911) would have been delayed."

Poems used in the novel

"Peonies" is translated by Charles Egan, this poem is from *Clouds Thick, Whereabouts Unknown: Poems by Zen Monks of China* by Egan and Chu, 2010. Copyright © 2010. Reprinted with the kind permission of its publisher Columbia University Press.

"The Boat Towman Haoz" is from "The Yangtze River Tow Men" by Liu Bai, published by Probe International on January 1, 2010. Reprinted with the kind permission of the publisher.

"Goose Goose Goose" is a poem known by every Chinese child. I took the liberty to translate it myself.

"The Water Song" is a famous poem that has so many wonderful English translations; it was difficult for me to choose. I settled on the translation by Mr. Lin Yutang, whose work I love and admire, and whose great novel *Moment in Peking*, published in 1939, inspires me.

Other significant resource books:

天下合川 *(Hechuan Under the Sky):* My cousin Qiang's wife Li, who works for the Hechuan city government, acquired this book for me. It proved to be a valuable resource for my research of the city's rich history, culture, and customs.

炸响辛亥革命的惊雷: 四川保路运动历史真相, 郑光路著 *(The Thunder that Struck the Xin'hai Revolution: True History of the Sichuan Railway Protection Movement* by Zheng Guanglu): I relied on this book for my research of the history of early railways in China and the Railway Protection Movement.

Chinese Words in the Novel

The pinyin system from the People's Republic of China is used for most spellings and pronunciations of Chinese words in this book.

ACKNOWLEDGEMENTS

I thank the Midwest Writing Center for believing in me. I have met so many amazing people through the organization and learned so much about the craft of writing through its excellent workshops and conferences. Many thanks to Ryan Collins, for telling me that, since I write, I am a writer, and to Susan Collins, Mary Davidsaver, Rochelle Murray, Jodie Toohey, and other board members for their constant encouragement and support. I also thank Skylar Alexander Moore and Sarah Elgatian for their assistance in promoting this book. This work would not be here today without the Midwest Writing Center.

I thank Misty Urban for her constant encouragement of my writing and masterful editing of this book. She elevated the book to a whole new level. "What's at stake?" I'll continue to ask myself that question—thank you, Misty!

I thank Chris Xi for the beautiful cover art that tells the story of the book so well.

I thank Jenny Parvin for her advice on publicity and my website.

I thank Jeanne O'Melia for proofreading this book and for her support.

I thank Galen Leohardy for his unwavering support of my writing from the very beginning and for spending countless hours reviewing my manuscripts, including this one. You are my *de facto* English professor, Galen! Thank you.

I thank my writing group for cheering for me at every step of the way and for their excellent critiques, which helped to shape the story. I am grateful to Becky Langdon for introducing me to this group, for her encouragement and guidance in many aspects of writing, from grammar to Twitter, and to Elaine Olson for the words of affirmation that give me confidence and the questions that make me dive deeper into my stories, and I am grateful to Terry Haru for his attention to details and sharp editorial eyes that always push me to be a better writer.

I thank my early readers of this book, friends who spent their precious summer reading time on this book and who gave me encouragement and honest feedback: Feng Chen, Hui Guan, Michelle Hendricks, Susan Hendricks (Michelle and Susan even bought me a bottle of champagne to celebrate), Tom MacKay (who took meticulous notes and gave me some great insights), Dan Moore, Beth Vogel, and Terry Giglio Voss.

Many writers shaped me in my writing journey with their encouragement, teaching, and generosity of time and advice, among them: Leslee Goodman, Felicia Schneiderhan, Tom Strelich, and Kali White VanBaale.

I thank many writer friends I met in the incredible #WritingCommunity on Twitter for their good cheer.

I thank those who are always in my corner, no matter what I do or where I am:

Jim Long and Yingjun Wang read my first-ever short story written in English and told me that the story did not put them to sleep. I took that as a good sign and carried on with writing.

My best friends from high school, the three others of our Gang of Four: Guan Xin, Liu Lin, and Zhu Zhu—I can always share my happiness and sorrows with you, no matter how far apart we are. Special thanks to Zhu Zhu, who helped me develop the vision of what the front courtyard and back garden of the Han Family House should look like.

My classmates from my elementary school, middle school, and high school in Kangding 康定—you guys are always so proud and supportive of me: I hope I make you proud still.

My friends from Ames and Iowa City—many of you are great examples of the hardworking, self-made immigrant story, and you are my inspiration.

My friends and colleagues at Black Hawk College, especially colleagues of NSE and ASDP, and the ladies from Building 2: you know who you are, and I'm lucky to work with you.

My extended family of aunts, uncles, and cousins who told me stories that became part of this book. Special thanks to Guo Li, my cousin Qiang's wife, who gave me a copy of 天下合川 *(Hechuan Under the Sky)*, which provided many details about the city of Three Rivers.

I am grateful to my adopted families, the Collinses, Mullinaxes, and Rouws, to Linzy Jr, Pam, Karen, Mary, Paula, Tina, and others who have always been supportive and encouraging.

I thank my immediate family: my parents, to whom this book is dedicated, and to whom I promise to read the book in Chinese. They taught me the value of books and hard work. I thank also my siblings and their families: Xiaoqian, Kevin, Kiki, Zipeng, Qiong, and Gudong, all of whom cheer for me and support me with their love and patience.

And to my guys—Conan, who's unfazed after learning that I have no plan B, and Ari, the best present I have ever received. What can I say? You fill me with wonder, peace, and joy. Thank you for your love and patience, for all the lessons you teach me every day, and for the time and space you indulge me with so I can write. I love you guys, "no matter what."

ABOUT THE AUTHOR

 X.H. Collins was born in Hechuan, China, and grew up in Kangding, on the East Tibet Plateau. She has a Ph.D. in nutrition and is a biology professor at an Illinois community college. She lives in Iowa with her husband and son. *Flowing Water, Falling Flowers* is her first novel. To learn more about the author and her work, visit her website at https://xhcollins.com/, and follow her on Twitter @xixuan_c, Facebook @xhcollins, and Instagram xixuan_c.

Photo © Giraffe Photography 2019

Made in the USA
Middletown, DE
11 October 2020